The Light of Dark Things

Rebecca McCullough

The Light of Dark Things

Croft

This book is a work of fiction. Any references to historical events, real people, or real places are used fictitiously. Other names, characters, places, and events are products of the author's imagination, and any resemblance to actual events or places or persons, living or dead, is entirely coincidental.

Copyright © 2025 The Light of Dark Things
by Rebecca McCullough

Cover Design by Rebecca McCullough

Interior Design by Rebecca McCullough

ISBN: 979-8-9920700-2-6

First Edition

I would like to thank Miss Bonnie for being my first reader.

And to Sydney, for sticking it out.

This book is also dedicated to anyone who has ever run away to join a traveling show, no matter how briefly. You live in a world of danger and joy and freedom.
And magic.

Many of us come to visit.

Some of us come to stay.

The Light of Dark Things

CHAPTER 1

Her shoes were wet again. Or still. It didn't really matter, at this point her feet were already blistered and pruney. What would a little fungal infection hurt? She'd been walking for she didn't know how long and her legs ached. Her back was also starting to put up a fairly loud complaint, but Kaylen couldn't stop. If she stopped, she would not just want to sit down but lie down and if she did that, she knew she would fall asleep for hours and then the people following her would catch her for sure.

Stupid, stupid, stupid to make them wait so long. They had been near to starving and driving her crazy with their incessant keening. It got into her brain, that noise, driving out all sensible thought until she had to let them feed or bash her skull into the nearest hard surface. Kaylen knew better than to let them go so long between feedings. She and they had been joined for as long as she could remember and she knew how to judge their moods and needs. This time she had just been caught out was all. And because of that little slip, she had been half-mad when she finally released them. It was almost a fatal mistake. They could and did protect her, but when they were that hungry even their caution fell away and maybe they didn't clean up as well as they should have.

Kaylen had known immediately that she had misjudged. Not about the food source, never that, her marks had shown clear and true, but about how tied that individual had been to the community. She knew better than to hunt sociopaths, they were simply too well-connected, too embedded with society. They had evolved into craven wolves among a flock of retarded suburban sheep. Society had become such a drone of constant subterfuge that the average human could watch a murder being committed and be so concerned about posting the video on social media they would neglect to call the police. Unfortunately, lassitude was contagious, and Kaylen had fallen into the same droll, unobservant existence as the other meat. It had nearly cost her dearly.

She tripped over a root and went sprawling, tearing her jeans and scraping her knee on a rock. "Damnit," she swore, rolling over and assessing the damage. It wasn't bad. It was just one more inconvenience.

Gods, it felt good to sit, to just stop moving for a minute. Kaylen felt her body starting to relax and jerked herself up. She couldn't stop, not yet. She didn't know how much evidence she had left. She lived as much off the grid as possible, but she knew a girl wandering alone through the woods not too far from a murder scene would be suspicious under the best of circumstances. And with the way her luck had been lately, she would get the one cop who was actually good at his job.

So thinking, she started trudging again. It was mid-morning and she had been walking since last evening. That had been another slip-up. She should have waited until the middle of the night if not the early morning. Kaylen knew well that hunting during the dinner hour was a fantastically bad idea, but she had been so out of it by the time she ran into the bastard that everything had happened too fast for her to think it through. She hadn't planned on running headlong into a serial killer, it had just happened. That was the problem when they got to starving; they took over and hunted down the tastiest morsel they could find. And killers were always the best.

Kaylen didn't know exactly what they fed on because she had long ago discovered it wasn't simply meat and bone. Something else drove them to only seek out bad people. Actually, evil people was a better description. They especially liked the ones who had committed multiple crimes. She didn't know how but feeding off these miscreants also held them over for a longer period of time. She didn't know if it was because the food had caused so much suffering that the residual feeling had built it up like fat marbled through a thick steak or maybe pain and suffering was like a protein shot, but they always went the extra mile if a particularly vile human was in the vicinity. Sometimes they even wanted to hunt that person if they had just recently fed. It was like an addiction.

She came out of the woods and stood on the edge of a paved road in serious need of a makeover. It had an abandoned feel to it. Kaylen could see patches here and there stretching in both directions where county workers had put Band-Aids on an open gash and hoped for the best. It was the kind of road where you took things that needed to be forgotten. The kind of place a smart cop might come trolling, in other words.

Her path had taken her slowly, but steadily uphill and looking across the road, Kaylen understood why. This side was an easy incline. The other side was nearly straight up. She would have to use the trees and roots to climb if she wanted to continue in her current direction. The thought of dragging her already exhausted body up the side of a mountain made her want to sit down again. Maybe jail wouldn't be so bad. Of course, given what they had done to the son of a bitch, she was probably looking at the death penalty. If this state still had it.

So, straight was out. Did she want to go left or right?

Left went slightly downhill and curved away out of sight about a hundred yards farther on. Kaylen could just make out the sign warning people to cut their speed. Right led uphill and was straight and clear for as far as she could see.

She crossed her arms. Was it to be the attic or the basement?

If she wanted to keep hoofing it, right seemed the more logical choice as towns were typically found in valleys. Given that logic, if she wanted to hitch, left would be more likely to lead her to a town or at the very least a bigger road. Of course, she wasn't guaranteed a ride in either case and since she had been standing here all she had heard was birdsong leading her to believe she was hell and gone from any budding metropolis.

It was her feet that decided her, she just didn't feel like walking uphill anymore. Kaylen turned left and started off again. She walked close to the tree line, though, in case the wrong type of car happened to swing by. A local police officer, say, or maybe fucking Ranger Rick out doing his morning rounds. Would such a person stop to help a girl who looked like she'd spent the night slogging through a swamp and the morning crashing through every bush and vine out here? Does a bear squat in the bushes, boys and girls? No, Kaylen didn't want to meet anyone local for a ride if she could help it. Her goal was a long-haul trucker or even a family on that ever-popular cross-country excursion. People with places to go and things to do a long way from here.

As she approached the sign, Kaylen noticed a trio of white rectangles with red arrows attached to the post. Each rectangle was a little bigger than an index card. Someone had attached them one above the other in a neat row. Kaylen stopped and looked at the arrows. She knew what these were. Circus arrows. She had put up plenty of these herself last summer when she had spent a couple of months with a mud show touring the southwest. The pay had sucked and the sleeping arrangements had been questionable, but it had gotten her to a new town every other day or so and feeding her companions had been a breeze. For the first time in a long time, she hadn't worried about an escape plan. And given the people she had been traveling with, nobody was much into backstory share time.

It had been a good thing, but the show had run into a bit of trouble outside Phoenix. One night the boss made them break everything down, pack everything up, paid them enough to keep them from lynching his ass, and told them all to get lost. Rumors were pretty rampant that he had spent time with a hooker who was not only far below legal age, but might not have been as much of a working girl as she let on. All Kaylen knew was that the cops had shown up at one of the shows and started asking questions. From what she had gathered from the others as she helped pack, sometimes just the cops showing up was enough for a show to scatter like roaches when the lights came on.

A roadshow. That was the ticket. People who wouldn't ask a lot of questions because they were used to a roustie being there one day and gone the next morning. If she were a performer, it would be different. Everyone took notice if an act up and split in the middle of a season, but rousties were a dime a dozen. And the concessions were always looking for butchers to run the stands.

Hoping the show was still at the end of these arrows and hoping she was close to the lot, Kaylen faded back in among the trees. She would follow the road, but now that she had a destination, there was no point in putting herself in at any undue risk. If the show was still here, and if she could get a couple weeks' work, or at least a ride to the next state, she could take a few deep breaths. If nothing else, she could take some time to formulate some kind of plan. She could afford that for a little while; they had eaten very well last evening.

CHAPTER 2

Detective Adam Slate glanced around the meticulous living room and frowned at a technician who was two inches from stepping on a piece of evidence. Not that it would be difficult to botch something in here. The living room was meticulous if one was able to unsee the ripped apart lumps of flesh and bones that had once been a man.

Slate had seen his fair share of carnage. He had worked five years homicide in Tampa's less illustrious neighborhoods and had worked many a gang retaliation message killing, but this blatant shredding of a human body was new to him. It was like something out of a Predator movie. There were pieces of this guy on the ceiling for Christ's sake. Contrast to the awesome brutality of the murder was the orderliness of the rest of the house. Hell, of the damn room.

The occupant had apparently enjoyed a monochromatic palette. The carpet, where it wasn't dark maroon, was a rich cream color. The couches, three set up in a cozy semi-circle around an annihilated glass coffee table, were a light gray. Except for the one that was as shredded as the victim. This one had drying blood and tissue gauged all the way into the springs and was splattered a muddy brown where expelled fluids had dried.

The walls were stark white with black and white scenery photos placed here and there as accents. The walls were completely untouched by blood. How the killer had gotten blood and gore on the ceiling and hadn't left a single drop on any of the walls was nearly impossible in Slate's mind.

The rest of the house was decorated in similar fashion. Monochrome, simple, almost Spartan. The drapes were the only real color point in the whole place and seemed totally out of character with everything else. They were a deep and vibrant crimson, so red they looked like screams. They gave Slate a creeping feeling every time he turned his back on them. Every window in the downstairs had a pair of those heavy drapes.

"Chief's on his way," Sargent Carter muttered on his way into the living room. Slate nodded to show he heard but didn't move out of Carter's way, forcing the other man to slink around his six-foot frame.

Slate couldn't stand Carter and the feeling was openly mutual. The two of them usually managed to stay out of the other's space, but on a case like this the whole cavalry had shown up. This was a sleepy little mountain town, not a crime hardened city. Most of these cops had worked from eighteen to retirement and never seen a murder, let alone a butchering. Slate knew the chief wanted to handle this as carefully as possible to avoid a panic.

Carter stationed himself next to what looked like the victim's left arm, although it was hard to tell without the hand attached. "Man, this dude pissed somebody right the fuck off."

"What are the neighbors saying?" Carter and the other uniforms had been canvassing the area, more to keep people away than to glean any real information. If someone had something to say, they usually came right up waving a banner, that had been Detective Slate's experience. What he wanted to know was who wasn't around. Idiots came back to watch the cops; real killers knew how to lay low for a bit.

"Nobody heard nothin' but the music. Which was loud, damn near blew my eardrums when I got here. Neighbors said that wasn't out of the ordinary. Apparently, Coleslaw here liked to show off his surround sound. Only reason they called us in the first place was because it was still playing when the kids got up this morning. They heard it while they were waiting for the bus."

"Any girlfriends that might have an extra boyfriend or maybe a husband that wanted some payback?" Because this much rage was someone with an axe to grind.

"Not that anyone ever noticed. Little old lady across the street," he thought for a minute, "Mrs. Wilson. She told Lawrence in a hush hush way she thought Lenoy was gay." Carter raised an eyebrow. "Could be a hate crime, maybe?"

Slate shook his head. Hate crimes were, by and large, crimes of opportunity. This was not that. A cursory examination had shown no forced entry, no struggle, no surprise. The two tables in the entryway still held their vases of dried flowers. If Lenoy, Martin Lenoy to be exact, had been surprised into a struggle those vases would have been the first thing to crash. "No signs of forced entry. If Lenoy was gay and worried about haters, do you really think he'd let them in the front door?"

"Could be someone he knew brought a friend over. No way one person made this mess."

Carter was probably right about that. If the damage had been done post mortem, Slate could maybe believe a single perp, but the arc of the blood splatter said Lenoy had been alive for some if not most of his torture. "They would have to be big, and armed."

Lenoy was small but well built. Detective Slate had seen a picture of the man standing on a dock holding up a good-sized trout. He put his height at about five nine, five ten, maybe one seventy, but a solid one seventy. His biceps were bulging as he held up his prize but not because the fish was huge. Slate opted the man could easily lift two twenty.

Solid, strong, and gay or not, armed. They had found two handguns and a rifle so far and nobody had given the basement a thorough going-over yet. This wasn't the type of guy you got the drop on; Detective Slate would bet his badge on that.

"Armed? Sure, Detective. How armed would someone have to be for you to let their buddy cut you into little pieces? Or tear into pieces is what it looks like to me." Carter scratched his stubbly chin. "I'd rather eat a bullet any day."

"Maybe he did. They could have gut shot him, immobilized him, turned up the music and had a party. I've seen things like that before."

"Yeah, but something like this would have taken time, man. And patience. Look at the way that arm was ripped. Looks like the damn thing was pulled off his torso like someone would yank a leg off a chicken. Who the hell could do that?"

Detective Slate's stomach rolled at Carter's grotesque yet eerily apt description. Suddenly the smell of blood and shit doubled in Slate's nose and his eyes focused on a picture of trees at dawn on the far wall until the nausea passed. Damned if he was going to upchuck on a crime scene. He wasn't a rookie for fuck's sake.

Something by the picture caught his eye. Moving carefully around the forensics guys and their equipment, Slate walked over to the wall. He pulled on a pair of disposable gloves as he went. He heard Carter following him and prayed the clumsy fuck wouldn't track bloody footprints everywhere.

Something white was sticking out from under the picture. It almost blended perfectly with the wall and if Slate hadn't been focused so hard on not puking, he would have missed it entirely. He gently tilted the bottom of the picture away from the wall. A white rectangle fell from where it had been hidden between the frame and the wall. It fell lazily through shafts of morning sunlight to land face down on the carpet.

Slate squatted down, his knees popping, and was reaching for the picture when an ashen-faced officer walked into the living room from the direction of the kitchen. "Holy fuck, you guys. You gotta see what I found in the basement. I think, I think I tripped over your ah, over your- ". He turned and bolted for the bathroom down the hallway. They heard him retching violently.

"Don't tell me there's another one down there," Carter groaned. "I thought I told them to survey the basement already."

"They did," Detective Slate said standing up with the picture in his hand, "but the man who did this wouldn't leave anything lying around for prying eyes." He handed the picture to Sargent Carter.

CHAPTER 3

"Looking for work, huh? Sure you ain't runnin' away?" The big man, Marco, spat a line of tobacco juice next to Kaylen's sneaker.

"I ran away a long time ago. Besides, I'm legal."

"Barely, if I'm a day. Ah what the hell, you'll probably cut and run after the first paycheck anyways." He held out a grimy hand. "Welcome aboard."

Kaylen shook the hand and then fought the urge to wipe her own hand on her jeans. His hand had looked dry but had been wet and clammy when she touched it. She settled on putting her hands in her hoodie pockets instead.

Marco set off toward the tent where three rousties, two men and a woman, were breaking down gear. Kaylen saw other people, performers and concessionaires it looked like, lending a helping hand. Perfect. Just the kind of low grade just-getting-by show she had been looking for. "Guess anybody can drag stakes and fold canvas. You got a pair of gloves?"

Kaylen held out her hands. "What you see is what you get."

He spat again. "Always hate a runner. Get this through your head, I don't care what you do or who you fuck when you ain't workin' but you steal from me and I will get full payment, we clear?"

The look he gave her said exactly the payment he expected. "Perfectly," Kaylen replied coolly. Her arms began to tingle as her marks rose to the surface. This man was not bluffing.

"Good. Get over there to Mabel, she'll set you right." With that, he stomped off to a couple of guys working on a truck. The hood was up and both men were looking at the engine as if it were an alien artifact. She could hear Marco berating the men as he approached. The younger of the two shrank back from his wrath but the older one stood his ground.

"Don't let him get to ya. Marco's always madder'n pissed on rooster. One of those little bandy fucks that think they own the world."

Kaylen turned to see a thin, pale woman with scabs on her face and a good case of meth mouth. Her arms had lost their tingle with Marco's departure, however, and that made even a well-traveled drug addict a welcome sight. "I know the type. Keep your head down and stay out of their way."

"You got it right, girl. Name's Mabel. You ever work a road-show before?"

"Kaylen. Yeah, I worked on one for a couple of months last summer. Down around Arizona, New Mexico way."

Mabel's eyes gleamed. "You was on the Hollister show, eh? Ol' Tommy got caught bangin' a fourteen-year-old wannabe hooker, way I heard it."

"Don't know if that's true but he kicked us all out of there in a hurry after the cops paid a visit," Kaylen confirmed.

Mabel was nodding as she led Kaylen to the row of pulled stakes. "Yup, yup, grab everything and haul ass when the popo show." She cackled. "Getcha a couple of these and drag 'em to yonder flatbed. We got us a late start today on account of a couple of the trap girls was out boozin' last night and didn't come home 'til dawn. Usually that shit don't matter none to us gazoonies but Marco's shackin' with the one and he went out lookin' for her two-timing ass. And you know how it is when the boss ain't around." She shrugged as if the answer were obvious.

Kaylen grinned at her and the grin felt good on her face. She most definitely knew how it was. When the lot boss was gone, ain't shit getting' done. Might as well expect a bunch of toddlers to paint the Sistine Chapel as have a crew of less desirables take it upon themselves to breakdown the show and load up. Some things simply did not occur. Not in this universe, anyway.

"Here." One of the men handed Kaylen a pair of gloves before she picked up the first stake. He was lean and jittery, with a mop of greasy black hair, but his eyes were kind. The eyes really were the windows to the soul. Eyes, hands, and shoes told a story most people missed entirely. Those three things could tell you all you really needed to know about anyone on your first meeting.

"Thanks, I'll give them back when I'm done."

"Don't worry about it. We've got a whole bucket full. People buy 'em, then quit and leave 'em. My name's Roger." He held out his hand. Unlike Marco's, Roger's hand was dirty and cal-lused but dry and his shake was firm but not a warning that he could make it hurt if he wanted.

"Kaylen." She pulled on the gloves and picked up a stake in each hand. She had forgotten how heavy the iron bars were. Her muscles quivered for a second, then remembered they had done this a time or two before. She followed Mabel to the flatbed, drag-ging the stakes alongside her. Roger picked up four, gripping two in each hand and fell into step next to her. *Fresh meat on the lot,* Kaylen thought. *All the boys have to show off.*

"You hangin' for a while or just 'til pay?"

It was a fair question and one no townie would ever dream of asking. "Don't know for sure. I just gotta get out of here for a while. Might come back in a bit."

Roger nodded emphatically. "I hear that. Never hurts to get some clear air once in a while. Change of scenery."

They all loaded their burdens into the stake slot and ambled back to the tent. Other people were already folding the large canvas so it could be rolled and stuffed into huge bags for transport. "You know how to strap canvas?" Mabel asked.

Strapping or weaving canvas referred to lacing sections of canvas together if the tent was big enough. This one apparently was, although just barely from the look. "Sure, I did all the set up and tear down on the Hollister show. Except for king poles and stake driving."

Mabel nodded. "Us ladies don't do that either. The boys can handle that shit."

"Just because you weigh less than the sledge doesn't mean you can't swing it, Mab," Roger quipped.

"And ruin my model body?" She stood in what Kaylen assumed was supposed to be some kind of alluring pose but she only came out looking like a badly positioned mannequin. "Ah fuck it, who'm I kiddin'? My modelin' days are way passed."

"You mean they never were." Roger dodged the swipe she took at him, tripped over a stake, and went sprawling. Mabel voiced her cackle again and one of the other guys yelled at them to 'quit fucking around and get this shit done.'

Mabel gave him the finger before picking up another couple of stakes. Kaylen watched Roger get limberly to his feet like a cat before grabbing her own share of iron. Her leg muscles, pushed passed exhaustion, found new pockets of strength as she dragged the stakes behind Mabel.

The morning wore on. Stakes gave way to side poles, side poles to cables, and finally, after Marco had tromped all around the lot like a tyrant surveying a conquered land, they all loaded up into the trucks and were on their way. Kaylen hitched a ride with Mabel in the truck hauling the bunkhouse trailer. Thankfully, Mabel was not driving. That privilege went to a dark-skinned fellow by the name of Fred who had a deep, soothing voice and a cool cat vibe. He was the crew cook, among other things, and Kaylen liked him immediately. His serene vibe settled her nerves as much as the knowledge that she was putting real miles between her and the latest feeding ground.

Kaylen kept awake until after they stopped at a service plaza right before hitting the interstate. While all the drivers fueled up, she, Mabel, and pretty much everybody else who wasn't fueling up, went to the McDonald's inside the plaza and ordered food to go. Kaylen was fumbling in her pocket for the money she had hastily grabbed off the dresser in her rented room, when Mabel stopped her.

"We don't pay," she explained. She pointed. Marco was standing at the counter next to the cash register while crew members gave their orders. "We give the orders and Marco pays the bill." She grinned her gapped-toothed grin. "They do that just in case they don't make enough from the shows to pay us."

Kaylen left her money in her pocket and shrugged. "Hey, free food is free food."

"That's what I say," Mabel confirmed.

As they were walking across the parking lot back to the bunkhouse truck, a wave of dizziness came over Kaylen. She staggered, caught herself, and then felt a hand steadying her.

"Come on, now, girl. Don't be passin' out in the lot and givin' us carnies a worse name that what we got."

Relief swept over her at the sound of Fred's baritone. "It's alright. I just got a little dizzy there for a second."

"Uh huh. Come on, let's get you in the truck and get some food into you. You ain't nothin' but a rail, girly." He looked over a Mabel. "Yo, you made sure she drank water, right?"

"I look like a fool to you, Fred? Of course, she drank water. Drank damn near a whole gallon."

They reached the truck. Fred helped Kaylen into the back seat and handed her the bag of food and soda she almost dropped on the tarmac. "Eat up and then crash out, you want my advice. We got two hundred miles to roll and set up when we get there."

Kaylen nodded. She would eat because her body needed fuel, but she wasn't the least bit hungry. Right now her body was screaming for sleep, craving it. Mabel climbed in the front seat and Fred pulled out of the space, following the flatbed with all the equipment. This was the way shows traveled, caravan style, just like the gypsies and road troupes had been doing since the Roman days.

Kaylen chewed and swallowed, not tasting the food. She listened to Mabel and Fred gossip about people she hadn't met yet but would if she stuck around long enough. Her mind began to fog over as the scenery turned into a blur of various shades of green. She handed her half-full drink to Mabel to secure in one of the front seat cup holders, stretched out in the back seat and was asleep in two minutes.

Fred glanced at the rearview mirror and saw nothing but the front of the bunkhouse. "She finally out?"

Mabel glanced over into the back seat with a couple of fries sticking out of her mouth. "Down hard." When she spoke, one of the fries felt out of her mouth and into the backseat footwell.

"Dammit, Mabel, was you raised in barn? Lookit my truck."

She waved a hand. "Don't get grumpy. I'll sweep it out at the lot. I always do."

"Yeah, yeah. So, you think runnin' from the law or what?"

Mabel considered this. Having had her share of John Law occurrences, she was more than an expert in the field of avoidance. "I think so. She don't act like a runaway. Too wide around the eyes or somethin'."

"Think she did somethin' or somethin' done to her?"

"I can't tell. I should have got a hit off her. I ain't been on the pipe since last night and I'm pretty clear, but when she walked up all I got was nothin'."

"Nothin'?"

Mabel shrugged. "It was weird. I can usually get a glimpse, 'specially if they're worked up or tired and she was both, but when I peeked at her all I got was fog." It had been more than that, but even thinking about what she had felt when she peeked into Kaylen's mind made her want to get high and stay that way for good. When Mabel had peeked into Kaylen, something in that fog had peeked back.

CHAPTER 4

"What the good Christ have we got here, Slate?"

Slate looked up from the box of, for lack of a better word, trophies he had been sifting through. Chief Nickerson was standing in the open doorway of the little room tucked discretely in the corner of Lenoy's basement. The detective hadn't heard him approach because the entire room, even the floor, had been sound proofed. "We got a mess, Chief. You better call the FBI on this one. No way all these ladies are local."

He picked up the box, it was big, the kind a mid-sized kitchen appliance might come in and put it on the steel table in one corner of the room. The table had already been cleared by forensics. Chief Nickerson came to stand next to him while Slate poked through the box again.

It contained several pairs of women's panties, each labeled with a name and a photo of the lady unlucky enough to be wearing them when they encountered Mr. Lenoy. Cut sections of hair, both scalp and pubic, in plastic baggies, again labeled with a photo. At the bottom of the box were scrapbooks, small ones, each with a different woman's name on the cover, each with a chronological account of how Lenoy found them, caught them, brought them here and what he did to them. Each scrapbook contained a pictorial record of it all. The last page in each filled book described how and where he disposed of the body and included a picture of what was left. Looking at them reminded Slate of the science journals he used to read in grad school. The scrapbooks, like the house, were meticulous in their attention to detail.

After flipping through the second book, Chief Nickerson tossed it back into the box and turned away. "You ever see anything like this shit? The sick bastard recorded everything like some kind of Mengele experiment. Wasn't he afraid of getting caught?"

Slate put down the book he had been reading. The names, he decided, must be names Lenoy gave his victims. They were all fairytale princess names. "I think he was counting on it. These books would have been his get out of the death penalty card. They're an FBI profiler's wet dream. The feds would fight tooth and nail to put Lenoy in a safe, high security mental hospital where they could study him for years."

"There's our tax dollars at work. Wouldn't they know he'd only be fucking with them?"

Slate raised an eyebrow. "Even if they did, do you think they'd care?"

"Maybe not, but I sure as hell do. Those women, hell those girls, have families somewhere looking for them. They aren't hookers or runaways. Did you see the first picture of the blonde? That was one put together woman. Looked like a corporate lawyer or something."

"Airline comptroller actually. From Indianapolis. Don't know what her real name is, but he called her Rose, as in Briar Rose."

"Why is that familiar?"

"Sleeping beauty," Slate explained. "At least in one of the early versions of the story. Book says he drove to her apartment, grabbed her, drugged her, and drove her back here. Says the whole trip took him three days, most of it driving."

"So he was a patient sick fuck."

"Not just patient. He was smart. Harold, Lenoy could have gone on hunting for decades without getting caught and kept right on chewing the fat with Mrs. Wilson across the street and coaching little league while he did it." The thought chilled Slate. A wolf in sheep's clothing. No, a werewolf in a sport coat, the kind of monster that blends in, never stands out, keeps to himself. That is, until he came down to his little playpen and unleashed the beast on these poor women. What Slate had seen in the last pages of those books hadn't looked much different than what he had seen upstairs in the living room. Talk about an eye for an eye.

"But somebody must be looking for this woman, whoever she really is?"

"I'm sure we can ask Google and find out all about her. The thing is, she was living several states away and he moved fast. Too fast to make a mistake maybe."

"Well, I guess Bundy got away with it for a while. But you'd think with all the cameras and forensics and other fancy shit we have, somebody would have clued in to this fucker," Chief Nickerson growled.

Slate shrugged. "I said he was smart. And the easiest people to fool are the ones who know everything. You told me that when I came here."

Nickerson nodded. "I did, I remember. But this isn't some two-bit car thief or a hopped-up junkie breaking into people's houses for fast cash. These women had lives, Adam. They had jobs and homes and people who would look for them."

"I'm sure they did." *But that doesn't mean Lenoy wasn't slick*, Slate thought. His father used to say you couldn't beat a man at his craft. Lenoy and his chosen craft seemed to prove that rule emphatically.

Chief Nickerson took a deep breath. "How many books are in that box?"

"Eight in the box and he was working on a nineth. Guys found a book upstairs in his office. He had already found his nineth victim. Little redhead in Tucson."

"Arizona? That's a helluva long haul."

"She's pretty hot from what I've been told."

Nickerson shuddered. Slate remembered a line from an old movie, he thought it might have been the Ten Commandments with Charlton Heston. Something Biblical and epic in any case. That wasn't important, the line was the thing. 'Beauty,' some long-ago actress has stated, 'is but a curse to our women.' Slate thought the women who had seen this room would have felt the same way.

Chief Nickerson shook himself and took a deep breath. "Well, tragic as this all is, the feds'll take it over. And we can't get sidetracked. No matter how much he deserved it, we can't let some vigilante get away with murder, justified or not."

Slate nodded. "We're going over everything up there with a fine-toothed comb, Chief, but it's weird. Predators, especially serial ones like Lenoy, have a heightened state of awareness. An almost supernatural sixth sense about shit, it's what makes them so hard to collar."

"Your point?"

"If Lenoy was as good at what he did as he seemed to be, why would he open the door for another killer?"

The chief mulled that over for a minute or two. Slate let him take his time. Harold Nickerson wasn't the chief of police because people liked him, that was how he got the job, he kept it because he was smart. He was also a country man, born and raised, and he liked to look at things from every angle before passing judgement. "What if whoever did this went fishing?"

"Fishing?"

"Yeah, you said the boys found a new little notebook. What if you and Carter are kicking around the wrong theory? Lenoy might not have opened the door for a couple of guys wanting to tell him all about the Book of Mormon, but if a cute little number walked up wanting to use the phone or maybe get directions somewhere?" He let the thought sink in.

"And if he was already hunting someone he would have been in a hot stage." Slate let the idea roll around a little. Sure, that he could see. Not a couple or even three guys coming up to the door. A girl, slim like the others and needing help of some kind. A little cutie in cut-offs and flip flops. Hell, why not? Summer was on its way and the days were getting warm. Just enough of a lure to get in the front door. Maybe she had a can of mace or pepper spray or something. Maybe she had a gun. People could get anything these days. Just a 'hey, can I use your phone, my cell died' and in she would be. With his physique and predatory skills, Lenoy wouldn't have thought twice about letting her in. He wouldn't do anything, not to her, not with how methodical he was about his victims. But the thrill of having her in the house where he kept all his trophies hidden behind pictures, they had found several more, or under rugs, two photos under the foyer rug alone, would be enough enticement to let her in. And once she was in and had incapacitated or detained him somehow, all she would have to do was let in her accomplices through the back door. The back yard was fenced and very private. No one would have been the wiser if a couple of guys had hopped the fence and strolled in.

"I'll ask around if anyone remembers seeing a strange girl wandering around the past couple of days," Slate said. He was talking more to himself than to Chief Nickerson. "Maybe selling Mary Kay or organic shampoo or something. She would have been around more than once to get the lay of the land."

"Unless she was just some chick somebody paid to knock on the door and then walk away before the party started."

Slate shook his head. "In Tampa, yes. You could pay street girls to do damn near anything and they'd keep their mouths shut, but not here. This is a small town, your town. You know this place is about as quiet as a church social. Nothing happens here without half the grocery stores and all the salons knowing about it."

Chief Nickerson had to smile. It was true. "Alright, a stranger, but nobody too out of place or someone would have already said something, girl or not. Someone wandering around this neighborhood would get noticed."

"Which means she couldn't have been selling anything." Again, Slate spoke to himself. "Someone comes to your door, then goes next door, then on down the block, you talk about it. Mention she's pushing lip gloss or whatever to your neighbor. Maybe you notice her moving from door to door while you're getting the mail or washing the car."

"No one said anything about someone like that?"

Slate shook his head. "If they did Carter didn't mention it." He tried not to convey the way he felt about Carter's ineptitude while performing police work and failed miserably.

"Look, I know you two don't see eye to eye, but Carter is a decent cop," Chief Nickerson explained patiently. It was not the first time he had given this speech to either man. "If people started telling him and the boys they saw some chick walking around, he would have mentioned it. Maybe not to you, but I talked to him on my way down here and he didn't mention anything."

Conceding the point, Slate moved on. "I'll talk to that Wilson lady myself though, just in case. Sometimes people need a little memory jog."

"If you're going to do anything, do it fast. I'm going to call the Bureau and you know how they are about territory." Chief Nickerson conveyed all his disgust on the word *Bureau*.

"You gonna hand this over without a fight, boss?" Slate fought hard to hide his disappointment. With women from out of state, they had to call the feds, but Slate had never had a good experience with government employees in his line of work.

"It's the easiest way for you to get free rein, if you're careful." The Chief turned away to go make his phone call. He paused in the doorway and turned back. "Remember Slate, the easiest man to fool is the one who already knows everything."

Slate thought about this as the chief walked away. The problem was, he didn't know anything and so had no idea where to look first. How could a girl subdue Lenoy for one thing? Sex was the obvious answer but a sweep of the bedroom showed nothing had happened in there since the last time Lenoy did laundry. Mace or pepper spray made sense if you were dealing with the average criminal, but a serial murderer who kidnapped his victims, raped and tortured them for days before killing them, dismembering the bodies and hiding the remains? He just couldn't accept that. And the untouched foyer didn't hold with a mace attempt. That shit burned and whoever got a face full would have taken out all the decorative furniture and half the framed pictures.

Although, they never would have caught Ted Bundy if his tail light hadn't gone out, Slate thought as he followed Chief Nickerson upstairs.

CHAPTER 5

Kaylen stretched in the camp chair Roger had loaned her and stared up at a star jeweled sky. Her body ached in about a million places and she was so tired she could barely raise her head, but she was content for the moment and that was something. They were fed and quiet; she was fed and clean.

After the show reached the next lot, Kaylen had helped unpack everything and set-up the tent and the ring and the seats and everything else a circus needed. She hadn't helped with the rigging but was intrigued by it as always. She stopped in her own work several times to watch the riggers hang lights, trapezes, ropes and equipment for other various aerial acts, safety lines, and cables. She had wanted to learn how to rig when she was on the show last summer, but by the time the guys agreed to teach her, the show was bust.

While the crew set up, Fred got started on dinner and by the time everything was in place he was ringing the bell. Kaylen hadn't had much appetite earlier but she had two big helpings at dinner, amazing both Mabel and Roger with her capacity for spaghetti. They had talked and laughed about trivial things, no one going into any detail about anything. That was something Kaylen loved about these shows, you only had to tell enough to get by, nobody wanted the whole story. After all, when you hired the outcasts of polite society how much truth did you expect to get?

When dinner was finished, the crew took turns taking showers in the bunk trailer. The trailer had three small living compartments with two bunks each and a much bigger living compartment up front in the gooseneck. The trailer also had a shower setup crammed between two of the compartments for the crew's use.

Mabel was down a roomie so she offered Kaylen the bottom bunk in her compartment. All the compartments had storage for various belongings as long as you didn't have much. Kaylen didn't even have a toothbrush so she was okay in that regard. Hot plates weren't allowed because according to Roger one night some idiot had almost caught the trailer on fire while trying to make a grilled cheese or something, but you could have a microwave if you bought your own. Too many items had been stolen over the years and the show owners got tired of replacing them.

Since Kaylen was sparse on everything and would be unless she could hitch a ride into town in the morning, Mabel had offered her a set of clean clothes to put on after her shower. She also shared her toiletries with Kaylen to a certain degree. Kaylen would knock her own teeth out before sharing anything that had been in Mabel's mouth. She would just have to put up with dirty teeth and bad breath until she could get her hands on a new toothbrush.

Now she was sitting in a camp chair listening the others joke and boast while they were circled around a briskly burning campfire. They had traveled two hundred miles north and the night still held the chill of winter here. Kaylen didn't mind though. Her feet had finally dried and her shoes were drying by the fire and that was all she cared about. She was warm enough in her hoodie anyway.

Mabel hadn't waited long after they settled for the night before producing her pipe and works. She was rather controlled for a meth addict and Kaylen wondered at this until she noticed all the others seemed conservative in their vices as well.

She looked over at Fred, sitting to her right and smoking an impressively large joint. "Hey Fred, how do you guys keep your addictions in check?"

Speaking this line anywhere else would have caused a shocked silence followed by a lot of loud accusations and denials. Here everyone just kept doing what they were doing. They were all addicts in their way, including Kaylen.

"Have to, girly. Don't ever know when the boss is gonna park us somewhere that we can stock up. Good thing to keep prepared in case of emergencies."

Being prepared and an addict sounded like an oxymoron to Kaylen, but there were plenty of functioning alcoholics who went to work on Wall Street every day of the week, so who was she to judge? "Do you think we'll get into town tomorrow or should I hitch a ride? I need stuff like toothpaste and deodorant."

"I wondered what that smell was," Roger chirped. He and Mabel were passing a crack pipe back and forth.

"Why don't you do me a favor and fuck off?" Kaylen said smiling sweetly.

"Oh damn, girly got some balls on her," Fred laughed. He choked on smoke and got coughing.

That got Kaylen laughing. Being normal like this always took Kaylen by surprise. It only happened after they were sated and never for long. Pretty soon, long before they started their keening, she would start worrying about how to get them fed. It would be worse this time because she had almost gotten caught the last time. But that was worry for later. Right now, she wanted to enjoy a night with people who were too screwed up themselves to pass judgement on anyone else.

"Stop calling me girly," Kaylen gasped when she could talk again. "I have a name."

"Yeah? And I bet you're smart enough to know not to use it too much if you're lying low," Fred commented. He waved a hand. "Ain't nobody here using their real names." He pointed at Mabel and Roger. "Look here. That's Unstable Mabel and Roger Rabbit so watch out for him." He continued around the circle. "That's Trips 'cause he used to drop acid, Tony as in Soprano. Thinks he's part of the fuckin' mafia."

"Yo, I done told you my old man was in the Family."

Fred waved this away and continued. "Donna as in Summer 'cause she's the disco queen when she's been drinkin' and that skinny fella is Edward as in Scissorhands on account of he's so thin and pale. Me? I'm Fred as in Flintstone. Favorite cartoon." He looked back at Kaylen. "So, what you want us to call you, girly?"

"I'm not particular. I'm sure y'all will come up with somethin'. Just not girly."

"I'll think about it," Fred said solemnly, garnering another round of laughter.

"He'll give you a good one," Mabel confided. "He named all us."

"So, you're like the black godfather of the circus or something like that?" Kaylen asked. She was starting to feel dizzy from all the mixed smoke in the air.

"Something like that. You want a hit?"

Kaylen waved away the offered joint. She didn't mind it now and then, especially when the keening got bad, but tonight she was happy just for silence in her head and in her bones. "I'm happy to sit here and listen to you guys. It's been a long time since I was invited into the group."

"Well, that's what makes us so great," Roger exclaimed. He spread his arms wide and nearly knocked Mabel out of her chair. "We're all so fucked up we can't judge anybody else."

"I'll drink to that," Donna said, raising her glass.

They all raised their various drinks. "To the Circus Crew of Fucked Up Outcasts," Roger toasted. They all drank to that.

#

The next morning Kaylen was helping Tony scrub down the concession trailer when Fred sauntered over. "Hey, Rails, want a ride into town?"

Tony and Kaylen both looked over, not knowing who Fred was talking to. "You want her or me?" Tony asked.

Fred gave him a cool look. "If I wanted you, I would have said Tony get your white ass in the truck."

"Guess that means I got a new name." Kaylen handed her rag to Tony.

He shrugged. "Fits good. You're skinny as a rail. Maybe blow apart if you sneeze too hard."

Kaylen flipped him off and followed Fred to the truck they had driven yesterday. She was wearing Mabel's clothes and small as the other woman was, the jeans kept sliding down Kaylen's almost nonexistent hips making her hitch them up every few strides. The shirt fit okay but it had several holes and Kaylen was afraid of tearing it further if she moved too fast.

"I thought you said Marco said no leaving on a show day?" Kaylen asked as they pulled off the lot.

"That only applies to rousties workin' the show. Since you ain't got nothin' to do yet, I figured today would be the only time for you to do some shopping." He gave her a stern look. "You got cash? I'll spot you some only because Marco will pay me what you owe before he pays you. It won't be much though. He never pays full until you're here at least three towns."

"I've got enough to get me started if you take me to Wal-Mart."

"Poor man's Macy's."

"Hey, Fred?"

"Yes."

Kaylen knew what she wanted to ask, but didn't know exactly how to phrase it. People, especially men she had learned, had very firm ideas about others staying in their place. Since she didn't have a place yet, Kaylen figured it would be a good time to ask about finding her own spot. "Do you think any of the riggers would want to teach me?"

"How to hang, you mean?"

"No, how to perform the perfect blow job." She waited for him to stop laughing before continuing. "I'm serious. I climb really good and I'm strong. I can lift my own body weight with no problem." Well, maybe not today, but once her muscles stopped complaining about yesterday's exertions she could.

Fred considered. "We talkin' straight?"

"Sure."

"In that case it'll be a while. They'll teach you. Hell, Jack's the best rigger I've ever seen, but rigging is a trust job. You'll be hanging shit that could cause a bad accident or even kill someone if you do it wrong, you dig?"

Kaylen nodded. She dug it alright. And she was the newcomer, the stranger. It would take a while for her to build enough trust for someone to show her the ropes, literally.

"I don't have any plans."

"Alright. Then my advice is: don't ask about hanging, don't even bring it up. Rigging pays twice what setup does and that's the first thing they'll think of. They'll think you want more money and won't care about doing it right. You'll probably start with concessions. Everybody who wants extra cash does. They won't let you around the tills for a while, but they'll let you run the stands. They can keep a count that way, find out if you're chipping. You know how it is in this business if you worked it before."

Kaylen sighed. "You're right. Last summer I worked for two months before I could wear the rigging guys down. Then the owner broke up the show so it didn't matter. I've done concessions before and run the stands. I've papered towns and set arrows too. That's how I found you guys. I followed the arrows."

"Didn't you see the signs up in town?"

There was a choice to be made here. Kaylen could lie and say she had but didn't think much about them at the time or she could tell a version of the truth. If she lied, Fred wouldn't question it, but she thought somehow he'd know. Like when he had been right there when she almost fainted in the parking lot. And Mabel. This morning without even asking, Mabel had known Kaylen didn't like coffee creamer. She hadn't even asked. She had set a cup of black coffee in front of Kaylen and said, 'here you go, sugar, black just like you like it' and walked away on her own business. These people were different. Not just broken, but different. It would be unwise to lie any more than she had to. "I saw the arrows on the road. When I was walking away from town."

There was a significant pause before Fred said, "Fair enough. This trouble you're in, is it coming for you?"

She didn't bother to ask how he knew she was in trouble. He did and that was the point. "I don't know. I hope not. What happened was my fault, yes, but not all my fault. I don't think anyone would believe it though."

"How bad?"

"Bad enough that I only stopped by my room long enough to grab some cash and then booked it cross country on foot."

He whistled. "Okay, we can keep you low for a while and send people away if they come looking, but only until they get pushy. Don't take this wrong but just 'cause you joined the campfire jamboree don't make you family."

"I understand." She did too, more than Fred ever would. What she was, what she had, was a deal that kept her safe but also kept her alone. Fuck all that Avengers and Justice League bullshit. The power to choose life and death didn't make lifelong friends. It made lifelong chains and razor wire topped fences keeping you and everybody else separated forever.

Perhaps feeling guilty, Fred reached over and patted her knee. "Sorry, honey, it's just how it has to be."

"It's okay, Fred. This trouble is mine own and I don't want anyone to get hurt by it."

"Kipling reference. Nice. An educated fugitive. I like it. By the way," he added as they pulled into the Wal-Mart parking lot. "You might want to get some antiseptic and Band-Aids for that knee."

Kaylen waited until they were walking to the store before asking, "How did you know about my knee?"

"Mabel told me," he said off-handedly. "I got a ton of groceries to buy. Just wait for me here or outside when you get done." He freed a cart from its mates and walked in the direction of the grocery section.

Frowning, Kaylen obtained her own cart and headed for pharmacy. Mabel told him? But how would Mabel know. Kaylen had changed clothes in the shower compartment and had slept with all her clothes on so Mabel couldn't have seen her knee. She would have noticed Kaylen's ripped jeans yesterday but the hole wasn't big enough to show the scraped skin underneath.

These questions nagged at her while she bought necessities. Toiletries and a bag to store them in were first, then a backpack to give her an idea of how much she could carry if she had to depart in a hurry. Next came underwear, sports bras, socks, a pack of cotton shirts, long-sleeved of course, and a couple pairs of jeans. She added a pair of cheap flip flops for the shower. The only extravagances she gave herself was a pair of good work boots and a heavy jacket. Her sneakers were almost new but after dropping a side pole on her foot during set up she knew sturdier footwear was a necessity and her hoodie wouldn't be much help if it got any colder. She also bought a cheap pillow and a blanket. While walking to the checkout she saw that clean wipes were on sale and grabbed a couple of containers. Those she could leave behind but she wanted very badly to wipe down her bunk before using it again after Mabel mentioned that when she didn't have a roommate she used either bunk depending on her mood.

Kaylen was sitting outside, enjoying the sun and people watching when Fred came out pushing one cart and pulling another. "I could have helped if you'd have told me to come look for you," she said when she saw him.

He reached into a bag and pulled out a faded blue baseball cap with a picture of Joe Cool on the front and stuffed it on her head. "Thought you could use one of these during teardowns if it starts to rain."

"And I'm sure Snoopy will endear me to everyone," Kaylen said dryly. Then she smiled. "Thanks. And I remembered Band-Aids." They started walking to the truck.

"Hope you got some good shoes."

"Boots and a jacket. I told you, I've done this before." She reached back and helped pull the food-ladened cart he was tugging along behind. "Do you always shop like this?"

"I have to. This is one of the biggest crews we've had in a while and I plan on keeping 'em well-fed while they're here. Helps keep them around longer." He gave her a look. "You get snacks and water and stuff? I know that little fridge in Mabel's compartment has got to be empty."

"Water for me and Mountain Dew for Mabel," she added with a shudder. "That stuff is pure sugar and it looks like battery acid."

Fred started loading the groceries. "They like it cause it helps with the meth cravings."

"Really?"

"It must. They all drink that shit."

"Huh." She started handing Fred items so he could store them. "I got a few snacks for me, but I don't eat much."

"We've all noticed."

They got the truck packed, put the carts in their little corral and loaded back up. "Hey, can we go through a drive-thru or something?" Kaylen asked.

"My cookin' not good enough for you?"

"It's fine. I'm just starving right now is all. I was going to get something in there but the precooked chicken looked highly questionable."

"Didn't look done?"

"Didn't look like chicken."

Fred roared laughter at that. "Tell you what, girly, you keep me laughing like that and I'll make sure the riggers teach you how to climb."

"I thought my name was Rails?"

"Keep eating all this junk food and I might have to change your name to Roll, as in jelly."

CHAPTER 6

"Are you sure you don't want any more tea? Cookies?"

Detective Slate smiled his most charming smile and put a hand over his tea cup. "No, really Mrs. Wilson, I couldn't."

The older woman shook her head and tsked. "Suit yourself, but if you ask me, you could use a little more meat on your bones." She sat on the sofa opposite him and smoothed her skirt. "I don't know what else I can say. I told that young officer everything I saw yesterday." She shook her head. "Terrible, that someone like that could have been living right across the street all this time. He seemed like such a nice young man, even if I we did think he was, you know, a little queer."

"We?"

"Me and Moira from next door. You should talk to her too. She lost her George not long after my Sam passed. We were friends before but after you've suffered the same losses it's nice to have someone who understands what you've been through." She lowered her voice. "She was the one mentioned Martin never had any lady friends over."

"That's what I want to ask you about, Mrs. Wilson." Part of being a good detective, Slate knew, was letting people prattle on for a while. Usually that was when you got the best information because people who babbled often forgot to lie. "Did you see a young lady around the neighborhood the last couple days or so? Or maybe a young couple?"

She thought about it. "Well, there's Kimmy Thompson. She's had a fellow around pretty regular. But she lives down the block and she's a good girl. Grew up here." She paused. "I did see a couple of boys last week. They were chumming with Walter McCoy two doors down."

"How old would you say they were?"

"Oh, they couldn't have done anything. They're just kids. Walter's only fourteen this year and they looked about the same age."

Fourteen was plenty old enough to commit murder, but Slate doubted Lenoy would have let a group of young teenage boys into his house. Before coming over this morning, Slate had read the reports from the first canvas. Almost every person interviewed had said Martin Lenoy was friendly and kept his place up nice, but he didn't entertain much. And no one had mentioned ever seeing a lady friend at his house. The consensus was that Lenoy was a closet gay who was afraid of persecution in small town suburbia.

"I agree, that's a little too young to commit murder. I'm more interested in a stranger. Maybe someone selling make up or cookies or something like that door to door?"

Mrs. Wilson sat back and looked out the large bay window that showed an impressive rose garden. After a few minutes she said, "I'm sorry. I can't think of anyone. We don't get many salespeople anymore since the Internet."

"I'm sure, but we have very strong reasons to believe whoever did this was an outsider. Somebody who had a plan."

"Was he really what they say he was?" Mrs. Wilson breathed.

Here was one of the problems of a small town. Even though the chief had told everyone on the force to keep his or her mouth shut, Nickerson knew word was already spreading about what they had found in the basement. You couldn't keep secrets in a small town. You might as well try to keep the wind from blowing. The first slip probably came from the officer who found the play room in the first place. From him it would have spread like lice in a kindergarten class. By morning the phones had been ringing off the hook at the station and Sylvia had been hearing all kinds of wild stories. People were calling Lenoy everything from Norman Bates to Hannibal Lecter. As far as the scrapbooks had shown, Lenoy had never eaten any part of his victims, but little details like the truth never got in the way of good gossip.

"What are they saying, Mrs. Wilson?"

"That he was some kind of monster. That he kidnapped those women and cut them up and did things to them." She shuddered.

"All I can say officially is it appears Martin Lenoy was a serial rapist and murderer. We haven't found any of the bodies yet because we have been told by the FBI to wait for their forensic teams."

"The FBI? That sounds serious."

And it's a plump piece of gossip, Detective Slate thought, *you'll want me out of here soon so you can call up Moira and get the mill grinding all over again.* He shrugged. "They have access to a lot more equipment than we do. And none of the women were from in state. The feds can cut through the red tape a lot quicker than we can."

"Such a monster in our little town." She brightened suddenly. "If it's a stranger you're looking for, why don't you ask Jurgen?"

"Karl Jurgen?" He made a note. "Why would he know someone?"

"He rents out that room he's got over the garage. He says he keeps the room for anybody but we all know it's the girls he caters to."

This was just the kind of information Slate had been hoping for. He had realized last night that whoever had killed Lenoy must have been staying in town somewhere. He had been on the phone all morning calling the few local motels. None of the them were doing much business right now in the off season and every person he spoke to assured him that the people staying in the motel were just passing through. Even so, Slate had sent a couple of uniforms to talk to the staff and the patrons face to face. He had completely forgotten about Karl Jurgen on Park Street.

Jurgen was a sixtyish bachelor who owned the hardware store. He did have an efficiency apartment above his garage and he did rent it out on occasion, but Slate found it hard to believe whoever had killed Lenoy would have rented an apartment. From what Slate knew, Jurgen wouldn't rent for any time less than a month.

"This girl wouldn't have been alone. She would have had a boyfriend or husband." *Or someone posing as one*, he thought but didn't add.

Mrs. Wilson waved a hand. "He likes the girls but he likes money more. He'd rent to a couple."

Detective Slate stood up. "Thank you, Mrs. Wilson. You've been more help than you thought. This at least gives me a starting point."

She rose with him and saw him to the door. "I know you have to do your job, Detective Slate, but if you want my opinion, whoever killed that monster did the world a favor."

He paused on her front step. "I'm sure the families of his victims would agree with you, but we still can't condone vigilante justice. If the persons who did this had suspicions or evidence they should have come to the police."

Mrs. Wilson eyed him with all the experience of her seventy plus years. "What makes you think they didn't? You always hear about cases where the cops say if they had just listened to that one person, they could have caught the guy before he killed again."

Detective Slate sighed. Unfortunately, she was right. Plenty of perps had walked free for weeks if not years because law enforcement refused to listen to peoples' suspicions or, in some cases, outright witness accounts of a crime. "I'm well aware of that ma'am, but they didn't talk to me."

"You would have listened?"

"I would."

"What if the person voicing their suspicions was junkie or a prostitute? Would you listen then?"

It was a fair question. And one he hated having to answer because he knew it would be a lie. He looked directly at Mrs. Wilson. "I would listen."

"I bet you tell yourself that when you look in the mirror while you're shaving in the morning." She stepped back into the house and closed the door.

What the hell was that all about? Slate thought as he walked back to his car. It was normal for the public to sympathize with vigilantes, especially if they took out a particularly bad apple. It was this empathy that made it difficult to prosecute a vigilante. And making such an arrest always came down hard on the police department. But laws were in place for a reason. So, somebody whacks a murderer, then where does it stop? Do clerks get to take pot shots at shoplifters? Does lynching make a comeback? Angry people making irreversible decisions based on emotion instead of evidence?

Slate put the car in drive and headed toward Park Street. No, he was a detective. It was his job to make sure he caught the bad guys. The right bad guys. He was man enough to admit plenty of cops were assholes and the precincts saw their fair share of corruption, but there were good cops too. Cops who really did believe in protecting the public and seeing justice prevail. He had and did work alongside men and women who would gladly take a bullet to protect an innocent. Too bad the media didn't hype those people or stories. The only thing the news wanted to report was when someone fucked up.

Knowing these thoughts would lead him down a dark path far away from the case he was working, Detective Slate made a conscious effort to focus his mind on how the killer had gotten into the house. She or they must have gone in through the back because there were too many eyes on the street. He had hoped Lenoy had a security system with cameras, but like most murders, he was confident in his superiority. A serial killer wasn't concerned about things like home invasion.

A scenario was beginning to form in Slate's mind. The girl or woman had come up to the back door with some kind of story to get into the house. She would have had to walk through the back gate but that wasn't a problem. There was an alley behind Lenoy's place and it was clearly a major thruway for neighborhood kids. Candy wrappers and empty soda cans had littered the lane. The gate in Lenoy's back fence hadn't been locked and it had been dusted for prints but so far the only ones they had found were Lenoy's. Of course, everyone knew if you wanted to commit a crime, you wore gloves.

So, she comes in through the back gate, walks up to the back door and says, for lack of anything better, her cell died and she needs to use the phone. Lenoy lets her in, maybe to keep up his friendly reputation, maybe because she's cute, and then what? She blasts him with mace? Zaps him with a taser? Where was she keeping it? In either case, he would have knocked something down.

The back door was sequestered in a tiny mudroom off the kitchen. This room contained a row of hooks with various yard implements. Hand clippers, a rake, a small shovel; things that would make a lot of mess if a guy got a face full of pepper spray. Next to the opening leading to the kitchen was yet another small table. Instead of flowers, this one held a bowl full of keys. If Lenoy had staggered back in that tiny space, those keys would have been everywhere. So, what, whoever axed the guy did a little house cleaning before they left? Not likely.

Jurgen's place was up on the left. His pick-up was in the driveway. It was Sunday and the hardware store was closed but that didn't mean the man would be home. Slate had heard enough fishing stories when he needed something for his house to know Karl's favorite pastime. The man spent nearly every free moment down at Clark's Brook. Of course, that could have less to do with fishing and more to do with a certain middle-aged divorcee that had bought a house down by the bridge last summer. As far as Slate was concerned, as long as they were happy and staying out of trouble people should get it where they could.

Karl was walking out of his house as Detective Slate parked behind his pick-up truck. "What can I do ya for, Detective?"

"I was hoping you could help with that mess we got down the street." Slate got out of his car and leaned back against it.

"Don't know how I could. I was at the store all day yesterday and I hardly ever get to that side of town. Heard all about it though."

"I'm sure everybody has heard something."

"Small town livin'," Karl grinned. He sobered. "Was he as bad as they say?"

"Worse. He was a serial predator. Took girls from all around the country."

"How the hell did he do it without anyone noticing? Thelma Wilson is like the FBI and the CIA combined. Nothin' gets by that woman."

"He had a soundproof room in his basement. If they were drugged and secured in his car, he could have driven right into the garage and no one would have been the wiser."

Karl sighed heavily. "Still. How could he be that evil and no-body knew?"

"Bundy was a nice guy as far as anyone was concerned. As long as you weren't a tall brunette."

"You know people are going to start up with how come none of the boys and girls in blue clued into that guy." He gave Slate a sidelong look. "Gonna be a lot of heat when the feds get here."

"Word travels fast. How do you know about that and Mrs. Wilson didn't?" They were getting off subject, sort of, but it was never bad to know the pulse of your town.

"Had coffee with Harold this morning. He's in a bad way about this."

"He's taking it personal. I told him no one knew about Lenoy. That he was good at hiding, predators are. It's what makes them the hunter and not the prey."

"Somebody knew what Martin was," Karl observed.

Slate nodded. "That's what I wanted to talk to you about. I think whoever nailed Lenoy was casing him for a while."

"Harold said it was pretty gruesome."

"Chief was right. Anyway, it had to be done by more than one person, but a man like Lenoy wouldn't let just anybody in and-,"

"And you were thinkin' maybe the someone was renting from me?"

Slate nodded. "All the motels claim their customers couldn't have done it, but we're double-checking to be sure. Mrs. Wilson suggested maybe you had someone here I might want to talk to."

Karl scratched his chin. "I am rentin' to a little girl right now. She's paid through the month so I imagine she's around somewhere. She's just a slip of a girl though, not really what I'd call the killin' type."

Slate pulled out his notebook. "She got a name?"

"Most people do. Her's is Kaylen."

Slate waited. When it seemed Karl wasn't going to offer anything else, he prompted, "Kaylen what?"

"Just Kaylen. Look, Adam, I rent the place for cash and don't ask a lot of questions. I keep a revolver by my bed and check the room from time to time."

"Don't you have them sign a waiver or something? Something to protect you in case someone falls down the stairs and breaks an arm or something?"

Karl shrugged. "I can get a pretty good read on people. Some of them I do make sign a waiver. Some I don't. I didn't with this girl because she was in some kind of trouble and it showed. She was runnin' from somethin'. She wasn't gonna sue nobody."

Knowing better than to get into a pissing contest with a man who thought he was protecting a damsel in distress, Slate veered the conversation away from questionable renting practices. "She around right now? I want to ask her some questions."

Karl crossed his arms. "I said she ain't the killin' type."

"I didn't say she was, but someone might have paid her to help them get into Lenoy's house." Slate held out his hands. "Help me out here, Karl. I just want to talk to her. I'm not gonna arrest her or anything."

The other man thought it over. "Alright, but I want to be there when you talk to her unless she asks me to leave."

It was the best he could hope for without pulling the authority card, so Slate nodded. He could read people too. If he got a weird vibe off this chick he'd just keep an eye on her until he could get her alone and then take her for a ride down to the station. This man wasn't just some random guy in a big city; he was a staple of the community and someone Slate would be doing business with for years to come. Slate didn't want to make an enemy out of him.

"Come on, follow me."

The two men walked up the outer stairs to the apartment above the garage. Karl pulled out his keyring and selected the proper key. He was reaching for the knob when he paused. "That's odd."

"What?" Slate asked from behind him.

"Door's open."

Slate slid in front of Karl, drawing his sidearm. "Stay behind me."

"You don't think she's hurt, do you?" Worry etched deep lines in Karl's face.

Slate didn't answer. He edged the door open with his foot and made a quick sweep of the room beyond. A combination living room and kitchen. Another door was wide open and directly across from him. He could see a neatly made bed. No signs of a struggle. No signs that anyone was around either. The apartment had an abandoned feeling and Slate holstered his handgun. He walked into the room and moved aside to let Karl in.

"Doesn't look like she went far. That's her backpack in the corner there." Karl pointed to a tattered backpack flung in the corner by the television. The pack may have started out dark blue, but it was faded to a shade of denim. Slate picked it up and began going through its pockets.

"Are you sure you can do that? Don't you need a warrant or something?"

Slate shrugged. "Door was open and it's obvious she isn't around. I consider this abandoned property." He looked at Karl. "I won't take anything if it makes you feel better."

Karl hmphed and walked into the bedroom. Not finding anything of importance in the backpack, Slate put it back on the floor and followed Karl.

The bedroom wasn't much help either. A quick look through the small dresser showed socks, underwear, a few bras, a couple pairs of jeans, and some t-shirts. A heavy jacket was the one item hanging in the closet. The bathroom held various toiletries but nothing that would help identify this girl. No prescriptions or even over the counter items like allergy medicine or pain killers. Whoever rented this room was used to living as much off the grid as possible. It gave Slate a disquieting feeling.

"How long did she rent from you?" He was looking at the neat way the bed was made. It reminded him of hotel beds. The room was like a hotel room. Clean, with minimal clutter on any surface. It was this observation that led Slate to believe she had worked as an off the books maid somewhere.

"Last month up to now. She paid in cash and she paid up front." Karl was scratching his chin and looking at the dresser.

"What is it?"

"That dresser isn't sitting right." He pointed. "See, the indentations in the carpet are a little off."

Pulling on a pair of gloves, he tried to keep an extra pair in his pocket during investigations, Slate moved the dresser away from the wall. A manila envelope fell from where it had been hidden behind the dresser. Slate opened it up and poked through the contents. "There must be three grand here."

"She'll be back then," Karl said confidently.

Slate wasn't so sure. The room felt like it was already forgotten, something in the past. Nothing was out of place in here except the open front door. Who walked out of a place with three grand hidden behind a dresser and left the door open? Someone running who wasn't planning on coming back, of course. Slate felt his stomach drop at the thought of the money. Someone who could leave that much behind would be hard to find. Clearly, this girl knew how to get by on nothing. And just because they found three thousand dollars didn't mean she hadn't taken a significant amount with her.

He needed to go back to the station and think about his next move. Meanwhile, Karl was looking at him. "What are you going to do with that?"

"For now, I'm going to put it back, give her a chance to come back and get it. I am going to take a few things out of the bathroom though, so that we can get a fingerprint or two and try to figure out who this girl is." He went back into the bathroom to gather a few items.

"I'll lock the place up. Could be she stayed over with a fella or something."

"And left the door open?"

Karl shrugged. "Young people get excited and forget things, Adam. You were young too not so long ago."

The two men went back into the living area. Slate looked at the kitchen, cleaned up and waiting for the next occupant. "How well do you know her?"

"I try to give my tenants their privacy," Karl said hotly.

"I didn't say you didn't. What I want to know is what kind of feel you got from her. Did she seem like a runaway or maybe she was in trouble with the law or something? You said she was in trouble. Did she act like she had something to hide?"

Karl thought about it. "She's a nice girl. Polite, but not overly friendly. She doesn't act flighty, but she's cautious. Didn't keep the shades drawn or only go out at night or anything like that, but she has an edge to her." He shrugged. "Yeah, I'd say she was hiding something. Or hiding from something."

"Abusive boyfriend maybe?"

Karl shrugged again. "Maybe. Wasn't my place to pry."

Accepting the stalemate, Slate asked, "She mention a job?"

"Nope. But I never asked either. She went somewhere most days though; she didn't just bum around here."

"She must have gotten money somehow and cash like that screams waitress."

"Had to be somewhere close if she was waitin' tables. She didn't have a car or even a bicycle." Karl thought for a minute. "She could have picked up a few shifts at Millie's or Frostie's. They're both close enough to walk."

"I'll try Frostie's first. That's a lot of cash to get from tips at a breakfast and lunch place and given the way Millie is with her girls I doubt she'd hire a stranger even if it was for cash." Slate was back at his car, eager to be gone. He had wanted to go back to the office and think, but it was still a while before noon, the perfect time to ask around the local watering hole in private.

Karl was standing a few paces away. "I know you got a job to do, Detective, but if Martin was as bad as everyone says he was, why don't you let this girl go? Sounds like she did the world a favor."

Slate got into his car. "I wish I could Karl, but you know it doesn't work that way."

"It don't, but sometimes maybe it should."

Slate backed out of the driveway without comment. The truth was, sometimes it did. A lot of times, actually. And this one would be easy to let go.

Here was girl with no identification, no ties, no concern about money, who had rented a room in a town where a serial killer just happened to reside and one night she just happened to what, exactly? Turn into a werewolf and rip the guy apart? It was looking more and more like she had been there alone and Slate had only gotten on her trail because he was working on a hunch. Who was to say whatever federal idiot they sent to clean up this mess would act on the same intuition? As far as his own office was concerned, it was a random attack and the killer may never be found and plenty of his coworkers, not to mention townspeople it seemed, were perfectly okay with that, so why couldn't he let this girl go back to wherever she came from?

"Because I want to know how you did it," he said aloud at a red light. That was the bottom line. How had she done it? Karl himself stated that she was just a little thing. How could a slip of a girl overpower a maniac and rip him up like that?

Slate realized as he drove through the intersection that he didn't give a shit about the why, people had all sorts of whys and he'd heard almost every variation. He wanted the how. How had she found out about Lenoy in the first place? How had she gotten in? How had she killed him in such spectacular fashion and then how had she gotten out? All without anyone on that street noticing her, a stranger, wandering in their midst. Why not just make an anonymous phone call? It was true that most went un-investigated no matter what cops said on camera. They had to deal with more than their fair share of crackpots, but if she had persisted someone would have taken a ride over to Lenoy's. It would have spooked him, put him on his guard, a random check like that. He would have been more cautious, maybe not hunted for a while, try to find out where he had slipped, who had found him out.

"And then he might have gotten the drop on her," Slate muttered. That made sense as to why she wouldn't have called the police. It was the same reason many battered women didn't go to the cops. That's logic. Go to a place where people are supposed to protect you, find out all they can do is slap a restraining order on the guy who's been using you as a punching bag, which would piss him right the fuck off and then you end up in the emergency room or the morgue because now the bastard has nothing to lose. What a fantastic idea.

Slate shook his head as he parked in front of Frostie's. No, if the lady under suspicion had any sense at all she wouldn't draw attention to herself.

Jack Kennedy, like the president, stood behind the bar with a remote, channel surfing. He gave Slate a rueful grin. "Want a beer? I just put out all the glasses."

"Little early in the day, don't you think?" Slate slid onto the stool closest to Jack.

"For a cop? Never. I get beat cops in here twenty minutes af-ter I open. Of course, they've been on the night shift so this is like their downtime." He left the t.v. on some talk show with the volume turned way down and leaned on the bar. The room was mostly empty. Lunch was still an hour away and the only person in the place was a diehard who was drinking a beer at the far end of the bar and talking to a bored looking waitress. "If you ain't drinkin' what do you want at this early hour?"

"I need to ask about a girl."

Jack raised an eyebrow. "What makes you think I can hook you up with the kind of 'girl' you need?"

Slate waved a hand. "Be serious, Jack." He lowered his voice. "This has to do with that murder yesterday."

"Good riddance to the freak is what I say. He didn't get any of my girls, did he?"

"No one local that we know of and the girl I'm asking about isn't a victim. You haven't had anybody in here the last couple weeks or so working off the books, have you? Karl Jurgen says she's small, kinda quiet."

"What's she got to do with Lenoy?" Jack crossed his arms over his chest. Slate noted the protective stance and began to tread more carefully. What was it about this girl that made everyone he talked to immediately run to her aid?

"Nothing I'm going to discuss here." He gave a sidelong glance at the waitress and her patron. "I just want to know if she worked here and what her story is. Karl said she rented that apartment of his for a month or so, but she's not there now and it doesn't look like she's coming back. Left her stuff and a substantial amount of cash. That's not the kind of person who's going to be easy to locate so right now I just want to get a feel for her."

Jack leaned back against the counter behind him. "You're not gonna sic the feds on her, are you? 'Cause I'm pretty sure she's got problems enough without that shit."

'She's in trouble', Karl had said. Here was confirmation. "I don't plan on helping the feds any more than I have to. If they pick up her trail on their own that's fine with me but I don't intend to point them in this direction. This is my case."

Nodding, Jack said, "Fair enough. She came in here about a month or so ago looking for open shifts. Didn't want nothin' permanent, she was up front about that from the start, but said she wanted to make a few bucks while she stayed in town."

Slate made notes, then asked, "You didn't ask her for identification by any chance, did you?"

Jack shrugged. "Honestly? I thought she'd stick around a day or two, get enough cash to go get high and then I wouldn't see her until she needed her next hit."

"You always hire like that?"

"Adam, this is a bar, not a four-star restaurant. I get what I can so Nancy doesn't have to work. She's busy enough with our kids, she don't need to come in here and deal with these kids." He jerked a thumb at the end of the bar. "So, this girl comes in here and she's definitely worked a bar before. That first night she made a bundle. Of course, being the new girl, I expected that. But then she did it again and again. People liked her, even though she was quiet, not like the other girls. This one didn't get into people's faces, didn't ask about their problems, she'd listen but she wouldn't ask, got 'em their drinks quick, and kept 'em full." He sighed. "She was good for business. I'm sorry to hear she won't be around anymore."

Slate tapped his pen on the bar. He liked this less and less. The person he was looking for would know how to disappear and then, presto, reappear somewhere else and fit into a spot like a key in a lock. She'd been at this a long time. Longer than any little girl, for sure. "How old would you say she is?"

"Said she was legal to drink and I believed her after I talked to her a bit, but to look at her you wouldn't think she was much more'n eighteen, I guess. That girl's gonna get carded until she's fifty."

"And you didn't ask for identification with her serving drinks?"

Jack gave him a put-upon look. "Adam, even in this little burg the cops have better things to do than ask my staff for their ID. She kept sober and showed up on time. I don't give a shit if she was sixteen. She knew her job."

"She have a name?"

"Kaylen, spelled with a Y. She was specific about that."

"No last name?"

"Hell, the first one was probably somethin' she made up. Why bother with a last one?" He gave Slate a look that said this should be the obvious deduction.

"She say anything about where she came from or where she might be headed since it sounds like she wasn't planning an being a permanent resident?"

"Nope." Jack came closer to Slate, presumably so the waitress, who had cocked her head in their direction, couldn't hear him. "Girl like her though, would know how to get around. She was real comfortable with the workin' guys who came in here, guys who spent a lot of time on the road. You ask me, she hitched a ride outta here when she left."

Perfect. She could be anywhere at this point, especially if she got picked up by a long-distance trucker. "Do you really think she would do that? If she was as small as you and Karl say she should have been more cautious."

"Small don't mean defenseless. I'll tell you something else about that chick; something about her told you to stay away."

That got Slate's full attention. "What do you mean? Did she say or do anything?"

Jack shook his head. "No, wasn't nothin' like that. It was like a feeling you'd get, Nancy felt it too. Like something about that girl was measuring you, checking you out, seeing if you were a threat."

"Makes sense. A lot of runaways develop a sixth sense over time. Comes with the territory. Same as cops."

"It wasn't like that though," Jack insisted. "When you looked at that girl it was like something was looking back at you. Even when her back was turned."

CHAPTER 7

"So, you got a thing about sunlight or somethin'?"

Kaylen rolled her eyes. She had been stuck working with Roger and while she normally didn't mind his almost constant babbling, it was worse when he was high. Today he was getting on her nerves. She'd had a headache since morning and been on edge, barely eating breakfast and then stumbling through the first show's concession rush. Thankfully, Tony was used to working with people who got through most of the first half of the day hungover and he covered for her. He did this on the promise that she would eat lunch, which she did, and that she would take something for her head, which she did not. She didn't like painkillers of any type and tried to avoid them because they made her queasy. She explained this to Tony who suggested she help Roger clean up after the second performance. She agreed and that was how she and Roger came to be cleaning up trash together.

"I just have fair skin and I don't like sunscreen."

"Oh, you one of those organic everything people? Tony said you don't like pain meds." Roger was leaning on the trash can watching Kaylen pick up the scattered leavings of popcorn bags and empty soda cups. Marco insisted on a neat and tidy lot.

"No, I just don't like sunscreen." And what was the big deal anyway? Her head was pounding, it was hot with not a hint of a breeze, she was going to make less money today, and now Roger insisted on playing twenty questions.

"What about the pain meds?" He was like a dog chasing a rabbit.

"I haven't eaten much today and they make me feel sick if I take them on an empty stomach." Right now, bending over was making her sick. What was wrong with her? She had slept good last night despite Mabel's visit to Roger's compartment next door and had not drunk or smoked anything before bed. The day had gotten hot, but the morning had been clear and cool. Maybe the last couple days were catching up to her.

"No kidding, Rails. Fred named you right. You anorexic?"

"That's a pretty big word for you, Roger."

He stood up straight and stretched, all male bravado since he'd gotten laid. The fact that it was Mabel and it was a trade fuck for meth didn't seem to make any difference to him. Well, he was named after a rabbit. "Just making conversation."

"Why don't you stop talking and help me clean this shit up?"

"I'm more of what you'd call a supervisor today," he grinned.

More of an asshole, she thought. Well, fine, she was almost done here anyway. After she got the rest of this picked up, she'd have a shower and go back to bed. She didn't feel like dinner and felt even less like socializing. She just wanted silence and sleep.

She was dumping the last handfuls of trash into the can, Roger was sitting next to the tent in the shade and playing on his phone, when Edward came trotting over. He was covered in sunscreen, making his pale skin even paler, almost translucent. "Did you guys see the news?"

Roger yawned and leaned against the canvas. "Didn't have to see it. We all heard Aliyah and Frank going at it last night. She finally threw him out. Again. He was sleeping in the truck this morning."

"Not them, you stoned idiot. The real news."

Roger, looking indignant at being insulted, stood up and snapped, "I don't really give a fuck about the outside world unless it has something to do with me, Eddy."

"Don't call me that," Edward said absently, "and this does affect us, sort of. You know that place we worked last week? Where we picked up Rails here?"

"Yeah, sure."

Kaylen listened to the conversation and felt a sinking in the pit of her stomach. She knew what was coming.

"Well, it turns out that little shithole was home to a serial killer." Edward announced this as if he were the ringmaster.

Roger's mouth dropped open. "It weren't."

"It were. And he was a pretty sick fuck if the news got it right. Look, I've got it right here on my phone. Come on, Rails, you've got to see this."

"No thanks," Kaylen breathed. She suddenly felt like she was going to vomit. She took a few deep breaths. The moment passed. She wanted, needed, to get away from them. But they were standing between her and the back lot and she couldn't go around the front of the tent because of the way the stakes were tied.

"Look at this shit," Edward was saying. Roger was crowding next to him, the two of them gaping at Edward's phone. "Ain't that wild? And we were just there. Sick sombitch got hammered that last night. Bet the boss won't book us there again anytime soon."

"Scroll down for more pictures. How did they get these? Dirty cops always selling out to reporters, that's what I say." Roger's face was avid, excited by the prospect of blood and gore.

Kaylen felt her gorge rise again and knew she wouldn't be able to stop it this time. She turned and puked into the trash can. She hadn't eaten much at lunch and now that was what came up. She heaved a couple more times, voiding bile that burned her throat as it passed through.

"Damn, Rails, I would've thought you had bigger balls than that. Blowing chucks over a few crime pics," someone tsked.

Kaylen looked up with puke on her chin to see Marco standing straddled legged and arms crossed, grinning. She wiped her chin angrily with her gloved hand, felt her marks rising hot and fast on her arms, and said, "I haven't been feeling good all day, asshole."

Marco's face darkened. Edward and Roger looked up from the screen and backed away, putting themselves behind Kaylen. Marco was not one to be crossed and they all knew it. He might just yell at a woman, or maybe worse, but if one of the men got between him and her that guy would pay a dear price for trying to play hero. "What did you say to me, bitch?"

Kaylen squared her shoulders, her marks burned on her skin under her long sleeves. "You heard me."

"Think you're tough, do ya?" He spat on the ground between them.

It was like this sometimes too. Sometimes part of them rose inside her and her anger slipped the leash. "I think I've got the right to be sick."

"Pukin's one thing. Snapping at the boss is another. I can leave your skinny ass right here on this lot and no one would be the wiser."

"Then do it."

Edward and Roger turned to her with wide, staring eyes. Was she really calling Marco's bluff? Not that it was a bluff. He had left plenty of gazoonies on lots before and would do it again. But in those cases, it had always been him making the move. No one had ever pushed him to do it. Not openly, at least.

"You want to think real hard about your mouth, girly, or I'll teach you what it's good for," Marco growled. He took a step toward her.

"Like you've taught other women? I'm sure the cops would be interested in knowing you were around Dawson with a traveling show the time that fifteen-year-old was raped outside a gas station, was it?" Actually, it had been a laundromat. The town was Dayton and the girl was closer to seventeen. Kaylen knew all this, as she did everything about the prey once her marks were clear and burning, but it wouldn't be good for anyone to know that. It was better for them to think she had gotten close than that she was dead on balls accurate.

Marco gave back the step he had taken. "What are you? You couldn't know about that, nobody knows about that."

Except me, you, and these two now, Kaylen thought. She felt Edward and Roger shift their gazes to Marco. They were likely dying for this little episode to be over so they could go spread the gospel.

"Let's just say my hunches are little better than Mabel's. You still want to teach me to swallow?"

He threw his hands at her. "I don't want nothin' to do with you. Stay the hell away from me." He turned to leave.

"That mean I've still got a job?"

He didn't answer, just stomped off around the tent. Kaylen felt the marks under her sleeves begin to disappear. Her heart slowed to a normal beat. Her hands were hurting. She looked down and saw that she was gripping the rim of the trash can so tightly, her gloves had indentions in the fingers. She let go with effort.

"What the hell just happened?" Roger nearly shouted.

"Are you okay?" Edward asked. He came over to her cautiously, acting as though he were ready to catch her if she fainted or fell down.

She nodded and stepped back from the trash can. She wobbled and Edward caught her elbow, steadying her and guiding her to the tent where she could sit in the shade. A light itching rose to her arms and then was gone. If she thought anything about it, she thought it was them giving an afterward twitch at Marco's abrupt departure.

"Did you see that shit, Eddy? She called him out. Sweet Jesus Christ! Rails called out Marco. Did you see his face?"

"Don't call me Eddy. And stop dancing around like that. You want to make her throw up again?"

Roger stopped his capering and stared down at Kaylen. "How did you know all that stuff? Are you really like Mabel? I mean, sometimes she gets a good one but most of the time her hits don't pan out, if you catch me."

Kaylen began to realize two things as she sat in the shade and got her bearings back. The first was that she had just made a powerful enemy by not keeping her mouth shut. The second was that this was one of the few places where psychic ability wasn't only accepted, but often encouraged. Everyone thinking she was psychic would make hiding the truth a lot easier and so she nodded her head. "Sometimes I get a flash, is all. It's not always true and what I said to Marco was probably close but not perfect."

"Close enough to scare the shit out of him," Edward commented. He was rubbing her upper arm in an attempt to be comforting, but she really wished he'd stop. She didn't like to be touched. "How are you feeling? Better?"

"Much, but I think I want to get cooled off and lie down for a while."

He put a wrist to her forehead. Kaylen accepted this because she knew he was shook, he and Roger both were, and taking care of her was calming his nerves and giving Roger something to focus on besides running through the crew and opening his big mouth.

"Wait until I tell Mabel and Trips. They're never gonna believe this." Roger started toward the back of the tent.

"Hold it right there, Rog," Edward called. "Come over here. Now, look, don't go runnin' through the lot tellin' everyone what happened back here. All it's gonna do is make a bad situation worse. Let things calm down a while before running your mouth, you dig?"

Roger's grin sagged. "But it's about time we found out something good on that bullying prick."

"And you can share it with all your friends," Edward went on patiently," but Marco's pissed right now. What do you think he'll do to you if he catches you talking about him?"

Roger paled. He swallowed nervously and glanced around. Apparently, it hadn't occurred to him that Marco would be looking for a target to vent his frustrated rage upon. "Okay, right. Let things cool off. I dig. I'll go help Tony with the stand."

"He going to blab to Tony first?" Kaylen asked when Roger vanished behind the tent.

"Probably, but not for a while yet. Roger might be an addict and a dingbat but he has a very strong sense of self-preservation. He'll keep quiet for a while. Until tonight anyway. Once he's high, all bets are off, but the good thing about that is no one pays much attention to him when he's high."

"Even Mabel?"

"Even Mabel. They have a, what do you call it? They talk about it in that Spiderman movie."

"A symbiotic relationship?"

"That's the one. They feed off each other so it ain't like a parasite 'cause it goes both ways."

Kaylen, having a long experience with her own symbiotic buddies, knew it didn't. She also knew it wasn't like the Spiderman version. In that, it was destructive and dangerous but also funny and heart-warming. They made it clear they only kept her safe because she could get them what they wanted. And they had no problem making her life hell if she didn't hold up her end of the deal. "Can you help me get back to the bunkhouse? I think I'll be fine from there, but it's a long walk."

"No problem." He helped her up and slipped an arm around her waist to steady her. Kaylen had been thinking more along the lines of walking next to her in case she wobbled again. She didn't like the implications this might lead to. Edward was nice and he was more compassionate than the others, but she wasn't looking for a bedmate, even an occasional one, and she didn't want him reading too much into helping her stagger across the lot.

Fortunately, Mabel met them halfway to the trailer. "Oh, honey, what's wrong with you? You look like a beat up rag."

Kaylen had no idea what that was supposed to mean, but Mabel was taking her away from Edward and that was the important thing. "I think I got overheated or something," she mumbled.

Edward let Mabel take her reluctantly. Kaylen could feel his fingers trailing off her shirt and her heart sank. This was something she didn't need on top of everything else. Meanwhile, Mabel was steering her to the bunkhouse. "Let's get your stuff and you get into the shower to cool off. Then I'll get Fred to make you a plate so you can just relax tonight. Keep away from the boys for a while."

"Mabel, you should have been someone's mother."

Kaylen felt the other woman stiffen against her. "Already tried that, darlin'. It didn't work out."

"Oh, Mabel, I'm sorry. I didn't mean to hurt your feelings."

Mabel kept them moving. "Don't worry about it. You couldn't know. Girls like us, we can't pick what we want to know, now can we?"

Kaylen sighed. "Did Roger run his mouth?"

"Roger ain't said nothin' to me, but a like knows a like just the same." She helped Kaylen up the steps into their compartment, then waited for Kaylen to gather clean clothes and her shower bag. She walked with her around to the other side where the door to the shower compartment was.

"Are the others going to treat me different?" Kaylen asked.

Mabel shrugged. "Why would they? They're used to people like us around here. You need me to help you back?"

"No, I'm feeling better. I can manage. Thanks, Mabel."

"No problem. Dinner's almost done. I'll have Fred make you a plate. Don't you worry yourself." She strode toward the cookhouse, picture of a woman on a mission. Kaylen hoped her earlier comment wouldn't send Mabel into a downward spiral. They never showed her the good in people, only the bad. Only the things that made the meat tasty. It was a compromise, Kaylen supposed. If she knew that the people they hunted had some good in them, it would make it harder to let them feed.

She went into the shower compartment and closed and locked the door. All the compartments had locks on them but only this one had a lock to which Marco didn't have the key. Kaylen didn't know why the lot boss couldn't open this door on a whim and hadn't asked. It was one of those things you just knew to accept and move on about, but now, after her revelation, she wondered.

She wanted a cool shower but the water spigot was a long way from the trailer and the hose had been baking in the sun all day. She had been lectured about taking long showers and about wasting water. The latter was mostly due to the fact the hose draining the shower wasn't very far from the trailers and so a lot of people taking showers resulted in a large mud puddle by the time the show moved on. A puddle like that made for muddy boots and dirty floors and so should be avoided. Not to mention, if the ground near the tires of one of the other trailers got saturated enough, that trailer might get stuck, making more work for everyone on leaving day.

The water wasn't warm, it was scalding. Kaylen was forced to wait a minute or two before she could step under the shower head. Her skin was always sensitive after her marks appeared which was another reason she wanted a cool shower. Her arms prickled at the hot water and there was a brief moment of pain. Kaylen bit her lip to keep from crying out. The trailer walls were thin and she didn't need the cavalry rushing to see what was wrong in here. The pain abated after a few seconds and she was able to scrub herself and wash her hair. This was something she hadn't done since coming here and she worked her nails deep into her scalp to remove the build up of dirt and oil.

Kaylen ran her hands down her belly and thighs, shuddering as she remembered the pain of meeting that serial killer face to face. Her marks were a direct indicator of how bad someone was. As far as she had seen, Marco was a bully and a fighter, but the girl in Dayton had been the only time he had really crossed a hard line. Her marks reflected that, showing only on her arms. When she had approached and then entered the killer's house, her whole body, with the exception of her face, had been on fire. The marks had started on her feet and snaked their way to her shoulders, covering her like tiger stripes. The marks were dark and were of a definite tribal persuasion.

Once, she had been at a biker rally working a knock down bar. Her marks had come and gone, flowing like water over her skin with the questionable clientele. Halfway through the night, she had removed the hoodie she had been wearing because it was exhaustingly hot. She had gotten many compliments on her marks that night, as men and women noticed them. Several people asked who her tattoo artist was and where his studio was located. She had deferred all requests saying he was retired. No one seemed to notice that the marks came and went or that they occasionally changed their patterns.

The pain had been immense when she had followed the killer into the living room, driving her to release them, to let them pass judgement and sate themselves. It was an orgasmic experience, releasing them. Her body twitched and jerked with pleasure at the instant relief of the burning as soon as they were free. Feeding them was often better than sex. It created a wave of sensation followed by a blessed nothingness that left her feeling hollowed out and sated herself, floating on the absence of feeling. It was dangerous. It lulled her into a lassitude, making her want to curl up and sleep for hours.

It was because of this reaction that she planned her hunts accordingly. She knew she would be useless for an hour or more after they gorged themselves. It was the reason she tried to make sure she could stay at the feeding ground for a couple of hours without fear of being discovered. The abruptness and brutality of their most recent feeding hadn't allowed her that luxury. Kaylen was certain that was why she had been feeling so crummy the last week. Her body, driven to run after the killing, had suffered a kind of shock and was having a tough time getting over it.

On top of that, she had found sanctuary in a job that thrived on manual labor, which wasn't helping her overstressed body.

Turning off the water, she stood in the shower stall and listened to the outside world. Voices outside walking passed, someone laughing, something heavy being dropped in one of the trucks. The sounds of everyday life, in other words. She reached for her towel and saw the marks appear, almost sluggishly on her right hand and wrist. They showed themselves then hid, then showed again. It was as if they couldn't make up their minds.

Frowning, Kaylen closed her eyes and fell into herself, reaching for them. She hardly ever did this, hardly ever needed too. They came to her aid when they felt her threatened or came to the forefront when they were hunting. She didn't have to look for them to take care of her; they did that instinctually. She found them with the very deepest part of her mind, curled up and sleeping, annoyed at her intrusion. They had awoken earlier, when it seemed they might need to take action against the loud male, but when he had retreated so had they, returning to their near comatose slumber.

Kaylen withdrew. The less contact she had with them the better. They had their place and she knew hers. The marks flickered again. A warning maybe? Someone they thought hadn't done enough but could if given the right motivation? She didn't know. She had never really thought much about her state of being. She simply was and they were. She accepted it and didn't question that there could be something more to their clan than protection and nourishment. That they might actually serve a purpose had never occurred to her. Whether they did or not, it wouldn't change what she was to them.

She finished toweling herself off and got dressed. No one had come banging on the door even though she must have been in here for half an hour or more. She wondered if Mabel had spread the word that she wasn't feeling good and should be left alone. Kaylen smirked at what that would mean in the group mind. They would all just assume she was pregnant. Well, let them think that, it might get her out of lifting heavy equipment like speakers and electricity cables.

Kaylen was reaching for the door when one of those flashes she got sometimes popped into her head. It was a flash, there and gone, a blip on the radar.

She saw a man and knew immediately that he was a cop in the way he carried himself. A cop, or worse, a detective, someone whose job it was to find people, to find secrets. He was tall and dark haired, not strikingly handsome, but good looking. He was wearing sunglasses but she knew the eyes behind the dark lenses would be busy, taking in everything, seeing everything. There was a coldness about him. A righteousness that so often condemned the innocent and the guilty. He was standing outside the place she had rented before meeting the local murderer. He was tapping his fingers on the roof of his car, thinking, trolling. His head snapped around suddenly and she knew, *knew*, he saw her looking at him.

Kaylen stumbled back against the sink in the tiny compartment, breaking the connection. Her back slammed into the edge of the sink sending a spasm of pain up her spine. She was shaking. She turned around and gripped the sink, looking at herself in the mirror. It showed white-rimmed green eyes looking out of a drawn face. Dark smudges marred the pale skin below her lashes.

He was looking for her, whoever he was. Had he seen her well enough to recognize her if he saw her again? She almost laughed at that. Recognize her? He didn't need to recognize her. A like knows a like and if he got anywhere near her, he would know her for sure.

"It's alright, you twit. He can't find you. Don't panic like some teenage birdbrain." Talking to herself calmed her down. She let go of the sink and took a deep breath. "He can't know you hooked up with the circus. You didn't even know you were hooking up with the circus until you saw the arrow."

True, but he would know the circus had been in town and everyone knew if you wanted to run away, you ran away and joined the circus.

"That's stupid. Kid's stuff, no one really does that."

Didn't they? If you wanted to disappear, really disappear, what better way to do it than with a traveling show that was used to hiring on people of questionable reputation? And if you were a detective investigating the brutal murder of a citizen in a small town? A citizen that kept to himself and maybe didn't participate in the local church socials or school bake sales but had far more questionable hobbies. Wouldn't you wonder how someone could kill this man and then vanish? Where could you go if you didn't have a vehicle, something he undoubtedly knew if he was at her old apartment? You had to hitch a ride, get out of town, way, way out of town. And who traveled from town to town, never too close so they could get a better bang for their buck? Why, the circus of course.

"I could be in real trouble here." She jumped as someone pounded on the outside door.

"Alright, prima donna, some of us want to clean up too if you don't mind."

"I'm on my way out." She grabbed her stuff and opened the door.

Tony was standing at the foot of the steps with his shower bag in one hand and a towel draped over his shoulders. "You fall asleep in there or what?"

"Or what," Kaylen said. She smiled at him to show she was only playing with him. "I've been out for a while so the water should be hot again."

"Like I want a hot shower after a scorcher of a day," he tromped up the steps and shut the door.

Kaylen walked to her compartment. Mabel had brought her a plate of food, but looking at it made Kaylen's stomach do a slow cartwheel. She put the plate in the tiny refrigerator and grabbed a can of ginger ale. She had bought these yesterday at a gas station while they were moving the show. Her stomach had already been feeling decidedly unhappy and she didn't want to spend the whole night worried about upchucking. She wasn't normally the nauseous type and pregnancy was out of the question, but she had bought the ginger ale anyway.

Feeling claustrophobic, she left the compartment and went to sit on one of the picnic tables set up a little away from the tent and trailers. There were four tables strategically placed under the sprawling branches of the large trees that dotted the lot. The place looked like a park of some sort. Trips had said there was a playground down the lane a bit, but Kaylen hadn't bothered to explore. She was perfectly content to stay close to the trailers.

A slight breeze had picked up and Kaylen sat on the table with her feet on the bench. She sipped her soda and thought about the man she had seen. He was looking for her, that much she knew, but what was he? If he was a local cop or even detective, she wouldn't have much to worry about. If he was a federal agent of some sort, she could have a lot to worry about.

Seeing someone the way she had seen him wasn't new to her. She had glimpsed people and places before. Sometimes she ran across them in person, but mostly she didn't. The strange part about this time was that he had looked back at her. She shivered, remembering those dark glasses and that stone jaw. He wouldn't want to hear her side of anything. As far as he was concerned, she was no better than guy they had fed upon.

Anger flared up inside her, surprising her with its vehemence. That this guy should hunt her down like an animal, like a coyote killing chickens, when a real predator, a wolf, lived in his sleepy little town, galvanized her. She finished her drink, crushed the can on the table, and hurled it as far as she could. If the jerk looking for her was any good at his job, they wouldn't have found anyone to eat. He would have discovered long ago that the guy in the big house with the perfect décor was hiding a nasty secret in his basement. Of course, if he couldn't find a serial killer living a few blocks from the police station, she really shouldn't be worried about him showing up at a show, should she?

"Hey, Rails, thought you knew better than to litter," Fred's baritone rolled across the open ground like thunder.

"I was gonna pick it up on my way back," she grumbled.

He sat on the table next to her, the crushed can in his hand and gave her a long, measuring look.

Kaylen matched his stare for several seconds before turning away. "See something green?"

"Nope, but I do see white and purple and blue. When was the last time you slept, Rails? I mean really slept."

"Last night." And that was true. She hadn't had a bad night's sleep since coming here.

"You sick?"

"If I was, would it matter?"

He blew out a breath. "Don't guess it would, but it would be nice to know if we have to keep an eye out for you to drop whenever the weather gets warm."

"I'm not sick. And the hot weather normally doesn't bother me. It's the cold I can't handle." She was quiet, not sure how to proceed. She didn't know these people, but she felt she should tell someone something, if only to keep them off her back. Before she could begin, Fred spoke again.

"You knocked up? That's what everyone's saying."

"Only because I'm a girl. If I was a man y'all would think I got some bad scratch or booze and leave it at that."

"True. But you ain't a man."

"I'm not pregnant either." She ran a hand through her damp hair. "I don't know what I am. I'm usually pretty sturdy. I feel like I could sleep for days, but when I do, I don't feel rested. I'm not hungry, but I don't eat much anyway so that doesn't worry me. I just feel," she thought a minute, "jittery."

"Jittery like you're twitchin'? If you are you need to take a small hit. Stoppin' shit like that cold turkey is liable to kill you."

"No, nothing like that. I don't do anything heavier than pot and I haven't done that in a while. I don't drink enough to have the dt's."

He leaned back a bit and looked around the quiet spot they were sitting in. Farther down from them, where the hill the show was on flattened out, a group of kids were playing frisbee. Kaylen envied their carefree energy. She never had much of a childhood, having met them when she wasn't more than eight, but before they came she had good memories. Before they came and she was marked as different by the other kids and weird by their parents. Her mother tried hard to make up for this lack of social acceptance, but in the end there was only so much a mother could do.

"Is what you said about Marco true? He really rape a girl in Dayton?"

"I said it was Dawson."

He waved a hand. "You meant Dayton. We never worked a town called Dawson but I remember Dayton clear as day because Marco was so hot to get the show off that lot and down the road." He looked at her. "If what you said is true, he has plenty of reason to want to get gone."

"It was true," she whispered. She looked at him, willing herself not to cry, not to seem weak. She wasn't, not really, but she was so tired and she felt so bad and now this guy was after her. It was all too much to deal with all at once. She needed to get her head straight, take some time for herself and decide what to do.

"That's the case, you don't go anywhere alone, you hear? Marco's got a reputation and he earned it. You may have spooked him today, but he'll get over it and when he does, he'll be looking for payback."

"Payback for what?" As if she didn't know.

"Calling him out in front of the boys. Hell, for knowing he committed a crime. How did you know anyway? Was it like Mabel?"

She nodded. "I couldn't prove anything and it felt like it was a long time ago anyway. And she wasn't as young as I said. I think she was closer to seventeen or eighteen and it could have started out as mutual. That's the problem. I see a little, feel emotion, but I don't get the full story."

Fred was nodding. "Same as Mabel. It's why she drinks and drugs. Story she told me was that she used to be really good, really reliable. Could go to Atlantic City and come home loaded. Always knew when someone was lying and usually what they was lying about. But then, ah shit."

"Something happened to her kid, didn't it?"

"How'd you know about her kid?"

"It was an accident. I said she should have been someone's mother when she helped me to the compartment and she said she tried that once and--."

"It didn't work out. Yeah, that's what she tells everybody. What she told me one night after drinkin' a whole damn bottle of whiskey, I thought she gave herself alcohol poisoning, I really did, was something different. I'm gonna tell you because you are strong the way she used to be. That's what she says anyway." He took a deep breath. "What happened was this. In her life before this one, she had a husband and a son and a house. Stay at home mom, bake sales, Tupperware meetings, June Cleaver and all that happy horseshit. And she could catch a glimpse now and then.

"One day she was sittin' home making dinner and a cop car pulls up. It's the highway patrol and they want to know if a Mrs. So and So lives here. They have come to regretfully inform her that her husband and son have died in a head on crash with a semi. Driver had fallen asleep at the wheel and the truck crossed the line. Your life is over, so sorry."

"It must have killed her," Kaylen breathed.

"You've seen her, seen how she is. She says she's made peace with what happened, it was an accident. The truck driver didn't make it either. Apparently, it was a real mess. She says she can forgive him and all that. What she can't get over is that she could see enough to pull the neighbor's kid out of the street to keep her from getting run over by a delivery driver, she could pick the right numbers on a roulette wheel, she could tell every woman she met if they were pregnant and how far along they were, but she never got a hint about her husband and son. Not a peep."

Kaylen thought about this. She herself had never gotten anything like a precognition. She saw people and places in real time, never anything that had or would occur. "Maybe it was a kindness."

"A kindness? How you figure that?"

"Well, if she saw an accident but couldn't tell when it would happen, what would she have done? Kept her husband and son home forever? Made sure they were never in a car together? Maybe not knowing is better than never living."

He thought about it. "I can see what you're getting at, but I wouldn't share this enlightenment with Mabel if I were you."

Kaylen shook her head. "I won't. If she can't come to it on her own than maybe it's better that she feels the way she does. We all have to know what we can live with and it's not like I've got a kid or ever been married so who am I to spread enlightenment?"

"Walk in someone else's shoes, live a day in their life?"

"Pick your metaphor and stick with it," Kaylen snipped.

"More fun to mix and match. I like variety."

"Don't let Donna hear you say that. I haven't been around her much but that woman seems a bit territorial to me."

He grinned. "We got a casual sort of thing going, but she does like her toys."

Kaylen yawned. "I think I'm ready for bed." She slipped down off the table.

Fred fell into step next to her. "You eat dinner?"

"Not yet."

"Eat before you sleep. It will help. Meatloaf and potatoes are good comfort foods."

The meatloaf didn't sound appetizing at all, but she could probably stomach the potatoes. "I'll try. My stomach does feel better." They were at the bunkhouse.

The others were sitting around in their camp chairs in their customary circle, swapping stories and swatting mosquitoes. Fred waved to them and gave Kaylen a stern look. "Dinner before bed, savvy?"

"Yes, boss."

She did try to eat, but her stomach clenched on the first bite of meatloaf. She managed the potatoes though. She put the leftovers in the fridge and curled into a ball under her blanket. Sleep was close but it stayed away long enough for her to picture the cop or detective or whatever he was and his dark glasses. She shivered and pulled the blanket up over her head. She prayed he was a local and that he wouldn't remember runaways often joined the circus.

CHAPTER 8

Detective Adam Slate was having his own week of restless nights. However, his nocturnal troubles had nothing to do with exhaustion brought on by shock or days of manual labor. He wasn't having visions either, except for that weird thing that had happened when he went to collect the girl's things from Karl's apartment when it became clear she wasn't coming back.

He had been standing by his car, letting his mind go blank and trying to feel out his next move when he felt eyes on him. He turned to look and for just a second, so fast he still didn't believe he had seen anything, he had seen a girl, or maybe woman was a better word, looking back at him. He didn't get a good look. All he knew for certain was that she was small and wet and she was holding something in front of her that looked like a towel. Then she was gone. It was as though she had never been there. He decided he was obsessing about her so much he had simply imagined she had been standing there.

His current lack of sleep was the sole responsibility of the federal government. The FBI had shown up just as planned. Slate had worked with federal agents in the past and found them, if not cordial, at least human. Not so with this bunch.

His first interaction with them had been when a woman in a high-powered suit and low heels marched into the station and demanded everything they had on the Lenoy case. She was direct and curt and Slate pegged her for a super bitch from the first breath. She did not disappoint. While the chief was still explaining that he was under the impression it would be a cooperative, interdepartmental investigation, the bitch queen's partner, King Dick, came striding in. They were like a power couple from Hell.

After forty-five minutes of arguing with them, Slate decided to wash his hands of the whole mess. What did it matter? They were going to take it all away anyway, that much was perfectly clear. Their forensics guys had already commandeered Lenoy's residence and were denying access to everyone who didn't have government clearance. They had also sent a team to plunder the evidence locker, the morgue, and the computer files already started on the case.

Detective Slate and Chief Nickerson watched the ensuing chaos over coffee mugs from the chief's office. "Damn agents. They really know how to make you feel like a piece of cowshit on their designer shoes, don't they?" Nickerson growled.

"Don't judge all agents by these assholes. I've worked with the feds before and it wasn't terrible. Wasn't great either." Slate sipped his coffee. His mind was elsewhere, backtracking a trail that had gone cold for all intensive purposes.

"You get any further than Frostie's?"

"Nope."

"Look I don't want to tell you how to run a case, but... Oh Christ are they really taking that whole hard drive? What could be on it that they can't copy?"

"You wanna take this outside, Chief?"

"No, no I want to make sure they leave the damn desks." He raised his voice to be heard through the closed office door. If the goon squad outside heard, they gave no sign. "Ah, hell, I'm just not as intimidating as I used to be." He walked around the room and closed all the blinds, then sat behind his desk.

Slate took a seat on the couch on the side of the small room. "You were about to tell me how to proceed," he said mildly.

Nickerson waved a hand. "No, I wasn't. What I was gonna say, was stay out of their way and keep your mouth closed about your little hunch."

"Come again?"

"Look, Adam, I know how the law works and I know what we're supposed to do here, but I've been asking around too. I talked to Karl and Jack and if this girl is your prime suspect then maybe you outta let it go."

Slate carefully put his coffee mug on the low table in front of him. "Are you saying I should let a murderer walk?"

"I'm saying you need to think about justice. You and I both know what would have happened if those yahoos out there had caught Lenoy. He wouldn't have gotten the death sentence. They would have worked it so he was sent to a federal lock up for observation and study. He would have got three squares a day, stellar healthcare, and all the reading material he could ever want. Could have gotten a PhD that you and me and Johnny Taxpayer would foot the bill for. And for all that, he'd play those idiots for the dumbasses they are." He gave Slate a steady look. "She did us and all those women a favor, Adam."

"And what if she decides to do another 'favor' to someone else?"

"I don't think she will. I think she had a connection to Lenoy somewhere. Something you might never find. But I think this was her one shot and it's done now, so let it be done."

"I can't."

"You want to see her stand trial, be found guilty, maybe get a death sentence?"

"She is guilty," Slate snapped.

"Really? The Bible tells us an eye for an eye. By my count, Lenoy owes seven more deaths he'll never pay for. What has this girl done?"

Slate balled his hands into fists. "Vigilantism is not the law."

"And what is? Giving kiddy fiddlers a few years in the pen and then sending them back out so they can do it all again? Arresting the same damn rapist five times? What about murderers who get off on a technicality and then write tell-all books and host their own tv shows? Where do you find the law there?"

"You're the chief," Slate said in disbelief.

"I'm a man, son. And more and more often I feel like an old man. This world we live in doesn't care about justice, it cares about hype and six-figure reality tv contracts. It cares about sensationalism. I don't know when we lost our humanity but the world has lost it and just knowing what that little girl might have done makes me hopeful there are good people in the world fighting for what's right and not what'll get 'em the most likes on Facebook."

Slate hung his head. "Chief, I understand what you're saying, but where is it going to end? If we don't have justice and laws, how does civilization go on?"

"Son, civilization ended a long time ago. We might not be living the law of the jungle, not yet, but we are certainly living the law of social media. Which is worse, in my humble opinion."

That conversation had happened almost a week ago. Since then, Slate had spent his time answering the few questions the FBI agents had for him and spinning his wheels. He believed in the law and he believed in good people, but he had to admit there was something to the chief's cynicism. When was the last time he could stomach the news? When was the last time he read a newspaper that wasn't short on news and long on hate? He couldn't remember. Some days it all seemed so pointless. They were all rats running around a maze, too stupid to realize the gas had already started to flow and they were already dying.

Thinking like this was getting him nowhere. With all the excitement over Lenoy, the local hellraisers were keeping quiet. No one wanted to go under the microscope. Fighting with the local cops was one thing. They could arrest you for some minor infraction and then later on the whole bunch of you would go drinking at one of the town watering holes. The feds were a whole other ball of snakes. They could be decent about something minor or they might bring your ass in for a total overhaul. Given his experience with this crew, Slate thought that the overhaul would only be the beginning of the experience.

The lack of action was making him restless. The only thing he had done involving his private hunt for one missing young lady had been to confiscate all her belongings from Karl. He told Karl he was going to take them to the station and lock them up, but further contemplation made him change his mind.

The two agents in charge of the Lenoy investigation were Nazi's flying under American colors. Nothing could be logged into evidence without either or both of them going through whatever it was for a peek. Slate and Nickerson were of the strong opinion that the agents thought the local precinct knew all about Lenoy and were giving him a free pass. Maybe even helping him dispose of the bodies. They hadn't come out and accused anyone of this yet but they had both skated right up to the line on at least a dozen occasions.

Logging a backpack full of woman's clothes, not to mention a significant amount of cash and a burner cell phone into evidence was a sure way to make sure all of their FBI paranoia buttons were slammed down at once. So, he had crossed his own ethical line and brought the stuff back to his apartment. He was starting slow with both failure to further an investigation and tampering with evidence. If he wasn't careful, these few indiscretions would begin to multiply like rabbits.

As far as he was aware, no one on the FBI justice league had figured out that Lenoy's murderer could have been a drifter and certainly not a girl. They were pretty hooked on the theory that whoever killed Lenory had tracked him to his home, overpowered him in an as yet unknown manner, tore him apart, and then wiped away all the evidence. They were looking for another criminal mastermind, in other words. Or at the very least, a person who spent a significant amount of time watching the ID network.

A woman who lived her life off the grid and went, from what Slate gathered, ninety pounds soaking wet in a trench coat was far below their radar. They were looking for some ex-commando bad ass who moonlighted as a mercenary or something along those lines. In Slate's opinion, it would be more likely for a were-wolf to attack Lenoy than Rambo. He kept this observation to himself. It was their show and their monkeys.

"Which always brings me back to you," he muttered. He was sitting on the sofa, the contents of the backpack spread out on the coffee table. He had a glass of whiskey close at hand and was well into his second round.

He reached out and fingered the jeans, the shirts, the jacket. All the items were old, well-worn, and faded. Discount store clothes, consignment or Goodwill, nothing here over ten dollars, he bet his car on that. The jacket was heavy but far too big for the person Karl and Jack described. Was she trying to conceal her-self or had it been the only thing she could find cheap when the weather turned cold for a few days last month? He had found a few dark auburn hairs on the shirts and bagged them, but hadn't brought them in for testing yet. He knew from Karl that she was slim, green eyed, auburn haired and about five two. The only thing the lab could tell him about the hair was whether it was natural or dyed. Not that he would be going to the forensics guys. Ever since his toe-to-toe with the FBI Wonder Twins, he hadn't gone near the lab. That meant he could have all the finger-prints in the world, but couldn't do a damn thing with them.

Karl said her hair was cut short. Not like a boy's, but shoulder length. 'Just barely long enough for her to pull it back in a hoss tail' was how Karl described it. This description was enough to get him started, but it also would lead one to assume this little lady was more practical than princess. That made him think of the jacket again.

Try this one on for size, he thought. Lenoy was a predator and a patient one at that, but predators did slip up from time to time. Say he went after this girl on a lark or whim, something that didn't give him the chance to vet her out. Say something goes wrong somewhere along their encounter, maybe he rapes her and she gets away. From what Slate knew of her, getting away was what she was good at. Say she goes to report him.

Slate could picture it. A young, bedraggled woman staggering into a police station with no identification, no permanent location, no family, and cries rape. Would they believe her? Would they really?

They might take her into a room, take her statement, possibly put her through the humiliation of a rape kit if they got that far, which Slate seriously doubted, and then throw the whole report out as soon as she left the station. If a woman like that walked into any precinct with a healthy prostitution problem, the cops would assume that she was just a hooker who's john didn't pay for services rendered. Nine times out of ten, they would probably be right. This was the ten. If that was what happened.

Another scenario occurred to him and he thought this was much more likely. Say she was attacked and raped and got away. A person used to living off the grid the way she did wouldn't automatically go to the police. If she got a read on Lenoy at all she most certainly wouldn't. He was well-to-do, had a nice car, good clothes. If it came to her word against his, she'd not only lose, but would probably be arrested for falsely accusing the guy.

It was just the way the world worked. If she got it into her head that she wanted payback, she would have access to resources, illegal though they may be, that would make it easier for her to track Lenoy than it would be for the police. All she would need is a name. Or if she was really intelligent, a license plate number. It would probably be a rental. Slate doubted Lenoy would have been dumb enough to use his own car.

She could hack the local car rental places or say she had rented the car before and thought she left something in it and find out where that car came from and who rented it. Everyone wanted to help a damsel in distress, especially this one from what Slate had gathered. From there it would be a lot of sifting but in the end, she had struck gold. A drifter had nothing but time and she had shown she knew how to get money. Maybe Chief Nickerson was right. Maybe they should give this girl a pass and hire her onto the force.

Either of those situations could have happened and yet neither felt right to Slate. Hunting Lenoy down, for instance. Why go to his house? Why risk that exposure? Before being kicked off the case, Slate had found out that Lenoy was an avid hiker and frequented all the local trails. Why not get him out there? It would have been days or even weeks before his body was found with it being the off-season and the kids still in school. He would have been easier to take down on a trail as well. In his house, she would have been in his territory, not knowing where any of the rooms or hallways led. For all she knew, Lenoy could have kept a loaded gun on one of the tables by the front door.

The state of the body was another thing. Rape was brutal and devastating, no question about that, but was it brutal enough to cause the rage vented on Lenoy? There had been blood splatter on the ceiling for God's sake. A little thing like the girl he was looking for would have had to have been in a drug induced frenzy to do something like what he had seen in Lenoy's living room. And where was her blood?

That really bothered Slate. The lab guys and gal had taken swabs from all over that room and so far as anyone knew the only blood they had found was Lenoy's. No matter what kind of weapon she had used, there should have been some of her blood mixed in with his. What Slate had seen was messy and rage-fueled. The girl, if it had been her, would have cut herself at least once on whatever she had used to sever Lenoy's arm. It wasn't as though she killed him and then dragged him downstairs to cut him up cleanly on the same table he used for his victims. Whatever happened to Lenoy had been quick and hot, not calm and collected. His killer wasn't Hannibal Lector, she was more Aileen Wuornos. So, where was her blood? How had she gotten out of the house without leaving a track?

That thought cut through the mild buzz beginning in his head and Slate sat up straight on the couch. How had she gotten out of the house, hell the living room, without leaving a bloody footstep or three? How had she opened the door? The forensics showed clearly that whoever killed Lenoy had come in and gone out. They never washed their hands or went upstairs or downstairs.

"Gloves," Slate said, "she wore gloves and after she killed him, she took the gloves off and put on new ones. That's why we couldn't find any fingerprints."

Okay, sure, and did she put booties on her shoes to keep them nice and tidy, too? If so, where are the tracks from them? And here's one to grow on, she might be light but she still had weight. The lab guys didn't find any tracks, bloody or otherwise, how do you explain that?

"She floated out like a fuckin' ghost," he croaked to his empty house. "Besides, how the hell do we know there weren't tracks? Carter and his buddies had been runnin' all through there before I got there with the lab people."

You know the chief was right. Carter might be an asshole but he knows how to preserve a crime scene.

"Shut up." Slate knew all the voices in his head were his and mostly he didn't mind. He spent a lot of time on his own and was comfortable thinking in a conversational way, but this one voice reminded him of an ex-girlfriend he had in college. She had been pre-med working on becoming a forensic pathologist and it was her job to ask impossible questions. When the nagging in his brain started, it was always, always, always that bitch's voice.

He drained his glass and slammed it on the table. He wanted to go for a walk, get out of the house, get some fresh air, new perspective, something. Sitting here and looking at the leavings of a life stepped into and out of at the drop of a hat was driving him batshit.

The night air was still cool with spring even with summer around the next corner, but Slate didn't bother with a jacket. He started walking casually down his street, by the time he hit the corner he was speeding up, and after crossing into the darkened shopping district, he was running. He liked to run, not jog. It cleared his head, washed away the booze, and gave his body a much-needed release. The exertion set his mind free to travel distant roads while he thought about nothing. It was in this way that he usually got his best hunches when he was stuck on a case.

He ran down several streets, passing closed diners, boutiques, and the corner drug store. The town wasn't huge but it wasn't tiny either. It was very proud of its historic main street and its warren of side streets made for an interesting route. The streets were dark as the clock stretched toward midnight and wet with an earlier rain. Slate didn't care. He liked to run at night because he could go blocks without stopping for traffic.

Finally, gasping for breath and feeling like his legs were ready to dump him on the ground at any moment, Slate stopped at the edge of town where the sidewalk ended and the grass began. The business behind him was a diner that had changed hands at least three times since Slate had come to live here. Right now, it was a breakfast place that did a good trade in feeding the mill workers across the street and down the road a bit. Slate leaned back against the window to catch his breath. His arm brushed something taped there.

It was a poster, but he couldn't make it out in the dark. He pulled out his cell phone and woke up the screen. He didn't know why he suddenly cared what local entertainment the place was pushing, but he was here and why not?

The poster was old and not for anything local. It was a circus poster. A faint bell went off in Slate's mind. He had heard about a circus being in town, about a week, no more like ten days, ago now. Right around the time Lenoy was killed. He pulled the poster off the window and stared at. It boasted all the normal things that came with a small circus, trapeze artists, horseback riders, clowns.

Slate turned off the screen and tapped the phone against his chin. A circus. Popcorn and candy apples and balloons. And a crew to set it all up, of course. A crew of folks who maybe couldn't hold a nine to five, folks who were maybe hiding in a place that didn't ask questions. Folks who really had run away and joined the circus.

CHAPTER 9

Kaylen leaned against the side of the concession trailer and shifted her board on its straps. She'd been barking candy apples before the show and she'd have to load up and go out again during intermission, but for now she could take a break.

"How'd you do?" Tony was working the stand, as usual. He hardly ever butchered, even when Trips and Roger had been drinking and were laid up with hangovers. He'd haul them out and make them run the stands, hungover or not.

Kaylen shrugged. "Did okay. Sold about half. They're not a fun crowd, for sure."

"That's what Marco was saying. Sometimes we get 'em. Probably has to do with the weather. They should've called the show today. Only the diehards come out when it's rainy and cold like this."

The rain had started that morning, then had cleared up for a couple hours. About an hour before showtime the sky had clouded over again and a steady drizzle had begun. The wind picked up and the temperature dropped. Kaylen was very glad she had thought to buy a heavy jacket on her one shopping spree.

"You think we'll have to pull out tonight?" She didn't want to tear down in the dark and the rain and the mud.

"Who knows? Depends on what the bosses say. You feelin' better?"

Kaylen rolled her eyes. The current rumor going around the crew was that she was pregnant and had run away from an abusive boyfriend or husband. No matter what she said to dissuade them, the others continued to believe this story. "I'm fine. I keep tellin' y'all I'm not knocked up."

Tony held up his hands. "Alright, fine. Did you really take on Marco?"

This was the other story going around. Far from the truth, Roger had spun a tale of wonder that no one should have believed, but yet everyone seemed to.

According to Roger, Marco had come around the corner, throwing his weight around as usual, and Kaylen had stood up to him like Joan of Arc or some such nonsense and had yelled at him so completely that Marco had backed off and run away crying like a little girl. Fortunately, he had not gone into detail as to what she had said to him. Edward had neither supported or denied anything Roger said, making it more believable.

"Not the way Roger is telling everyone I did. He just caught me at a bad time was all. I guess my tongue was sharper than I thought. He didn't run away or anything. He just stomped off like he does whenever he throws a tantrum."

"Must have a switchblade of a tongue." Tony scratched his chin. "The last girl who mouthed off to Marco got a split lip for her trouble. Marco's avoiding you like you got the plague and are ready to share."

Kaylen shrugged. "Maybe he thinks I'm already somebody's punching bag and that dude might not like competition."

"You're giving him too much credit." He gave her a speculative look. "Are you somebody's punching bag?"

"I haven't been anybody's anything for a long time. You gonna load me up with apples or what?" She slid the board up on the counter and pulled her jacket tighter around herself.

Tony ignored the board. "Nobody's gonna buy more than what's there. Ten bucks says half the crowd leaves at intermission."

The wind picked up and blew the canvas around the front of the tent. One of the performers came out, looked around at the darkening sky and ducked back inside. Thunder rumbled in the distance. Kaylen huddled closer to the trailer.

Tony pulled the board into the concession. "Come around back and help in here. Tracy just poked her head out to check the weather. My guess is they'll call it at intermission or only have a ten minute or so break. Nowhere near enough time to run the bleachers."

Kaylen bounded around to the door and hopped up into the trailer, thankful to be out of the wind. She was closing the door as the first drops of rain started to fall. "Great. I love tearing down in freezing rain. Maybe we can all get pneumonia."

"Boss won't have us tear down tonight. He used to be a hard ass and made us move no matter what. Couple years back though one of the rousties slipped on a pole or something, I can't remember what, anyway the guy threatened a lawsuit 'cause we were tearing down in a thunderstorm. So, the boss pays all his hospital bills and gives him a hefty bonus and sends him on his way. Ever since then, he's real particular about the weather when we move."

"Good thing. I wasn't looking forward to riding two hundred miles in wet and muddy clothes."

"Fred would have made you change first. He don't like the front of the truck getting dirty."

Kaylen leaned back against one of the counters. "Why doesn't he pull the cookhouse? It's where he lives and Donna stays, most nights anyway."

"Trips can't pull anything bigger than the cookhouse and Edward has a few too many fender benders on his record for anyone to be happy about him hauling their stuff." Tony gestured to the concession trailer. "And I pull the candy trailer."

"Everyone has their spot."

"That's what keeps the circus rolling. You drive?"

"I don't have a driver's license."

"That's not what I asked."

She rolled her eyes. "Yes, I can drive. I haven't driven a trailer in a long time though."

Tony leaned out to call over to Trips who was standing just inside the tent. "They almost done?"

Trips ran over to the trailer and came inside. He cupped his hands and blew into them. "They're doing the dogs right now. Little yappers don't want to work. They can feel the weather out here. They want to go back in the trailer and get warm."

"Don't we all," Kaylen muttered.

"You want company, all you got to do is ask." Trips smiled, showing his lack of several teeth.

"I'll pass," Kaylen said dryly.

"Your loss."

Marco came over to the trailer. "Aren't we all nice and cozy in here. Trips, Tony, you two get out here and start securing the tent. Boss says we ain't going anywhere for a while. Real bad weather on the way. They called the show." He shifted so they could see the scant crowd leaving the tent and hurrying to their cars. No one stopped for a last minute snack. Marco continued his orders. "Rails, you clean up in here and shut the place down." He gestured to the cash drawer. "Clean it out and hand it over, Tony."

Tony emptied the drawer and closed the window as Marco headed off to give more instructions. "You got this?"

"I think I can handle cleaning up a couple of counters." She moved out of Tony's way. He and Trips pulled on their jackets.

He looked back over his shoulder at her. "When you're done in here come help us out and we can all get done and get dry."

Kaylen gave him a jaunty little salute. The guys went out into the darkening afternoon. The rain was still light, but more than the drizzle it had been earlier. Kaylen scrubbed the counters and the equipment, put the leftover stock away, closed and locked all the serving windows and shut off the lights. Taking a deep breath, she went outside. She folded up the outer counters and secured them so the windows would be safe from flying debris. After walking around to make sure everything was locked down, she went to see if anyone else needed help.

She was walking with her hood up and her head down, going in the direction of the back of the tent, when another wave of dizziness hit her hard. She staggered, tripped over one of the tent ropes and whacked her kneecap directly onto a stake head. The pain was enormous and immediate, but she felt it in a detached, off-handed way. Kaylen wasn't here at the moment in the freezing rain, ankle deep in mud, while the wind whipped her hair around her face.

She was in a car this time, sitting behind the driver's seat. Sun heated farmland flowed by on both sides. It was him again. She could recognize the set of his shoulders but more than that she could almost feel him. The prey always recognized the hunter. He was tracking her. She looked into the rearview mirror. He was focused on the road, but as soon as her eyes flashed across the reflective surface his head snapped up and he looked back at her. The car swerved and she put a hand out to keep from falling sideways and ended up sprawled out in the mud.

"Son of a bitch!" She rolled over, there was no point in trying to stay clean at this point. She was mud from tits to toes. Pain flared in her knee reminding her that she had slammed it into an iron rod a few seconds ago. It was the same knee she had scraped the day she had come to the circus. It had been stoic and had only voiced the slightest complaints over the past week, but now its patience was at an end. It wasn't whining about her abuse, it was screaming. It was swelling rapidly and it had a new cut to accompany the old scrape. Mabel was going to shit kittens over this. She had a thing about infections, Kaylen had learned.

She was struggling to get to her feet when Trips came stumbling around the tent. "What the hell are you doing, Rails? You hit one of the stakes?"

"No, I thought I'd take a mud bath, try to catch pneumonia too while I'm at it."

"Don't be a smartass." He leaned down and helped her up, slinging an arm around her waist to keep her from falling back down.

"I'm gonna get a rep for being a total pussy if I keep ending up on the ground."

"Well, a girl in your condition, you know. You shouldn't be out in weather like this."

"How many times do I have to tell you guys I'm not pregnant?"

"Don't you think it'd be better to be pregnant than a pussy?"

"Careful, Trips, I might actually think you have a brain in your head."

He laughed and helped her up into her compartment. "Don't let that rumor get around." He lowered his voice. "Hey, we still got a bit to do. If you sneak in and take a shower quick, you can get clean and dry before Marco gets wise to it."
"I think I'll do that." She winked at him.

He nodded and smiled, then closed the door. Kaylen looked around, grabbed the cleanest looking clothes she could find and her shower stuff. She snuck around the trailer to the shower compartment, took her shower, and hurried back to her own compartment as fast as her wounded knee would allow. She wasn't fast enough to beat Mabel.

"Now, what in the world are you doing messin' around the tent in this weather?" Mabel was standing with hands on hips and glaring at Kaylen. She was positioned between Kaylen and the steps to the compartment.

"I was trying to help. Jesus, Mabel, you of all people should know I'm not pregnant."

Mabel slung an arm around Kaylen's waist and helped her up the stairs. The door slammed behind them as the wind picked up, rocking the trailer. Definitely not tearing down tonight. Kaylen wondered if Fred would be cooking or if they were all on their own for dinner. He usually didn't cook on a teardown because they always hit a truck stop somewhere down the road, but no one was going anywhere in this.

"I know that, but somethin's sure as hell is wrong with you and you don't need to be out trying to get yourself hurt." She boosted Kaylen onto her bunk. "You want something to drink?"

"Depends what it is," Kaylen muttered.

Mabel waved a hand. "Nothing you can't handle." She poured Kaylen a healthy dose of cheap whiskey into a plastic cup and handed it over.

Kaylen took a sip to be amiable, she couldn't quite read Mabel's mood, and winced. "Damn, Mabel, this is some rotgut shit you bought."

Mabel poured her own cup and took a hearty swig. "I didn't buy it. Roger gave it to me in trade for a rock. I shoulda kept the rock, this shit's gonna give me an ulcer."

"Hey, what's the story on chow tonight? We on our own?"

"Nah. Fred'll put somethin' together. Probably Dinty Moore stew or something like that. Not great, but it's hot and on a night like tonight, that's all that matters."

"You going over to Roger's tonight?" For some odd reason, Kaylen hoped Mabel would stick around tonight. She was on edge and didn't know why. It wasn't the weird shit that kept happening with the cop, or whatever he was. It was something deeper, something even below them. And why were they adding their two cents, anyway? Maybe some questions were better left unanswered.

"Nope. He called me clingy and I told him he could fuck his hand for a while." She grinned at Kaylen. "Hope he bought some lotion."

"You love it and you know it," Kaylen laughed. Cheap or not, the whiskey was warming her up and calming her down.

"Maybe a little." Mabel took another swallow. "So, what's up with you anyway? You got a mental thing or something? What's it called when you get dizzy all the time?"

"Vertigo, and no I don't have a mental thing." Kaylen sipped the whiskey. "I don't know what's going on." She looked at Mabel through her lashes. "Can I ask you something? Something personal?"

Mabel leaned back against the scant counter. "I guess."

"When you feel things, do you ever see things?"

"Like what?"

Kaylen squirmed on the bunk. "Like, have you ever seen a person, but not just seen. Have you ever felt like you were right there with them?"

Mabel thought about it. Kaylen could see the other woman was troubled and she felt bad to be scraping against old wounds. Finally, Mabel spoke, "I've never had that happen before. I just get feelings about things, or I used to, and sometimes, if I really concentrate, I can see into a person a little. Not enough to read their future or anything like that, but I can see what's in the front of their mind, if you catch my drift."

Kaylen nodded. What Mabel was describing wasn't that much different from what she saw when they chose a victim.

"If I could see what was coming, things might have been different."

"I think that's true for all of us," Kaylen agreed.

Mabel shook herself and finished her drink, then refilled. "Anyway, what's got you so spooked about him? If you don't know him, what's the difference?"

"I think he's looking for me."

"Most of us got someone looking for us. That's why we're here. He won't find you, honey. And if he shows up, we'll send him on his way."

"I don't think Marco will go along with that."

"Marco won't say shit to a cop." Mabel checked the level in the bottle. "He'll be scarce if the popo makes an appearance."

There was a knock on the door. Mabel leaned over and opened it a crack. "What?"

A hand reached in holding a bowl of stew. "Here, Fred sent it over for Rails. Guess you're on your own, Mabel." Kaylen recognized Edward's voice.

"Thanks, Ed. You want a sniffer?"

"That the shit from Roger?"

Kaylen burst out laughing, almost dropping the bowl Mabel was handing up to her. She didn't drink much and the two or three little nips she had taken were making her fuzzy. And giggly.

"Hey, Ed, you do me a favor?" Mabel was reaching over to refill Kaylen's cup. "Would you go get me a bowl from Fred?"

"What's in it for me? It's freezing out here." Edward sounded irritated, something Kaylen thought was impossible.

"You come back here and you can stay with us if you want. No hanky panky or nothing, but we could all play cards or something."

He peeked in the door at Kaylen. "You mind me staying over, Rails?"

"As long as you bunk with Mabel, I don't give a shit."

Wind blew into the compartment, chilling all of them. "Make up your damn mind and shut the door," Mabel groused.

"Fine, I'll go get you some chow. You guys got cards?"

"Yeah, and ask Fred if he's got some bread or something to sop up this muck."

Edward arched an eyebrow. "Rails isn't complaining and you don't even have yours yet."

Mabel waved a hand. "Yeah, but I've had it enough to know what it tastes like."

"I'll tell him you said that." He ducked out of the door before Mabel could get a clean swing at him.

Kaylen grinned because it was expected, but she didn't want to play cards. She wanted to choke down what was in this bowl, it wasn't bad but her stomach didn't want anything on top of the liquor it was already trying to expel, and go to bed. She figured Mabel and Edward would leave her alone. Roger or Trips would harass her until she played a hand or three. Mabel was pawing through one of the two drawers in the compartment. She held up a battered deck of Bicycles and laughed.

"I knew the damn things were in there."

"Is it a complete deck?"

Mabel took out the cards and fanned them. "I guess I could check the suits real quick. Would be a pain in the ass if we were missing an ace or something." She sat on the narrow counter.

Kaylen could hear the slap of cards as Mabel organized. Her head was starting to spin and the food she had already eaten was decidedly unhappy. She put the bowl on the counter by the foot of the bunk. She had to stretch and lean down to do this and for a second she thought she really would throw up. Then she was leaning back again and the urge passed. She lay back on the bunk and closed her eyes. The steady beat of the rain on the roof of the trailer was soothing. She slid under the heavy blanket she had bought when it looked like the cold was going to stay a while and settled herself.

Mabel's head popped up next to the bunk and Kaylen opened her eyes. "I can tell Ed it's not a good idea after all. He won't mind."

"No, it's okay. Will the two of you fit on the bottom bunk?"

Mabel inclined her head. "We have before."

"Edward too?" Kaylen knew women like Mabel weren't picky when it came to bed warmers, but she was kind of surprised Mabel would sleep with multiple guys on the same show. Especially when the show was this small.

"No," Mabel drawled. "But Roger's been down here and he's a bit heavier than Scissorhands, don't you think?"

"I guess," Kaylen muttered. She was having a hard time following the conversation, simple as it was, and her eyes kept fluttering shut.

"Are you sure you're okay? You can barely keep your eyes open." Mabel was looking Kaylen over in a worried, fretting way Kaylen wasn't used to.

"I'm just more tired than I've ever been in my whole life. Not sure why."

"Stressed out, I bet. Stress does some weird shit."

"Maybe."

"Hey, me and Ed can go over to his bunk. Roger can stay in one of the trucks if he don't like it. Give you some peace and quiet."

Panic flared in Kaylen at the thought of being alone. "No don't go, Mabel, please." She hated the pleading quality of her voice.

The other woman rested a hand on her shoulder. "Alright, honey, alright. We'll stay in here with you." Mabel had no doubt had her share of people on a bad trip and was probably better than any shrink at handling paranoia. "It's okay though. That guy ain't gonna find you here, Rails."

"I don't think he's the one I should be worried about." With that, Kaylen dropped off into nothingness.

#

She was back in the woods, only this time her lungs were on fire and she felt a sharp, searing pain in her lower right side. She was limping again too, but the pain was radiating out and up from her ankle. It was raining and cold and dark as a mine shaft. Wind whipped the trees and every gust pushed her off balance.

Kaylen kept looking back over her shoulder, terror coursing through her at what she might see pursuing her. The night was so dark she couldn't see more than a few feet. This realization brought her no comfort as she realized that whoever was chasing her would be upon her before she saw anything. The rain and wind made it impossible to hear anything beyond the natural cacophony.

Her terror was new to Kaylen. She hadn't felt this kind of panic since she was a very little girl, since before they came. This was how she had felt when she had known she was alone, had known if something bad was going to happen to her it would be impossible for her to stop it. Then they had come, had promised to keep her safe, and she had stopped being afraid of people. Until this cop or whatever he was started following her.

Going to prison didn't scare Kaylen. She knew she wouldn't get the death penalty. Not at first anyway. No until they got hungry enough to start hunting the cell blocks. It was what would come after that. That was what scared Kaylen.

What would happen when the authorities reviewed the security footage? Where would they put her? Why, they'd take her to some high security institution of some kind, wouldn't they? Somewhere she could be studied, observed, experimented on.

How long before she really did go insane? How long before they abandoned her like everyone else? Because that was what they would do, of course. If she were locked up and unable to get them to prey, they'd have to leave her or starve. And would they leave without first punishing her? Would they really? Wouldn't it seem more likely that they would blame her for their hunger and lack of options? Kaylen wasn't sure how much or what kind of intelligence they had, but she had been driven to distraction enough when they were hungry to know they didn't have a problem sharing their discomfort with her.

She fell on the wet ground. The pain in her side flared, making her scream. She rolled over on her back and touched her side cautiously, afraid of what her probing fingers would find. They slid across a warm, sticky wetness, the tip of her index finger actually sliding into a ragged hole in her body. Kaylen cried out again in renewed pain and rolled over, trying to get back to her feet.

Someone hit her hard across the back with something long and heavy, like a crowbar. Or a tent stake. Kaylen felt something snap inside her and she fell flat to the ground, gasping in agony. Where were they? Why weren't they helping her? She reached down into her mind to find them and encountered only a strange blankness. The person above her hit her again, this time striking across her shoulder blades. Kaylen tried to scream, to call for help, but her throat was clogging up. She coughed up a mouthful of blood and used the last of her strength to roll herself over, determined to see who was killing her.

In the dark, she could only make out the form of a person above her. She strained to see any kind of feature that would help her identify her assailant. All she saw was the end of the metal object coming down fast, aiming directly for her chest.

Kaylen woke up screaming just as the metal point drove into her chest. She waved her arms around, still trying to fight off whoever was attacking her. Her hand struck someone and they grabbed her. She felt them groping, finding her other hand and pinning her to the bunk. Screaming, Kaylen arched her back, trying to buck the person off.

"Jesus Christ, get the fucking light on!" Someone yelled. Kaylen vaguely recognized the voice but in her terror she couldn't place it.

"I'm trying. The fucking power must be out."

Kaylen continued to struggle. She could hear the person on top of her beginning to pant. She took this as a sign of weakness and redoubled her efforts, using her feet to brace against the bunk and shove.

"Dammit, Rails, it's Ed. Stop freaking the fuck out. Mabel, get a goddamn light on in here."

"Here." A beam of light shot up toward the ceiling. "I found the flashlight." Mabel hurried to the side of the bunks and shined the light so Kaylen could see her and Edward.

Kaylen stared at them with insane, white-rimmed eyes. She was covered in sweat and breathing hard, her chest rising and falling so fast Mabel could barely keep count of the rhythm. Edward was panting as well. He was straddling Kaylen, trying to put as much body weight on her to keep her pinned to the bunk without hurting her. He looked as panicked as she did.

Mabel reached out and gently stroked Kaylen's sweaty brow. "Look, honey, look. It's just us. You're okay. You were just having a bad go is all." She continued to stroke Kaylen as Edward slowly released his hold When Kaylen stayed where she was he climbed off the bunk.

"See, honey. You're alright." Mabel was still stroking her head and Kaylen was getting her breathing under control.

Edward was poking around in the small refrigerator. He came back with a bottle of water. "Here." He handed it to Mabel.

Kaylen watched all this from where she lay on the bunk. She was fighting to regain some control over herself. She sat up, ignoring the water Mabel held out and put her legs over the side of the bunk. She hung her head low and took a few deep breaths. Her whole body was shaking from reaction or shock or both. Edward took Mabel's blanket off the bottom bunk and put it over Kaylen's shoulders.

"Don't worry about upchucking on the floor, honey; we've cleaned up worse." Mabel was gently rubbing Kaylen's back. Edward was leaning back against the scant counter and watching.

"I'm not gonna puke, Mabel," Kaylen croaked. She took the bottle from Mabel with a shaking hand and took a tentative sip.

"You get into some bad crank or somethin'?" Edward asked.

"No, I don't do anything stronger than pot. And I haven't had any of that since I got here." Kaylen took a deeper sip and shifted back on the bunk to rest against the side of the compartment. "Besides, the kind of dream I had would come from doing peyote or mescal or something like that."

"Must've been a helluva of mind fuck," Edward commented.

Kaylen shuddered. "I've never had a nightmare like that before."

"What do you think brought it on?" Mabel was standing next to Kaylen's bunk, looking like she was ready to pop up like a jack-in-the-box if Kaylen started getting wonky again.

"Don't know. I haven't felt right for a week or more now and I can't figure it out."

"You sure you're not—" Edward began.

"Do you want me to drop my britches and piss on a stick right here in front of you so you'll believe I'm not pregnant?" Kaylen said hotly.

He waved a hand. "And she's back."

"It got something to do with the guy that's following you, doesn't it? I told you not to worry about him," Mabel soothed.

"What guy?" Edward asked.

The women exchanged a look and Mabel said, "She got a feeling about a guy a few days back. Like my feelins'."

"Your's always come true or are they hit or miss like Mabel's?"

Kaylen shrugged. "I don't know. I've never had a feeling like this before." She took another sip and said, "I think he is coming, why else would I keep seeing him?"

"How many times have you seen him?" Mabel asked sharply.

"Twice. The second time was longer." Her hands started to shake again. "Mabel, I'm pretty sure he saw me too."

Now it was Mabel and Edward who looked at each other. He raised his hands and shrugged. "I got nothin' you two. This is strictly Twilight Zone as far as I'm concerned. Hell, I never even believed Mitzy and she could pick the ponies for every race."

Kaylen raised her eyebrows.

"Mitzy was a self-proclaimed psychic that was on the show last season. She's gone on to bigger and better things. Rumor is she's working a joint in some tourist place like New Orleans or Orlando or someplace," Mabel explained. She sighed, "If he really did see you, you keep yourself scarce at showtime, you hear?" she said sternly.

"How am I supposed to make money, Mabel?" Kaylen didn't really care about money, but she didn't want to be locked up in the compartment all day either.

"Wear that Snoopy hat you got and keep your head down," Edward advised. "Almost everybody here wears a hat so it won't stand out."

"Y'all only do that so you ain't got to wash your hair but once a month," Kaylen observed.

Edward shot her the finger.

"Alright children," Mabel drawled. "You feelin' better?"

Kaylen nodded. "Think I'm done sleepin' for the night though."

"Good," Edward said. "You about gave me a heart attack when you started screaming."

"As bad as my nightmare was, I think I should be more concerned about the fact that no one came to investigate what all the screaming was about."

Mabel stood up and stretched. "Rails, you worked a road show before. How many times did you ever see anyone come out to check on the rousties?"

"Good point, but I was screaming pretty loud. I probably won't be able to talk tomorrow. My throat is still on fire."

"If everybody didn't know that me and Ed were in here with you, they probably would've come. But I told Fred what was up and all the performers are parked on the other side of the lot. With the rain, they probably didn't hear nothin'".

"Hell, even if they did, they wouldn't give a shit unless the cops showed up. You know, don't know, can't say," Edward explained.

Kaylen sighed. He was right. If you didn't see or hear anything, you didn't have to go downtown to the little room with the bright lights and the endless questions. "I think I'll read a little with the flashlight if it won't bother you two."

"Won't bother me," Edward yawned.

"Me either." Mabel gave her knee a little pat, then slid herself onto the bottom bunk. Edward joined her a minute later, after getting Mabel's blanket from Kaylen.

Kaylen stayed sitting the way she was, and put the flashlight up against her shoulder after pulling her blanket around herself. She had a battered paperback in the drawer by her bunk but she didn't want it at the moment. What she wanted was quiet and light.

She took a couple deep breaths and looked inside herself again. She almost fainted with relief when her mind brushed against them, sleeping soundly wherever they hid inside her. They were still here; they hadn't abandoned her. She was shocked at the depth of her relief. Kaylen chocked it up to the nightmare in which they hadn't been around to save her. It troubled her to think she was so dependent on them she couldn't survive without them.

Her assurance that they were with her and sleeping caused an instant relaxing in her body. It was as though her terror followed by her reassurance had left her body entirely drained. She wondered idly if this was what people who lost a lot of blood felt like. That reminded her of her own wounds in the dream and she shuddered again, but even that horror couldn't keep her eyes from fluttering closed.

Kaylen fought hard to keep herself awake, but her eyelids felt like they each weighed a ton and she was sliding along the side of the compartment. Once on her side and warmed by the blanket, fighting sleep was futile. She contented herself to leaving the flashlight on and succumbed to fatigue.

CHAPTER 10

Slate looked down at the plate of greasy eggs and bacon and felt his stomach do a slow roll. He had ordered food because his body needed it after the night just passed, but he was an experienced enough drinker to know he should have stuck to pancakes this morning. He slid the plate away and concentrated on the toast and coffee. His stomach gave a warning lurch on the first bite, then decided to hold a temporary truce for the time being.

As he methodically chewed and swallowed, Slate thought about last night and the nightmare that had woken him. He had awakened screaming, drenched in sweat, and twisted in the sheets. The blanket had long since been kicked to the floor. In the darkness of the hotel room he had groped for the light, recoiling from the cold metal of his sidearm before clicking the switch.

He blinked in the sudden illumination and tried to get his bearings. It took several seconds. His eyes were seeing the ordinary trappings of any cheap roadside room, but his mind still saw the woods. His skin felt wet with cold rain, not sweat. He didn't hear the sound of traffic on the highway; he heard her screaming, shrieking, and then silence.

It had taken a hot shower and half a bottle of whiskey before he could fall asleep again. And he kept the light on this time.

What the hell was happening to him? First that crazy shit in the car when he swore he saw a girl sitting in the backseat and now this horror of a nightmare where he was searching for her in the woods in the middle of a raging thunderstorm. Searching for her while someone else hunted her. Hunted and killed her if that's what the silence meant.

Slate had never had a nightmare even close to that one in his entire life and he had had more than his share of sleepless nights. Nightmares came with the territory if you were a cop, particularly if you worked homicide. Experience taught you that vampires and werewolves were kindergarten teachers when it came to the vileness humans were capable of. At least monsters needed to eat; humans tortured and maimed for the pure hell of it.

The waitress came to refill his coffee. She was a sadly attractive woman well into middle-age who still thought she was in her prime by the amount of eye shadow she had on at this early hour. "How you doin', honey?"

"Little rough this morning. Any chance I could change out these eggs for some pancakes?"

She stood holding the carafe on one hip in what Slate supposed was her version of sexy. The cocked hip suggested it anyway. "No problem. Have to charge you for both though. Sorry, honey, but every penny counts around here."

He gave her the best smile he could with his roiling insides. "No problem. I come from a small town myself. I know how the rabbit runs."

"Bet you do, sugar. I'll get those cakes out soon as I can." She walked away with a switching of her hips he could have done without.

Slate looked out the window at the highway. He had been chasing this circus for more than a week and still couldn't catch it. The problem was, it was such a small time show it didn't have a website or a schedule anywhere. Mostly, he only had hunches and logical deductions to go on. Until the last lot he had found that was.

He located the spot, like all the others, by looking at a map, finding the most logical place for a circus to go, and then keeping an eye out for posters or those little read arrows taped to sign posts. He had missed them by two days. Still, policework was policework, and he canvassed the fairgrounds where the circus had set-up.

The grounds hadn't revealed much more than he already knew. A few discarded syringes, a couple burnt spoons, several roaches smoked down to nearly nothing, beer cans and cheap booze bottles. The trash pick up had been late to the fairgrounds and Slate had surveyed the nearly full cans. He took a glancing inventory of the cans and then walked casually around the fairgrounds in the area it was obvious the circus had set up their trailers. Halfway to the bathrooms he got lucky.

He stooped to pick up a work glove. It wasn't anything fancy and wouldn't have meant anything to anyone else, but the second his fingers closed around it he knew it was hers. The certainty had jolted through him like a low impact shock and his hand clenched around the glove spasmodically.

This had happened to him on occasion and it was something he never told a living soul about. If he had, his career as an officer would have been over and he would have twice weekly head shrinking sessions until the end of time. Cops and the Powers

That Be were all fine with intuition, but only to a certain extent. A hunch was one thing; you started talking about how you could track a person like a damn bloodhound and people started looking at you funny. Since he had never talked to anyone about it, Slate had never had to explain it and therefore, he just accepted it. Sometimes he could just touch something and all of a sudden it was like a location system was activated in his head. He didn't know why it happened or how, but he did know it was random. Why he could now locate her after finding her glove but couldn't with the backpack of her shit he had in his trunk was something he didn't have the time or the patience to explore. Not that it mattered to him anyway. He was a detective; he didn't really care about the why, just the result.

"Here, sugar. Nice and warm and just off the grill." The waitress was back, startling Slate out of his ponderings.

"Thank you," he said politely, even though all he wanted was for her to get gone. He noticed she had undone the top button of her uniform, revealing the top of a couple sagging breasts. This he didn't need.

"No problem. You want more coffee?"

Since it seemed like the fastest way to get her gone and keep her away, Slate held out his cup. While she poured, he asked, "You see a circus come through here anytime lately?"

She seemed to think it over a lot longer than the question required. "I want to say there was a show in town a couple days ago, but my circus days are a ways behind me now." She smiled to show this was a joke. "You lookin' to join up?"

He shook his head. "Nope, just looking for someone who might have run away and joined already."

She frowned. "Not a girlfriend, I hope. If your woman ran off with the clown show, I'd say it's good riddance."

"No, not a girlfriend. My sister," Slate lied easily, "I think she may have gotten herself in some trouble and I'm trying to help her out of it."

The waitress laid a hand on his arm. "Oh, sweetie ain't that somethin'. Let me go back and ask Clyde. He's got a couple of kids. If anyone knows if the circus was in town, it'll be him."

Slate smiled at her again. "If you would, that'd help me out."

She grinned at him, revealing a couple of missing teeth. "No problem. Back in a jiff." She sauntered off toward the kitchen.

The things I do for this job, Slate thought as he attempted to eat the pancakes.

#

His head wasn't much better by noon. Clyde had informed him via the waitress whose name he had intentionally forgotten that there had indeed been a circus in town not two days before Slate arrived. They did a couple of shows and then cleared out. Slate asked if anyone might have an idea of where they went and neither Clyde nor the waitress offered a valid opinion.

Despite finding the glove and having a temporary sonar light up in his mind, Slate hadn't been able to hold the link. This happened from time to time, especially if the person he was tracking was miles away. The momentary elation he had felt when he found the glove was a fading memory. Still, he had kept the glove and stuffed it in the backpack.

Frustrated and discouraged, Slate had returned to his motel room after paying for another night and had crashed out on the unmade bed for another few hours. The nightmare had not returned and he was able to get some actual sleep. It hadn't helped the pain in his head but it was making it a little easier to focus. He took some aspirin and while he waited for it to kick in, he glanced over the battered Rand McNally he carried in his car.

So far, the circus had been heading in a steady northeast direction. They stayed away from the big cities, preferring, apparently, to play the small to mid-sized burgs that clustered around the thriving metropolises. Slate wasn't sure about the logic of such a schedule and decided it must be a circus thing. Maybe they were territorial about their bookings or something. Either way, the smaller cities made it harder to locate the damn thing and also where it might be headed. He had also discovered that a five-hundred-mile jump for this little show was no big deal, furthering his irritation. It made him feel like circuses, at least little ones, and carnivals really were tailored for people living just outside the law.

Getting no clear idea of what direction to take from looking at the map, Slate decided to go out and get some fresh air. He grabbed his jacket and headed down to the stream that flowed behind the motel. He had been down here last night and had noticed a path that wound along the running water.

He started downstream, not really paying attention to anything and seeing everything. He didn't know if this kind of awareness was a cop thing or if it was just him, he had never asked another one, but it was the best way for him to find what he was looking for. He listened to the stream but he could also make out distinct bird calls, the road traffic up and to his left, the crunch of his boots on the path. He saw not just the trees and the dirt and the water, but he also noticed the glint of sunlight in the leaves, the splash as a trout hit the surface, the spill of ash from a cigarette or cigar. He smelled the green of the grass, but also the decay of leaves left in hollows from last fall. It was eerie, this too awareness that he had cultivated over the years, and it spooked him sometimes with its totality. He could walk into any crime scene if he was alone and almost see what had transpired there. If someone was with him, it wouldn't work. He didn't know if it was self-consciousness, or their energy, or what, but if another person was around he couldn't manifest this level of immersion.

He was turning around to head back, thinking he wasn't going to get a hunch on this one, when something pinged inside his head. Slate froze where he stood and closed his eyes, focusing on whatever had just happened. It was like a bell had rung, very softly, in the back of his mind. The ping came again, faintly, almost shyly. Slate cocked his head, looking for all the world like a man straining to isolate a specific sound. The ping came one more time and this time, Slate locked his mind on it.

Suddenly, he saw her again, really saw her this time. She was looking into a mirror, it had to be a mirror because she was checking her face the way women did before they went out, and he was behind the glass. She was touching her lips, which were a tad swollen, and examining her red-rimmed eyes. She had no idea he could see her.

Everything Karl had told him was true. She was a little thing; Slate bet she was a hundred pounds soaking wet. She wasn't as young as he expected. And neither Karl or Jack had mentioned how pretty she was. Even with dark circles under her eyes and hollowed cheeks, she would turn a few heads. Her hair was a rusty shade of auburn that highlighted her bright green eyes. A dash of freckles spotted her cheeks making her look younger than she probably was. The haunted look in her eyes gave her a mysterious air. It was no surprise to Slate how she had gotten such good tips at the bar.

He was trying to see something in the room behind her that might give him a hint about where she was when something behind her eyes looked in his direction. It was an odd sensation. It was being seen by something without eyes. Whatever hid within her had turned its full attention in Slate's direction and he could feel it marking him. Terrified, Slate snapped his eyes wide open and gasped in a harsh breath. What the hell had that been?

Slate rubbed the side of his head. His skin felt cold in the warm afternoon and bustling stream had taken on a gloomy cast. Something had put a finger on him while he was looking at the girl, something dark.

The ping in his head returned. Cautiously, Slate turned in a small circle. He didn't reach out with his mind again, too afraid of whatever was in the girl reaching out and finding him. When he faced north, the ping was stronger, beckoning to him. He could find her, probably by tomorrow if he drove all night.

He turned back toward the motel, walking with his head down. Chief Nickerson's voice was in his head talking about how maybe this time Slate should just let it go, let her go.

If whatever had seen him decided to pick a fight, would Slate have much more of a chance than Lenoy? What had that thing been? Slate didn't believe in hocus pocus bullshit but something had definitely been in the girl's eyes, behind the girl's eyes.

By the time he reached the parking lot, his mind was made up. The cop in him had won out. He would go find her. Not to bring her in. A girl like her wouldn't last long in prison and he would have a helluva time getting a prosecutor to believe a little thing like her could take out Lenoy. No, he would find her because he had to know what had marked him and why.

CHAPTER 11

Kaylen grimaced as Fred neglected to miss yet another pothole. She sat up in the back seat where she had been trying to get some sleep. In the front seat, Mabel snored against the passenger window. "How far have we got left?"

Fred's eyes flicked to the rearview mirror. Kaylen was sitting up behind him. "About fifty miles. If the trailer holds out that long. These are the worst damn roads in the whole country."

Her backside agreed with that observation. "At least we can set up after some sleep this time." Marco had announced that since this was a short jump, they could all take the rest of the night off when they got to the next lot and start setting up first thing in the morning. Usually, they arrived at dawn and Marco insisted on setting up all the trailers before anyone could get any sleep. The tent could go up but the rigging had to wait until the riggers had gotten enough sleep to do their jobs.

"You been gettin' any shut eye?"

"Not really."

"Mabel says you've been having some real bad dreams."

"Mabel is right." She yawned and leaned back against the side window, stretching her legs out on the backseat.

"Any idea what the problem is?"

"No. I mean I've always had nightmares. Just something you pick up when you grow up on the streets, you know. But this is different. It's the same dream, over and over."

"You know, they say if you're having the same dream again and again, it means something in your head is trying to work itself loose." He winked at her in the mirror. "Either that or it's a premonition or somethin'."

"I hope not. I keep dreaming I'm being murdered."

"Say what?"

Kaylen sighed. She hadn't told Mabel or Edward about the contents of the dreams. "I keep dreaming that I'm lost in the woods during a thunderstorm and someone is chasing me. Then when they get me, they kill me."

Fred's eyes were stern in the rearview. "It ain't this guy that's followin' you, is it?"

She shook her head. "No. I don't know who it is, but I think the guy following me is trying to help me." She lapsed into a contemplative silence.

"You don't like anybody gettin' close, do ya?"

Kaylen crossed her arms. "I thought I made that obvious."

"Yeah...but everybody needs a little body once in a while, if you dig me. Having somebody lyin' next to you might keep the nightmares away."

She shuddered and looked out the window. "I don't like being touched."

Hearing the warning underneath the words, Fred chose his own words carefully. Growing up the way she had, he was sure Kaylen had plenty of reasons to avoid a man's touch. "We ain't all bad, girly." He used his personal nickname for her, trying to ease her nerves.

He thinks I've been raped, Kaylen thought. *What would he think if he knew the truth? Better to let him think I've been violated than try to explain what happens when people get too close.* "I know. It's just easier for me this way. For now."

They drove in silence for a bit. Then Fred ventured a question, "I know we all agree that this guy lookin' for you is bad news, but if you're dreaming that he's trying to help you, don't you think he may want to get close?"

Kaylen gave him her severest stare. "That's a pretty big assumption based on a speculative conversation."

"There are a whole lotta big words in that sentence, but before you get your feathers ruffled, think about it. Why else would he be in the woods tryin' to save you?"

"Because he's a cop."

Fred waved a hand. "Like a cop gives a shit about people like us. My guess is, he's gonna be around a while."

"Well, he ain't got anything to pin on me," Kaylen snipped. "And if he's got other plans about pinning, he better keep his hand handy."

"I wouldn't be so sure about that." Mabel's voice made them both jump.

"How long have you been up?" Kaylen demanded.

Mabel stretched lazily. "Long enough to know Fred's right. This guy is going to be a pain in the ass."

"I hope you don't mean that literally," Fred drawled.

Mabel grinned back at Kaylen. "Always fun to try something new."

Kaylen raised her hands in defeat. "Okay, let's stop talking about anything in my ass."

"Yes, please," Fred begged. He eyed Mabel. "Jesus, Mabel, is there anything you won't do for blow?"

She sniffed. "Not much."

"That's a comforting thought," Kaylen mumbled. "Why do you think this guy is more than some cop lookin' for me so he can keep a perfect record?"

"Because I've got a feelin'."

"You said those were hit or miss."

"Yeah, but I've had this one for a while and usually if they don't go away, they come true."

"Perfect." Kaylen folded her arms and sank back into a brooding silence. Mabel and Fred started talking about the next lot and how everyone was hoping for a big crowd to make up for the shitty week they'd had.

It was all well and good for Fred and Mabel to make cozy little predictions, but Kaylen had more to go on after her incident in the truck stop bathroom. She had felt him looking at her while she checked herself in the mirror. Her lips had been chapped and swollen and she wanted to make sure it didn't look like someone had taken a whack at her. When she looked into the mirror she had felt as though she were being watched. Before she could focus on who was watching her, she felt them focus on him. The contact had been there and gone almost before it had happened. Her guess was that he had felt them looking at him and had broken the link. But they had marked him, nonetheless. And they would remember him if he came looking again.

Her marks had not appeared and she found that mildly comforting. But then again, this whole connection was new to her and she wasn't sure the marks would show unless she was close to him. She hoped they wouldn't but, in her experience, every cop she had ever been near had made her marks show themselves in one way or another.

She thought about Fred's assumption that she had been raped. She knew the others had come to the same conclusion, mostly because she insisted on staying covered up and never wanted anyone too close. The thought of a man trying to force himself on her made her want to burst out laughing. They would pull the bastard apart limb from limb just for the pure fun of it. They had done it before.

When she was a little girl, a man had tried to take her somewhere. She had been too young to know what he wanted, but she hadn't liked the look in his eyes or the way he kept pulling her faster down the alleyway beside the movie theater where she had been with her mother. She had wanted to show her mom what a big girl she was by waiting outside the theater bathroom while Mom went inside.

She had been sitting on a bench when a man showed up. He smiled at her and told her how pretty she was and asked if she wanted to see his new puppy. Kaylen had told him she was waiting for her mom and then they could both see the puppy. He took her arm and pulled her off the bench, telling her it wouldn't take a minute. Kaylen had tried to scream, knowing he was taking her somewhere she didn't want to go. The man had put his hand over her mouth and lifted her up, carrying her down the hallway and pushing out through a side exit.

In the alley, he had started telling her everything was going to be alright, that he wasn't going to hurt her, that if she was a good girl, he would bring her back to her mom real quick. Kaylen had struggled as best she could but she was just a little girl. A little girl who knew terrible things were going to happen to her if she couldn't get away. Her mouth was covered and she was having a hard time breathing. The man's hand smelled awful and it was clogging her nose.

Unable to scream, Kaylen started to pray. She didn't know a lot about God but she knew people asked for help of some kind when they got into trouble. She didn't just ask God for help; Kaylen's plea was open to anything that was listening.

That was when they answered. They were free then, not bound to her. They tore the man apart, spraying his blood across the alley and biting into his flesh, devouring huge chunks of his meat while a trembling Kaylen stood watching. When they finished, they turned their attention to the little girl.

Even from the beginning she hadn't been afraid. They talked to her like she was a person and not a child. They promised to stay with her, to protect her. If she let them in, no one would ever be able to hurt her. She could live her whole life and not ever have to worry about bullies or bad men or being taken away from her mother ever again. All she would have to do in return was make sure they stayed fed. And she wouldn't have to do anything, they would do all the hunting, all the killing, she would just have to get them close to their prey.

The child Kaylen had readily agreed to their deal. They had come to her at the most perfect time, saving her from rape and murder, promising to keep her safe from bad people. What child wouldn't have agreed to a guardian angel offering to protect them?

In their defense, they had never lied to her. They had kept her safe and they did look after her, as long as she kept them fed. It had taken months for Kaylen to realize the full price of protection. Yes, they kept her safe, but they also made her an outcast, a freak. She learned quickly to hide her skin so her marks wouldn't show, had learned to avoid mean kids for their own safety.

Despite what her current traveling companions wanted to believe, Kaylen had been with men in the past. Both relationships had been several months long and she had been satisfied as a woman by both men. Sex had never been the problem. It was the chasm that began to grow between her and anyone she wanted to be intimate with. A wall that she couldn't explain and they wouldn't understand even if she could. Eventually, Kaylen and her partners had parted company. The one had been a fling and not very serious from beginning to end. The other had been affectionate and light on her part and passionate and deep on his. She was pretty sure she had broken his heart and it was the only thing she regretted from the relationship. She hadn't intended to hurt either man.

After that, she decided to keep her physical needs to an as needed basis. Just getting close enough for a roll in the sheets, but lose my number and don't come looking after we're done. This philosophy had served her well for several years and she saw no reason to change it.

"Lot's coming up," Fred announced.

Kaylen shifted around and started putting on her boots. "I can sleep in the truck tonight if you want, Mabel. Give you a break."

Mabel waved a hand. "I'll just bunk with Roger."

"Nice to see you two are talking again," Fred snickered.

"About as much as you and Donna. What was that argument about last night anyway?"

"I guess the whole lot heard it, huh?"

Kaylen and Mabel both nodded.

He sighed. "Just the usual. Donna had a little too much to drink and wanted more than what we got. I told her how I felt and she didn't care to hear it."

"Can't blame her for wantin'. You're a damn good catch," Mabel commented.

"True, very true. But I told her from the get go, this boy ain't tyin' down to nobody never."

"So, what you're saying is this is like a monthly thing?" Kaylen asked, trying to keep the smile out of her voice.

"We get along a lot better than that," Fred drawled. "We only have it out about twice a season." He angled his head at Mabel. "Unlike you and Rog. You guys are a Friday night special."

"We do our part to entertain y'all." She reached for the door handle. "You need me to back you up?"

"Yeah, I wanna put the bunks up against that barn right there."

She gave him a little salute and hopped out of the truck.

Fred swung the trailer around and started backing up, watching Mabel in the side mirror. Kaylen was sure Fred could back the trailer with no help. She was under the impression that he wanted Mabel out of the truck for a minute.

She was right.

"I don't mean to tell you your business, girly."

"But you're gonna."

He nodded. "My feelin' is that if you keep dreamin' that this guy is trying to help you, maybe give him half a shake before you write him off?"

"That your professional opinion?"

"It is. Course if you want him gone, we can do that too."

It's not you getting rid of him that I'm worried about, Kaylen thought. She said, "How about we let him catch up with me first before you guys start making wedding plans?"

"I think your time's about to run out."

CHAPTER 12

"Man in the house."

Kaylen jumped as Tony opened the concession trailer door. She looked over her shoulder. "You sure?"

He nodded and put his cotton candy board on the counter. "Trips saw him saunter in. Can't hide a cop no matter how hard they try."

"Marco's already on it, then?"

Tony shrugged. "He's watchin'. No point gettin' the guy's attention if he don't make the first move. Could be he's just curious and here to watch the show like everyone else."

"Ya think?" Her voice betrayed her doubt.

Tony lowered his voice. "You want to get to your bunk? Lay low? Fine with me, I'll cover no problem."

She did and she didn't. All day she had known he was going to show up. She had spent a restless night. No nightmares, they seemed all over, but a tingle of excitement had been running through her. It was like being on the edge of a storm, waiting for the first blow. She wasn't sure if her anxiety was because she was afraid of what he would do now that he was here or because she wanted to meet him face to face and see what would happen, if he would recognize her. "I think I'll stick it out. He's never met me, so he might not know who he's looking for."

Tony started refilling his board for the intermission run. "Sure he hasn't seen a picture?"

"Nobody has a picture. Besides, I'm not exactly sure why he would be after me. I was runnin' but not from anything any-one would follow me this long for." The lie was easy enough. She doubted the crew would kick her out if they thought she was wanted for murder, it would probably raise their respect, but there was no point in bringing it up unless he did, as Tony would say.

"Well, if you want a look before the break, he's standing next to the bleachers by the front flap. Didn't bother to take a seat. Dead giveaway." Tony's smugness was catching. It was cute to watch him fuss over his cotton candy bolstered by his sighting.

Of course, Kaylen had been down this road before. The cop was making sure they all saw him and knew him for what he was. If he hadn't, he would have been able to blend in with the rest of the townies. He wanted her to know he was here. Honestly, Kaylen was shocked Mabel hadn't come running in already to say a cop was in the tent. "That's okay. I can wait. I doubt he'll come up for a soda at intermission. Maybe he's just a town cop catching the show and he'll go on home after."

Tony gave her a look that said, 'fine have it your way' and continued with the cotton candy. "Alright, get on over here. I have to spin some before the break."

Kaylen slipped out of his way and started filling the candy apple board. After that she filled a soda board. Tony kept his peace, spinning the candy and watching the ebb and flow of the rest of the crew hanging around the entrance. Everyone wanted a peek.

She had just finished when the crescendo of the last act echoed out of the tent. Tony was tying up the last bag and hanging it by the window. He whistled for Trips and Edward. The three of them would run the stands. Roger would come and help her in the trailer. Mabel was in the ticket booth and usually helped in the trailer if they got busy, but she and Donna had to help Fred with the other trailer. That one sold the circus version of real food, popcorn, fries, hotdogs, stuff like that. It was a big house tonight and everybody needed to pull his or her weight.

"Ready to rock 'em?" Roger asked, pushing his hair out of his eyes and resetting his cap.

"Totally. Most won't come to us though, with the guys running the stands."

"You know how it is. They come out for a smoke and then get a soda 'cause the line at the other is too long." He leaned against the counter.

"If that's true, why does it take two of us to run the stand?"

He raised an eyebrow. "Maybe I'm supposed to keep an eye on you."

"More likely the other way around," she laughed.

Roger grinned and nodded to the window. "First customer, Rails."

Kaylen turned around, grinning herself, and felt all the muscles in her face go soft. The cop was standing at the window. Kaylen froze, her mind locking up, her tongue stuck to the roof of her mouth. Roger, oblivious as always, walked up behind her and put a hand on her shoulder. She jumped, flinging her hand up and catching Roger square in the face.

"Jesus, Rails!" He stepped back grabbing at his nose.

Kaylen turned to Roger. "Sorry, sorry. I didn't mean to whack you, Rog."

"What is wrong with you? You never seen a man before or somethin'?"

She put her hands on her hips, finding her footing, "Well, not around here I sure as hell haven't."

They stared at each other, then they both burst out laughing. They kept at it until a throat cleared behind them. Kaylen turned around, steeling herself, and put on her best I-can-sell-ice-to-Eskimos smile. "What can I do you for?"

The cop gaped at her. It was such a change from the shocked expression she had greeted him with to this winning smile, it put him completely off-balance. "Yeah, can I get a drink?"

"Coke, Diet Coke, Sprite, Lemonade, or water?" She rattled them off with the speed of an auctioneer.

"Sprite."

"You heard the man." She put just enough emphasis on man to get Roger cackling again. "That'll be two bucks."

Slate handed her a five. "You two always have this much fun?" Slate tried to keep his voice jovial. His heart was rabbit-thumping in his chest. It was her. He knew she was here, but he had thought he'd have to ferret her out. He didn't think she'd be right out front in public like this. He was as thrown as she had been.

She rolled her eyes. They were even more green in the afternoon light then when he had seen her before. "Most days. We do have our moments." She handed him his change.

"Keep it," he said, reaching for his cup.

Shrugging, she put it in the tip jar on the counter and said, "You keep tipping like that and you can come back after the show."

He nodded. "I might." He moved away so the next customer could get to the counter.

Kaylen watched him go from the corner of her eye. She felt them stirring, taking notice, then rolling over and going back to whatever they did when they didn't need something from her. Giving her head a little shake, she turned to the dad in search of cotton candy for his little rugrat. As she served him, she had no doubt the cop would stick around. She could handle him two ways. She could either stick with the herd and make it damn hard for him to single her out or she could wander away from the group and give him the chance to approach. By the end of intermission, Kaylen had made her decision.

#

"You sure about this?" Fred was smoking next to the cookhouse. He was in the shadows and had no doubt been there for a while waiting for Kaylen to pass by.

"The worst he can do it try to take me in for questioning, which he won't. Not this far from his jurisdiction."

"Has a helluva jurisdiction if he's federal."

Kaylen blew her bangs off her forehead. "I haven't done anything that would make the Feds take notice of me."

"I don't like it." He crossed his arms. "You've been runnin' from this guy for weeks and now all of a sudden you want to go for a midnight stroll?"

"It'll be the fastest way to get rid of him, don't you think?"

"I think if you'd had any sleep in the last few days, you'd know how crazy this is." He crushed out his cigarette. "At least let Mabel go with you."

Deciding Fred deserved better than her usual aloofness, Kaylen softened, "Okay, look. You know how I said I get feelings like Mabel only mine are more reliable?"

He nodded.

"I got a feelin' about this guy now that I've seen him. Besides, weren't you and Mabel the ones that said he might be here to help?"

"What we said was he might not be what you thought at the time. That don't mean he's Mister Rogers."

Even Jack the Ripper wouldn't be a problem for me, Kaylen thought. "I'll make you a deal. I'm gonna go over by the bathrooms where that swing set is. If I don't come back in a half hour or so, you and Mabel can bring the cavalry."

"He can get aways in thirty minutes," Fred drawled.

"What kind of idiot would do something like that? He knows you all saw him today and can describe him. He'll wait a while if he's smart."

Not having an argument for that logic, Fred waved a hand. "Have it your way. Thirty minutes and then I'll come lookin'. Cop or not, you better still be on a swing when I get there."

Kaylen smiled. "Thirty minutes."

She sauntered down toward the bathrooms. Now that she was alone, her outward cool abandoned her. What was she doing? She should be running away from, not toward this cop. She flexed her shaking hands as she walked. They wouldn't let him hurt her; she was fine. She just needed to find out what he knew and send him on his way.

Kaylen reached the swing set and sat down, casually pushing herself back and forth on the tips of her toes. After a minute or so, she addressed the shadow leaning against the bathroom wall. "I know you're there. You might as well come out."

Slate stepped into the light of the playground. He was on edge. He knew the others would be keeping an on eye on her. He also knew these people probably all had records and weren't big fans of the local establishment. "Pretty observant."

She tossed her head. "Not much to it when you've been on the streets. You've been lurking around since the show."

"Lurking?"

"You prefer skulking?"

Slate approached her cautiously. This was not going the way he had expected. "You been with the circus long?"

Her eyes flashed in the halogen light. "Look, I'm on a time limit here so don't waste your time with stupid questions. Why are you following me?"

"Who said I was?"

She got up. "We're done. Better clear out before the boys help you out."

He held up a hand. "No, wait. Listen, I've got some questions for you."

"Unless you got a federal badge, I don't have to tell you anything." She crossed her arms.

"You're right, but I'm not leaving until I get some answers." He put a fair amount of steel in his voice, thinking she'd back off a little. He was pretty sure her swagger was a show.

He was wrong. "Don't think you can bully me. I know my rights and you're a long way from home field." She spun on her heel and started walking back to the trailers.

Slate reached out and grabbed her arm. She whirled around and he saw that other thing flash behind her eyes. "Let go of me." She jerked her arm free. She started to walk faster. "Get out of here if you know what's good for you."

He shouldn't have touched her. That's what had set her off. He should have tried to charm her more, cajole her more. Waited until she was more at ease before scaring the shit out of her.

"I'm not leaving," he called after her.

She waved a hand and kept going. "You are tonight."

Cursing under his breath, Slate stomped off in the opposite direction. He shouldn't have approached her directly like this. He'd have to figure out another way to get to her. Not tomorrow. No, he'd wait until the next town, give her a chance to settle. He'd found her, now he could wait and bide his time.

Kaylen marched back to the trailers and flopped into a camp chair by the nightly fire. Fred gave her a speculative look but kept his mouth shut. Mabel had no such reservations. "So, what did the big man have to say?"

"Not much. Said he had some questions he wanted to ask."

"You give him any answers?" Roger asked.

"I didn't like the way the asshole asked," she snapped. "And why don't you mind your own business?"

Roger sulked. "Why you always got to take it out on me?"

"Cause you're the only one dumb enough to not to see she's pissed," Trips explained.

Kaylen folded her arms and her legs and glared at the fire. Mabel tapped her elbow with a plastic cup. Kaylen took it and sniffed. She raised an eyebrow at Mabel. Mabel shrugged. "Bottoms up."

Kaylen tilted her head back and drained whatever was in the cup. Red fire burned down her throat and bloomed in her chest. She fought the urge to cough and was rewarded with claps and hoots from around the fire.

"Damn, Rails, you must be pissed," Trips laughed. "That cup was half full of straight whiskey."

Kaylen held out the cup. "Refill please."

Mabel complied without comment. No one are this fire had any say in what someone drank or smoked. The bottle did disappear after she filled the cup, however. Kaylen was small and thin; Mabel had no intention of letting the girl give herself alcohol poisoning because some asshole showed up when she was already in a bad state.

Kaylen settled back against the chair and sipped the cup's contents. Seeing her relaxing, the rest of the group ventured their own questions, none of which had anything to do with what the cop wanted in the first place.

"How long do you think he'll stick around?" Tony wondered.

"Depends on how much vacation time he's got saved up. He could dog us for weeks if he feels the urge," Donna suggested.

"Wonderful," Kaylen snarled.

Donna and Mabel shared a look missed by everyone except Fred. If Kaylen had seen it, Unstable Mabel would have been bunking somewhere else tonight for sure.

"I wouldn't worry about it too much, Rails," Fred comforted. "Once he finds out you won't talk and we don't know anything about you, he'll find someone else to hunt down."

"You think?" Roger asked.

"Why not? Not all cops are stupid. He'll hit a couple of walls and be on his way."

"Well, in that case, I suppose this is the only excuse I'll have to get drunk," Kaylen quipped.

"Like you need an excuse for that around here," Mabel laughed.

CHAPTER 13

Slate watched the fairgrounds from his car. Everyone he had seen was moving very slow this morning. That wasn't surprising given he had watched their fire until well past two in the morning. He doubted they had spent the night drinking soda and talking about reality TV. She was especially moving in a way indicative of one helluva hangover. Interested as he was in her comings and goings, it was the big man throwing his weight around that held Slate's attention.

Even from this distance, he could tell the guy was an asshole. A small-town carnival Napoleon that was used to pushing people around. Slate had dealt with his kind before. He was going to be a pain in the ass right up until Slate flashed his badge. Then he'd go hide in his camper or whatever and bitch and moan to anyone who would listen, but he'd make sure to do it out of Slate's hearing. The interesting thing was that no matter how much he yelled and pointed at the other workers he steered clear of her.

Slate had been watching since daybreak and he had immediately picked up on the fact that the big guy avoided Kaylen at all costs. The man seemed to be somewhat in charge, but if he wanted her to do something, he sent someone else to tell her. Pretty odd considering she was maybe a hundred pounds soaking wet and hungover. The others didn't seem bothered by her at all.

Slate sipped his coffee and thought about his next move. After last night, it was clear he would have to have some kind of plan in mind before approaching her again. He could follow them around until he came up with something. They were open to the public and he wasn't bothering anyone or even on the property they occupied, so no one on the show had any cause to call authorities on him. No that these people would. They knew he was a cop. They would know that the local authorities would realize Slate was following the show for a reason and steer clear of the situation. Or they might even help him, which would be worse for the circus workers. He got the feeling they weren't too worried about consequences if protecting one of their own, but they didn't want any undue attention drawn to themselves.

He had called Chief Nickerson last night and had asked for an extended leave of absence.

"Found something, have ya?" The chief sounded particularly annoyed.

"Maybe." Slate chose his words carefully. "I found who I was looking for but I think it's going to be a dead end. I'll have to double back and pick up the trail somewhere else."

"They haven't tapped the phones," the chief said dryly. "Yet, anyway."

"Thought it sounded like they were still there."

"They've taken over the whole damn department. I don't even know why our guys and gals even bother coming in. They've stripped the entire evidence locker, cross checked all the files, and scavenged through all the computers. They just don't want to believe no one on the force had any idea about Lenoy. Or that we didn't have anything to do with his death."

"Are they looking for me?" It was the logical question. If the federal agents were that convinced the local police force had something to do with Lenoy's murder, the head detective would be the first person to look at. Especially since said detective had packed up his car with a lot of shit and taken an extended, un-planned, vacation.

"Not yet," Nickerson drawled. "I think they think you're pissed off about the way they've taken over and I've sent you out of town to keep the peace."

Slate's lips curved in a smile. "Now where would they get an idea like that?"

"Might've helped that me and Carter were talkin' a little loud about how much you just love government interference."

Slate laughed out loud. "Damn, you'll have to buy Carter a beer for me."

"Already did. What do you make of her?"

He waited before answering. "I don't know. To look at her, you would never think she could so much as kill a rat, but there's something about her. Something behind her eyes that I can't put my finger on."

"Could be guilt, but it's most likely general suspicion about a boy in blue."

"I don't think it's guilt. It's almost..." he couldn't finish.

The silence stretched out. "Almost?" Nickerson prompted.

"Like something else is looking back at me that isn't her."

There was a pause. "I would say maybe you've been drinking too much but I've been around a long time. Let me give you some advice before you go kicking a damn wasp nest. There are things in this world that are better left alone. If there's something about her that did what we saw in that living room, maybe you'd better leave well enough alone."

"I don't think I can at this point."

"If that's true, you had better tread careful. Whatever you saw might have been protecting her and that's why Lenoy ended up the way he did."

That had been a sobering observation and something Slate kept in mind when he got in his car and drove out here in the predawn hours. If Nickerson was right, he had better be damn careful. He didn't want to end up splattered all over a ceiling. Not that he believed in the supernatural. He was under the impression Nickerson might be saying she had a screw or two rolling around upstairs. Unstable people could be capable of some really weird shit.

His attention was drawn back to the circus. Kaylen was talking to a black man. Slate had seen him yesterday handing out plates of food after the show. Other people were putting cloth bags, they looked like laundry bags, in the back of a pick-up truck. Kaylen said something, then walked over to the bunk trailer and went into one of the compartments. A minute later, she was coming back to the truck with a backpack style purse slung over one shoulder. She and the black man got in.

Slate turned on his car. He had planned on approaching her again in the next town, but he wasn't about to let an opportunity to talk to her away from the main group escape him. Lady Luck was a fickle woman; only an idiot wouldn't drop everything when she offered a chance to dance.

He followed the truck into town, staying a prudent distance back. They had to know he was following them, but old habits kicked in and he didn't see any point in annoying her further. He watched them park in a plaza that had a laundromat and a grocery store.

The plaza also held a Dunkin' Donuts. He went through the drive thru and got coffee, smiling as always, at the thought of a cop eating donuts. He parked under a tree and waited for her to be alone. The guy with her was on high alert. Slate could see him marking where Slate had parked his car. Kaylen was walking resolutely into the laundromat with a bag in each hand. After a few seconds the guy followed, carrying more bags. Sooner or later they would have to split up. Either that, or it was going to take a long time to wash clothes and shop. He was about to decide to drive back to the fairgrounds, park in the shade, and get a few hours sleep when he saw the guy sauntering over to the grocery store. He gave Slate's car a glare as he walked to the store. Bingo. Slate finished his coffee and got out of the car.

#

"You just don't take a hint, do you?" Kaylen looked up from the book she was reading. She was sitting in plastic chair in the back of the laundromat in front of eight washing machines.

Slate settled into a chair a several down from her. "I thought I could try again."

Kaylen shifted to face him. "What do you want from me?"

"I want to know how you knew Lenoy."

She frowned at him. "Who?"

"The guy in," he looked around and lowered his voice, "the guy in the living room."

"Was that his name?"

"Look, I doubt we've got very long before your bodyguard comes back. If you didn't know him, how did you get into the house?"

"I didn't go into any house."

Slate ran a hand through his hair. "Okay, fine. You weren't ever there, but if you were, how would you have gotten in?"

"I would have rung the doorbell. And then I would have tried to sell him Avon lip gloss." She opened her book again.

"Listen, lady, I got nothin' to book you on and no evidence at all. I just want to know what the hell happened in that room. I'll be the first to admit the son-of-a-bitch deserved it, but I can't for the life of me figure out how a little thing like you could have done what I saw on that couch."

She shrugged a shoulder. "I guess you'll just have to wonder, won't you?"

"Did it have something to do with whatever's inside you?"

She closed her book with a snap. "What are you talking about?"

"Don't act dumb with me. I saw you, and I know you saw me. And one time I know something else saw me too."

Her knuckles were white around the book. "You should stay away from me. If you saw something and it saw you- "

"You know it did."

"Then you should stay far away from me. They get territorial."

"Who?"

"Whoever saw you peeking." She looked past him to the washers. "I have to change out."

"I'll help."

They pulled a couple of rolling carts over to the washers. "You must like to live on the edge. That's Mabel's laundry."

Trying not to grimace and only using his fingers, Slate pulled the rest of the wet clothes out of the washer. "You could have warned me." He had seen her bunkmate from a distance and that was close enough as far as Slate was concerned.

"Why would I care?"

They wheeled the wet clothes, carefully separated in the carts, to the dryers. It was easy enough; it wasn't as though anyone on the crew had an abundant wardrobe. "You always this amiable?"

"You always this persistent with someone who obviously doesn't want you around?"

"Only when I want to know something."

"Good luck."

He watched her put change in the dryers and start them up. "Why are you the only one doing laundry?"

She sighed, resigned to his relentlessness. "We take turns every time it needs to be done. That way everyone gets a chance to get off the lot."

"What about your bodyguard?"

"Fred? He's the crew cook. He gets to leave all the time because it's his truck."

He followed her to another set of chairs. "You got a name?"

She plopped down into a plastic seat. "I'm sure someone already told you."

"I want you to tell me."

She blew out an exasperated breath. "Kaylen."

"Detective Adam Slate." He held out his hand.

She looked at it. "You had to make your point that you're an important cop."

He dropped his hand. "Who's the guy in charge?"

"The show owner?"

Slate shook his head. "I don't think so, not unless the owner directs the crew. This is a big guy, loud mouth, obnoxious."

Her eyes took on a suspicious cast. "Why do you want to know about him?"

"Just seems like he's a real jackass." He was trying to get a read on how she felt about the big guy since it was clear the guy was nervous around her.

"He can be." Her voice was wary.

Knowing pushing her would only get her to shut down again, Slate changed the subject. "So, besides laundry, what do you do?"

"You mean besides serving soda to men who are stalking me?"

He smiled before he could stop himself. "Besides that."

"Anything that doesn't involve getting in the ring."

"You drive stakes too?"

She rolled her eyes at him. "You're not making friends here." She kept rubbing her left arm. She was wearing a long-sleeved shirt despite the warm summer day. He wondered if it was a nervous tic of some kind.

"Something wrong with your arm?"

Kaylen looked directly at him. "Don't worry about it." Back off, in other words. Slate took the hint.

"Where are you guys headed next?"

"Dunno. They don't tell the crew anything. We just pack up and set up."

"Doesn't sound like much of a life."

"Better than on the streets." She looked past him. "Fred, the clothes are almost done. I hope you didn't get any ice cream."

"No ice cream." Fred stopped between Slate and Kaylen and leaned on the back of a chair. "You two gettin' acquainted?"

"He won't take no for an answer. I told him we were all full."

Fred raised an eyebrow in Slate's direction. "She ain't lyin'."

Slate met the other man's gaze. "I'm not looking for a job and it's a free country. I can tag along if I want."

"Sure. Just don't tag too close." The dryers started to ding one at a time. "Let's get these clothes packed and head for the lot. Marco'll be pissed if we miss opening."

CHAPTER 14

The sound of the crowd cheering startled Kaylen from where she was leaning on the trailer counter. Her elbow came back and knocked her soda off the counter. Diet Coke splashed across the floor in a caramel puddle.

"Shit," Kaylen snarled. She grabbed a handful of paper towels and started mopping up the mess.

"Better get that cleaned up before intermission."

Kaylen looked over her shoulder. Marco was leaning in the trailer window. "Won't take a minute."

"What's that cop want?"

"Why would I know?" Kaylen tossed the wet paper in the trash can and got up for a wet rag from the sink.

Marco clucked his tongue. "Don't play with me girl. We all know who he's after. What'd you do, knock off a liquor store or somethin'?"

Kaylen stopped her wiping and looked up at him, her green eyes flashing. "Or something."

Try as he might, Marco couldn't hold that icy gaze, her explanation of his mistake in Dayton was still too clear. He looked back at the tent. "Boss finds out a cop's after you, he'll cut you loose."

"I doubt the boss even knows who I am." She rinsed out the rag in the sink and threw it in the used bucket.

"Don't matter. He'll find out and get rid of your skinny ass just to be rid of the cop."

"Maybe," her voice turned sly and she walked toward him, shoulders back and head high. "And maybe I might just tell this guy he might want to check out a rape in Dayton that's gone unsolved. Maybe he might think that's more important than anything I've done."

Marco's hand curled into a fist. "I don't know what you think you know about that, but I do know that cop ain't got no jurisdiction here."

"You think a cop that's following a circus around is worried about jurisdiction?"

Marco pushed away from the trailer and pointed a finger at her. "You just watch yourself, little girl. You ain't always gonna have the boys around to keep an eye on you."

Unperturbed, Kaylen leaned forward on the counter. "Lucky for me, I don't need anyone's protection."

The moment held as neither person dropped their eyes. Marco was mad, furious, but it was obvious he wasn't ready to take her on. Marco was a bully who only did anything if he knew the odds were heavily in his favor and he had plenty of backup. This little confrontation wasn't going the way he thought it would and he was off balance.

After an eternity of a few seconds, Marco looked away. He cleared his throat and gestured to the tent. "Better get your shit ready; full house tonight and they're all lookin' for munchies."

"I think I can handle it."

Marco snorted and stalked off into the evening light. Kaylen watched him go until she was sure he wasn't going to turn around, then she slipped farther back into the trailer. Her arms were on fire. She rubbed them through her shirt. Sometimes rubbing the marks made them go away. The rubbing seemed to sooth them back to sleep. They weren't hungry, not yet, but all these people asking about her was irritating them. They usually didn't strike out at people who annoyed them; it was too dangerous. Kaylen was afraid they were about to make an exception.

Trying to distract herself, Kaylen started getting the boards ready for the guys. Normally, Tony and Roger were already in the trailer helping her get things together, but they were both missing tonight. Frowning, Kaylen filled popcorn bags and lined them up neatly on Tony's board. It hadn't occurred to her until now that it was strange they weren't around. It was a decent crowd; the boys should be helping her. She looked over at the other trailer.

Mabel was laughing at something Trips was saying. Kaylen flicked the lights of the candy trailer to get Mabel's attention. Mabel glanced over and noticed Kaylen was alone. She raised her hands in a 'what gives?' gesture. Kaylen shrugged and shook her head. Trips craned his head around and then pointed back toward the bunk trailer. Tony and Roger were strolling up the path between the units.

"Bout time the two of you showed up," Kaylen snapped when they came into the trailer.

"Oh, don't get your panties in a knot, Rails. We had stuff to do," Roger drawled. One look told her exactly what stuff they had been doing.

"Marco's in a mood. Better not let him catch you two smokin' at showtime."

Tony waved a hand. "Marco's only got a hard on for you. And that cop that's still lurking around."

"Which is another reason you two should be discreet."

"Cop ain't after us," Roger offered. "Besides, havin' the popo around is why we need to take the edge off now and then."

Kaylen rolled her eyes. "You guys haven't seen Edward around, have you?"

"Worried about your boyfriend?" Tony teased. He had finished filling his board with popcorn and was grinning at Roger.

"He's not my boyfriend, but I don't want him doing anything stupid." Edward had been acting strange ever since the cop had shown up. More possessive over her and while Kaylen was annoyed at this new chivalry, she didn't need anyone to protect her, she also didn't want Edward to do something stupid and get into trouble.

"Okay, you tell yourself that," Roger laughed.

"I'm serious, you idiot. This cop is just looking for a reason to throw someone in jail."

"Wouldn't be the first time Eddy was in the clink." Tony raised an eyebrow. "First time over a girl though, I bet."

Kaylen threw up her hands. Her arms were burning again and she felt them waking up inside her. Waking up and cranky. "You don't need me here since the two of you are full of yourselves. I'm going to go find him."

"Okay, but if we see the bunkhouse rockin' we won't come a knockin'," Roger chanted.

Kaylen flicked him the bird and stormed out of the trailer. The men's laughter followed her out into the darkening sky. She felt Mabel and Trips' eyes on her as she stalked off, but she didn't care. This was why she preferred it on her own. She didn't like complications, didn't like people who would do stupid shit to try and impress her when she honestly didn't give a fuck.

She walked back toward the cookhouse, meaning to ask Fred if he had seen Edward tonight. The big man would be halfway through making dinner by now and if he was done, he might help her try to find Edward. Or he wouldn't. It didn't matter one way or the other to her. Kaylen was only interested in finding Edward before the cop did so that he wouldn't blurt out something the cop might find interesting. The man was too keen on what was going on between her and Marco already. A wrong word from Edward and the cop might haul her in on suspicion or something.

A noise to her left caught her attention. "Edward? Is that you?"

Ignoring the prickling on her arms, Kaylen walked behind the bunkhouse. The lot was small and Fred had parked the bunkhouse as close to the chain link perimeter as he could while still making sure they could get into the shower compartment. The result was a narrow passageway just wide enough to open the door. It was empty. Throwing up her hands, Kaylen swung around to head back the way she had come.

Marco was standing at the end of the trailer, blocking her path. "Well looky here. Shouldn't you be selling cotton candy?"

Knowing the best way to deal with a bully was head on, Kaylen threw back her shoulders and looked him in the eye. "The guys got it handled. I was looking for Edward. You seen him around?"

Unease flickered across Marco's face for a second before he rallied himself. "Now why would I know where your boyfriend is?"

"He's not my boyfriend and since you haven't, I guess I'll keep looking." She knew she couldn't turn her back on him so she started walking forward.

Marco seemed to hesitate for a second, unsure about if he should give ground, then she saw the resolution in his eyes and wished she hadn't pushed her luck. "You're not going anywhere, girly."

He reached for her, trying to grab her arms. Kaylen shoved him away. "The hell I'm not. Get out of my way."

"Fiery little bitch, ain't you?" He grabbed again. This time his hand locked on her wrist. He spun her deftly and slammed her up against the side of the trailer face first. "Now you're gonna git what you've needed all along." She heard the zip of his fly and felt him ripping at her jeans. Where the hell was that cop now?

Her arms were burning. She struggled to get away, wishing for her knife lying safely in the compartment. Marco slammed her against the trailer every time she moved, until her head was ringing and her nose was bleeding. Her vision was getting fuzzy as she felt her jeans and panties being pulled down. He grunted behind her, positioning himself. Kaylen braced herself for the pain she knew was coming. Then she felt the familiar pulling apart as they leapt out of her. Only this time it wasn't a pulling, it was a ripping.

Marco gave a choked scream from behind her. Kaylen turned clumsily, getting tangled in her jeans and falling to the ground. Marco was pinned to the fence three feet above the ground by one of them. It was holding him with a hand that looked like a giant pincher. It was smiling a jagged toothed smile into Marco's terrified face. Another one was crouching on the ground in front of the struggling man like a terrier waiting for a rag toy. Neither gave Kaylen any notice.

With grotesque delicateness, the one holding Marco extended a long, blue tongue and licked the sweat off the man's forehead. It snarled at him and squeezed with its pincher. Marco's breath was cut off immediately. He began to twist and buck violently against the fence with to avail. The creature looked at Kaylen who was fighting to get her jeans pulled back up before she could tangle herself further. It grinned at her, then looked to its companion. The crouching one glanced at Kaylen long enough to get her attention, then slashed out with a clawed hand. Something fell from Marco's contorting body to land in the gravel by the fence. Blood poured from the place where Marco's penis had been.

Snarling, the creature dropped the weeping, screaming man to the ground. They both gave him a long, calculating stare, marking him. Then Kaylen felt the rush of them filling her again, hiding within her slight frame. As always, she fell the strange juxtaposition of being alone and not alone in her own body. She tried to hold on to consciousness, but her head was throbbing and her vision was swimming. Somewhere, someone was screaming. She fought to stay awake. Someone was coming toward her, asking if she was okay. She wanted to say yes, she was fine, but

Marco needed help. Before she could say anything, she fell away into darkness.

CHAPTER 15

Slate took a long pull of cheap whiskey, trying to drown the thoughts in his head. On the bed, Kaylen moaned in her sleep and twisted the damp sheets in her sweaty hands. Another nightmare or maybe it was the same one. Slate didn't know, didn't care at this point. She had been in and out of consciousness since he had snuck her into this motel room yesterday evening. He wasn't sure she knew where she was or who she was with.

And what was he doing? He was a cop, a detective, and he had taken an assailant from the scene of a crime, told no one where he was going, and hidden her in a cheap, sleazy motel in crack town. He had a confused memory of pushing past Mabel, telling her to call an ambulance and that he was taking Kaylen away. He had carried the mumbling, unconscious girl to his car. The cook had been waiting for him. His only question had been where Slate was taking Kaylen. Slate told him he didn't know but away from here before the local boys showed up. The cook had given him a measuring look then helped stuff her in the back seat and given Slate his cell phone number. Slate had driven away without a second thought. He was risking his badge, not to mention his freedom, to hide someone he didn't know or trust.

That what had happened was obviously self-defense didn't change the fact that somehow she had castrated a man while sitting on the ground six feet away from him. Slate shook his head. No, she hadn't done anything. Those things had done for Marco.

Slate had seen the big man following Kaylen. He had crossed behind the tent and come up in the shadows trailing Marco, knowing the other man had something bad in mind. He came around the end of the trailer just as Marco was flung carelessly up against the fence by something that looked like it belonged in a Lovecraft novel. His cop's eyes had taken in the whole seen at once: Kaylen on the ground, her jeans around her thighs, Marco struggling on the fence, the larger creature holding the big man up with a pincher-like appendage, and a small creature crouching near Kaylen but looking up at Marco like a dog begging a treat. Then the smaller one slashed out and Marco got that sex-change he never wanted. Slate had blinked and the creatures were gone.

He ran to Kaylen. She was out cold and mumbling. He finished buttoning her jeans and turned to the screaming man on the fence. Marco was in so much pain and disbelief he wasn't even aware Slate was right in front of him. Not bothering to see if the son-of-a-bitch would survive his injuries, Slate scooped up Kaylen and headed for the parking lot.

Kaylen sat up suddenly and blinked at him. She had a confused, dazed look on her face. He went to the bed, meaning to coax her to lie back down. She threw her legs over the edge and staggered as fast as she could to the bathroom. He heard her vomiting in the toilet. He went in behind her and held her hair back from her face. Her knuckles were white where she gripped the bowl. She threw up until he was afraid she was going to rupture something inside herself.

Coughing up one final mouthful, she pushed away from the bowl and slumped against the bathtub. She looked at him with glassy eyes. Her nose was swollen and blood was crusted under one nostril. Her lips were swollen as well. "Where am I?"

"In a motel room. In a bad part of town so don't go wandering." Not that she had anything to worry about with those things around. He flushed the toilet.

"Don't tell me what to do," she grumped.

Deciding she wasn't going anywhere fast, Slate got up and poured some water from a bottle into a plastic cup. He handed it to her. "What's in the bottle?" The glassiness was leaving her eyes and suspicion was setting in.

"Just water."

"Why can't I have it from the tap?"

He sighed, got up and turned on the faucet in the sink. Water with a yellowish cast dribbled into the basin. "Satisfied?"

"If you drug me and try anything, it's your funeral." She took a swig of the water and swished it rapidly around her mouth and spit it into the toilet bowl.

Slate flushed the toilet again. "I believe you."

She carefully sipped the water and watched him. He soaked a washcloth with water from the bottle and handed it to her before sitting down on the floor across from her, resting his back against the wall. "How much do you remember?"

She smirked and dabbed gently at her nose and lips. "You mean do I remember that bastard trying to rape me up against the trailer during intermission, do I remember my friends taking care of him so he'll never rape anyone again, with his dick any-way, or do I remember you pacing back and forth at the end of the bed trying to decide what to do with me?"

He started. "You were aware of that?"

She shrugged, winced. "They were aware of it. We have a unique way of communicating important information."

He took a deep breath. "So those things are real."

She only looked at him.

"What are they?"

Her eyes slid away from him for the first time. "I don't know. They've been a part of me for a long time." She cocked her head at him. "You saw them?"

"I was trying to get to Marco before he got to you, but those things beat me to it."

She favored him with a disturbing smile. "Good thing. The worst you could do is put him in jail for what, like two years?"

Knowing she was trying to bait him, Slate refused to bite. "Where do they come from?"

"They live inside." She was picking at the bathmat with one hand and holding the washcloth up to her face with the other. It made her responses muffled.

"Inside your body?"

"No, inside the Twilight Zone. Didn't you see the little portal open up right before they showed up?"

Anger fueled by confusion and delayed reaction, forced him to snap, "Listen lady, if you don't talk straight to me I'll haul you down to the station myself and tell the local pd that you cut that guy's dick off just for the hell of it. I'll tell them you lured him to the trailer for sex and when he refused to pay you made him pay anyway."

She dropped the hand with the washcloth and leaned forward toward him. "Go right ahead and try. How hard do you think they'll try to put someone like me in jail?"

He leaned forward as well, getting within a few inches of her face. "They'll try a lot harder when they find out about Lenoy."

"If you think you can make them believe that I tore him apart in his living room with my bare hands, then I hope you have good enough insurance to get into a plush psyche ward."

They held each other's stare for several seconds. To his annoyance, it was Slate who dropped his eyes first. She was right. Cops might believe she would go after Marco, provided they found some cutting weapon at the scene, but they wouldn't buy her hundred pounds ripping apart a man who could snap her over his knee like kindling.

Kaylen held the washcloth back to her face. "Okay, fine. They live inside me somehow. When someone tries to fuck with me, they fuck them up first."

"Is that what happened with Lenoy?"

"Not exactly. Can we have this conversation out of the bathroom?"

Blowing out his breath, Slate got up and helped her to her feet. He led her to the bed, but she bypassed it in favor of the chairs on either side of the small table in the front of the room. She collapsed into the one on the right and leaned back, stretching her legs out in front of her.

Slate sat across from her and waited. He saw she was looking for a place to start and if he pushed her, she would only get defensive again. Outside, traffic passed on the road, people got in and out of cars, a horn honked. Life went on, in other words.

"My mom raised me by herself. When I was eight years old, we went to the movies. My mom needed to go to the bathroom. I wanted to feel like a big girl, so I asked if I could sit on the bench outside the bathroom. My mom said she'd be right back.

"After she left, a man came over and started talking to me. I knew I wasn't supposed to talk to strangers, but he grabbed my arm and pulled me out one of the side exits. I tried to scream but he covered my mouth and it was in the afternoon so there weren't very many people at the theater."

She was clenching her hands in her lap. That was the thing about trauma, it never really leaves, just takes a vacation from time to time. "Anyway, he was dragging me down the alley next to the theater, telling me to shut up, and I fell down and scraped my knees. When he reached down to grab me again, I saw them for the first time. There were two of them. They ripped him apart in that alley. Painted the walls as the saying goes. Before I could run back to my mom, they came to talk to me. They settled right in front of me in that alley filled with blood and gore and told me I never had to be afraid of bad people ever again. They said if I would help them, they would protect me."

Kaylen looked at him with pleading eyes. "They talked to me like an adult, you know? And they had just saved me from who knew what. I felt obligated to them. I thought they were angels."

She took a deep breath and continued. "They did take care of me. Always have. But their protection comes with a price. You see, they need to eat. And they feed on evil. I don't know if they are good or bad or if this is just what they are, but they feed on whatever makes people bad. And they need me to hunt."

She rubbed her hands together and placed them carefully on her thighs. "I don't know much about them, but I know they can't go far from me. When they get hungry, they start hunting. They can tell about people, you know, that's why I wear long sleeves. When I get close to a questionable person, marks show up on my skin. The more evil the person, the more marks show up. Sometimes the marks come and go. It's like they aren't ready to commit to killing that person. But when they get really hungry, they force me to go around and walk through crowded places until they find their prey. Then they stalk, or use me to stalk is a better explanation, then they kill and feed, and then they sleep for a while. That's how I learned everything has a cost." She gave him her disturbing smile again. "At least I'm not in bed with the mob. These things only prey on predators."

"Do you know why that is?"

"The darker the soul, the sweeter the meat."

Despite his attempts to remain calm, Slate shuddered. "That's why you live off the grid. How old were you when you ran?"

"Does it matter?"

"It does if someone is worried about you." He paused. "Is your mother alive?"

"She died a while ago. I didn't want to grow up in a foster home where bad things could happen, so I learned to survive on the streets." She shrugged. "It wasn't hard, with my little buddies."

"Did they teach you how to hide?"

She settled back into her chair, her shoulders relaxing. This was a subject she obviously didn't find threatening. "They don't teach, they just cover my tracks. I learned the same way everyone else does who lives on the street."

"I bet you're a quick study. From what I've been able to scratch up about you, you find out the best place to get cash quick where no one will ask a lot of questions. Not to mention finding the only place in town to rent that wouldn't raise a bunch of eyebrows. And leaving all that cash behind tells me you have no problem living broke."

"And you've deduced all this how?"

"I am a detective. It's my job to look for people."

"For criminals you mean?"

He shrugged. "I'm paid to solve cases."
"Why were you looking for me anyway?"

Slate thought about that for a minute. Deciding lying would only make her walk out, he said, "Okay, what we saw in that living room was pure butchery." She winced and he went on in a softer tone. "No matter what Lenoy was, we, I, couldn't let whoever did that to him walk away." He ran a hand through his hair. "Besides, I needed to know how you got in, slaughtered a grown man that by all accounts outweighed you by almost a hundred pounds, and got back out again without leaving a trace."

She looked toward the curtained window. "And how did you get started?"

This was a loaded question, a learning question. She wanted to know how he got on her scent, presumably so she could hide better the next time. "I did basic police work. I got a feel for Lenoy in the basement. Got to know what he was hunting for.

Figured he would only open the door for a woman. Then I canvassed the neighborhood, found out who would rent a room or apartment to a girl down on her luck in a small town and went from there."

Kaylen was watching him closely. "What did you find in the basement?"

"You didn't go down?"

"I just went in, let them do their thing, and left. I don't need to snoop around their prey because when they hunt, I see what draws them."

Silence fell. It was Slate who broke it. "How do you sleep at night?"

She laughed shakily. "With liquid or pharmaceutical help. Although that comes with its own complications. It sucks when you can't wake up."

"Tell me about it."

They looked at each other. Slate felt something pass between them. A shared understanding of the human capacity for brutality. He knew if he looked at himself in the mirror, he would see the same shadows he was looking at right now in her eyes.

She took a deep breath. "So, did they give me up right away or did you have to prod them a little?"

He grinned at her. "The only two I really spoke to were Karl and Jack and both of them tried like hell to stonewall me until I convinced them I only had your safety at heart."

"Did Karl give you my stuff?"

He rolled his eyes. "I've got your stuff in the trunk of my car."

"Shouldn't it be in an evidence room or something?"

"Only if you want a couple of federal agents picking up your trail."

Kaylen hugged herself. "They might come anyway now with what happened to dickhead."

"I doubt it," Slate said dryly. "From what I saw and from what I know about how cops feel about carnivals and circuses, Marco's going to start spouting out his story about monsters and the local guys are going to chock this up to a drug motivated attack that went wrong."

"Won't they notice one of the help is missing?"

"My guess is you aren't the only one who's going to catch up with the show in the next town."

"Does that mean you'll give me a ride?" She was trying to be coy, but he could tell she was still exhausted.

"Wherever you want to go if you'll answer a few more questions for me."

"Do I have to answer them right now?"

"How about we make a deal?"

She grew cautious. "What kind of deal?"

"Given what I've seen, do you think I'm stupid enough to force you into anything?"

"There's plenty of stuff you can do that won't physically hurt me."

"Fair enough, but that's not what I have in mind. My deal is this: I'll go get your stuff out of my trunk. You get cleaned up and start clearing your head. I'll go get you something to eat and then you need to sleep for a few more hours before we continue this conversation. Then we can go track down your circus buddies."

She thought about it. "Okay, you've got a deal. Not because I feel obligated to your for dragging me here, but I have a few questions of my own."

"Like what?"

"Guess you'll have to wait until I feel like asking. Go get my stuff so I can take a shower."

CHAPTER 16

Kaylen listened to the deep breathing coming from the chair by the door. She had thought he would never go to sleep. Not that she planned on trying to escape even before he positioned himself between her and the door. She had almost tried to convince him to share the bed with her. More for herself than for him. She wasn't worried about him getting the wrong impression, but given everything she'd been through the last couple of days, the thought of sharing a bed with a strong, protective male wasn't exactly disagreeable. However, she knew all of his hackles would rise if she suddenly decided to become friendly.

She had held it together until he left to get Chinese. In the shower, she let her emotions pour out. Her reaction earlier had been delayed shock from what had almost happened. This outburst was a release of all the frustration and fear coursing through her. What was she doing hiding out with a cop? And what if he decided to turn her in? He could and she knew it, despite his promises to do otherwise.

Her hands were shaking so badly when she got out of the shower that she dropped the towel twice. She wanted a drink but doubted if Slate's generosity extended that far. Digging around in her backpack revealed a bra, panties, a t-shirt and jeans. There were other clothes in there as well. He must have grabbed a couple handfuls of items and shoved them in the bag. Her money was neatly wrapped in a plastic baggie and stuffed into a jean pantleg. She usually didn't care about money, but right now she was looking for a getaway, a far getaway, and that would take cash. She couldn't run away through the woods on this one.

Dinner had been a painfully awkward experience. He had tried small talk which had then evolved into probing questions of her past. Kaylen had put up with this by giving only the most evasive answers and when he continued to pry, she told him to fuck off. That had pretty much been the end of their tenuous civility. She knew it was stupid to bait him, and worse to piss him off, but she'd had enough of him minding her business. She wasn't a child and despite what he wanted to believe she had gotten herself out of tighter spots than this. She could have talked her way out of being held by the local authorities. She wasn't without her own wiles and she had enough experience with cops thinking she was a common junkie running from her past to know exactly how to handle them. And with the lunatic story Marco had no doubt told them, Kaylen was certain she could convince the cops that she was nowhere near Marco when he castrated himself. But she couldn't do any of that with Inspector Gadget tagging along at her heels.

Sitting up in bed, Kaylen leaned against the headboard and thought about her options. She could try to convince Slate to let her go back to the circus in the next town. He had told her he had Fred's cell number and had already told Fred she was okay and that they would catch up with the show as soon as Fred knew where they were going. If anyone asked where she'd been, she could just say she had spent a couple of nights with a guy and he had brought her back but didn't want to get involved with the show drama so dropped her off a little way from the lot. She'd make sure she was suitably shocked by what had happened to Marco and the others would leave it at that. They would know something was up, but they wouldn't dig.

Mabel and Fred would know different, of course, but she could handle them in private. Edward would be wounded but.... Her musings stopped suddenly. Where had Edward been anyway?

When she asked Slate over dinner who had seen him taking her, he told her he had only talked to Fred and Mabel. Everyone else had gone to see what Marco was hollering about. Kaylen didn't deny that Edward had a little bit of a crush on her, so where had he been? If he had heard Marco yelling and seen what the other man looked like, he would have made the connection that it had something to do with Kaylen and he would have come looking for her, wouldn't he? She frowned in the darkness. Inside her, they shifted irritably in their sleep. They wanted peace and quiet. They had done their part and still weren't hungry, so they didn't want to be bothered by her unsettledness.

Kaylen folded her arms and tapped her fingers on her upper arm. She started going through last night one moment at a time, trying to pinpoint the series of events.

She and Fred had come back from doing laundry. Fred had parked the truck and left everybody's clothes bags in the back like always. Kaylen had carried her and Mabel's bags to the compartment where she had put hers away and thrown Mabel's bag on her bunk. Then Roger had come and gotten her to start prepping for the show. She had not seen either Edward or Marco. Not seeing Marco around wasn't odd; he was usually scarce at showtime. Edward should have been in one of the concession trailers prepping but he wasn't. He hadn't come to get the butcher boards before the show or at intermission when Trips and Roger had come to run the stands. He could have been sleeping off a hangover, they had all drunk a lot the night before, but Edward was as seasoned as the rest of them and knew how to get it together for a show. So where had he been?

Swinging her legs over the bed, Kaylen got up to get a drink of water. Slate was instantly awake. "What's wrong?"

"The cops are raiding the place, better hide the cards and booze."

"Very funny."

"That was fuckin' hilarious." Kaylen got another bottle of water out of the pack on the vanity counter. "Got a question for you." She heard him yawn.

"What's that?"

"When you were whisking me away to safety, did a guy show up that looked like Edward Scissorhands?"

"Nope. I only saw the cook and your roommate. The skinny, pale dude wasn't around."

Was that jealousy she heard in his voice or just annoyance at being woken up? "How long have you been watching me?"

"Long enough to know most of the players. Your boyfriend didn't come on the run when he heard the commotion."

"He's not my boyfriend." She took a sip of water, wishing it was whiskey.

"Does he know that?"

She whirled on him. "What does it matter to you?"

Slate stood up, turned on a light and stretched. He walked over and grabbed his own bottle of water. Kaylen moved aside to give him plenty of space. "It only matters because if your little friends are as picky as you say they are, could they have done something to him?"

Anger flared inside her. "They wouldn't do anything to someone like Edward. He's got his problems but he's not a psycho. They would have shown him to me when we first met if he was. They aren't shy."

He shrugged. "Maybe they read him wrong. Everyone makes mistakes."

"They do not make mistakes," she seethed. "They balance them. For instance, why do my arms keep itching every time you come around?"

Not rising to the bait, Slate drank his water and smiled at her. "Every cop has something they aren't proud of. My guess is that since they haven't ripped my dick off, I'm not worth their time."

"Then why are you so sure Edward did something?"

"He's MIA, isn't he? You all got pretty hammered the other night. Here's a theory." He sat on the end of the bed. "You guys get drunk, he likes you, and maybe you figure what the hell, you could do with a little comfort."

Kaylen snorted.

"Anyway, say you two wander off for some privacy, get close, and then you decide you're not interested but since you're drunk, you panic. It's pretty clear you don't like to be touched. These things protect you, just like always, and even if they didn't hurt him bad, just them showing up is enough to scare the shit out of anyone. Maybe he just runs off, thinks about it, figures he was just tanked and maybe he saw something that wasn't there. Either way, he might want to give you a little space while he thinks things over."

Kaylen was silent. He took her silence for anger and so was completely caught off guard by her outburst of painful emotion. "That would never happen. I have never been so drunk I didn't know what was going on." But she had been blacking out on and off the last few days. What if Slate was right? What if something had happened to Edward and she was responsible? "And he wouldn't have left me. If they had shown up, he would have tried to save me from them."

"Maybe that was the problem."

As his words sank in, he saw the resolve in her eyes. She slammed her water on the vanity and stomped over to the door. A second later she was putting on her shoes.

"Where do you think you're going?"

"I'm going to find him. To prove that you're wrong."

Understanding that he had struck a nerve, Slate cut her off when she came back to retrieve her backpack. "Hey, I was just speculating. He's probably just sleeping it off somewhere." He saw she wasn't going to buy it. "If we go back to the lot, we're going to attract attention."

"Fine, then we just tell them we spent the night in a motel and I was just coming back. And we know nothing about what's going on because I don't have a cell phone and you didn't leave a number because we're not exactly a thing."

"A cop might take that as solicitation."

"He'd have to prove it. And trust me, local cops don't care about people like me. He'll buy any line I give him."

Deciding she wasn't going to change her mind, Slate gave in. "Fine, but I'm going with you."

"Good, because I doubt Uber picks up in this neighborhood."

CHAPTER 17

"He's not there, is he?" Slate knew the guy wasn't but he thought it would be polite to ask.

Kaylen rolled her eyes at him. "Just because we haven't seen him doesn't mean he isn't in the bunkhouse or something."

Slate gave her a measuring stare and turned back to the lot. They were sitting in his car behind a row of dumpsters. They had an open view of the trailers. The tent had been taken down the day before, but the local cops still weren't letting the show leave town. Slate bet they'd keep them around for a day or two and then cut them loose. Unless they found a weapon somewhere or a witness, the authorities didn't have anything to hold them on. Besides, interviews would have shown that pretty much everyone thought Marco had it coming.

"Text Fred and see if he's seen him around."

"For someone you're not involved with, you're pretty involved," he groused, sending the message.

"For someone only interested in me as a case you sound pretty jealous." She ran her fingers through her hair and peered at the figures walking around the lot or sitting on the tailgates of trucks. Slate felt sorry for his earlier jab about her friends possibly hurting this guy. He could see it was eating at her.

"Hey, if something, drastic, happened to this guy, somebody would have noticed."

"Not if it happened in a spot no one would look."

"Do you think that's what happened?"

She threw up her hands, her control snapping, "I didn't until you mind fucked me. I've been blacking out and getting dizzy a lot lately okay? How the fuck should I know what happened if anything did?"

He reached out and put a hand on her shoulder. "Hey, look, I'm sorry. I didn't mean anything when I said that. Besides, if they only castrated Marco for coming after you the way he did. I don't think they would hurt this Edward guy just for the hell of it."

She shrugged his hand off and pressed herself against the passenger door, putting as much space between them as she could. "How would you know?"

"I don't. I just thought that if they attack out of hand, it would put you and them in unnecessary danger." He was about to go on when the phone buzzed in the cup holder. Before he could pick it up, she grabbed it.

"So?" Slate asked.

"He says no one's seen Edward for two days and the show boss raised enough Cain about getting a lawyer that the cops are letting them go today. He also says Marco's in a psych ward."

"Like that's a surprise."

She dropped the phone back into the cup holder and sighed, turning to look out the window. Slate gave her a minute to think over her options. In his opinion, this boyfriend of hers, or whatever he was, probably had a warrant out for something and was laying low somewhere. He'd come out when he wanted to. The way Kaylen was chewing her lowered lip made Slate think she was low on patience.

"The lot may be off limits, but if what you guess is even a slight possibility, he can't be far. We can park a few streets from here and walk to the other side of the lot. There's a couple abandoned buildings over there. He could be sitting in one and watching what's going on. I don't know much about any of the people I've been traveling with. They could all be wanted for murder as far as I know."

So, she was smart enough to know the company she kept. Slate turned on the car and pulled out from behind the dumpsters. "I saw a shopping plaza a street over. We can park there and no one will think twice about the car." He saw her relax a little from the corner of his eye. That was good. She was running on pure nerves and sooner or later her body was going to give up whether she wanted it to or not. "After we do a little scouting, do you want to go back to the motel with me? I don't know about you, but if I don't get some sleep, I'm just gonna drop somewhere." He hoped making the decision to stop about his weakness would lower her guard a little.

"If we find Edward and he's okay, I'll probably hang with him until it's safe to get back to the show."

Why had he thought offering her a real bed would be any kind of enticement? "Fine. Just so you are aware, I'm not leaving anytime soon."

She crossed her arms and shot green lightning from her eyes. "I don't need a babysitter."

"Or a bodyguard," he agreed. "But I told you, I want answers and I'm not satisfied with what you've told me so far."

"There isn't any more to tell. I went to the house, they fed, I left. End of story."

"I don't think so," he argued. "I think these things are way more perceptive than you give them credit for. For instance, how did they know about Lenoy in the first place? Everyone I talked to agreed he kept pretty much to himself. Not the kind of guy who would hang out at the local bar."

"I probably walked past him on the street or something and it perked their interest. When they're hungry, they go on high alert."

I bet they do, Slate thought, pulling into a space in the back of the lot farthest from the stores. Not many cars were parked here and the ones closest to his looked like they might belong to employees of the various shops. The dashboards, front seats, and back seats were sprinkled with fast food wrappers, clothes, empty soda cans, things of that nature. Young people working at throw-away jobs.

He got out and stretched, surveying the area. Nobody was paying them any mind. People were always in a hurry to get their business done these days. It made them less than observant. Kaylen watched him from the other side of the car with a little smirk on her face.

"What?" he asked, falling into step beside her as they started back toward the lot.

"You don't need a fancy badge or a gun for people to know you're a cop."

"You'd be surprised how many people don't know."

"That's because most people are sheep who are blind to the wolves in their little flocks." She cocked her head at him. "Must get frustrating, having to save people who nature so clearly doesn't want saved."

He blinked at her. "That's pretty cold."

"It's reality."

They walked the rest of the way in silence. Slate had to lengthen his stride to keep up with the brisk pace she set. For a little thing, she could certainly move when she was motivated. She only slowed when they approached the first building. Without waiting for him to make any decisions as to how to proceed, Kaylen marched right into the first doorway she came to. Swearing under his breath, Slate followed.

The door led into what looked like a lobby of some sort. Old, corroded metal chairs were stacked helter skelter in one corner, their plastic seats long since cracked and broken by time and weather. The remnants of a large desk sat in the center of the room and two doorways led further inside on either side of the desk. Kaylen stood for a second before taking the door on the left. Feeling all his instincts rise in the unknown territory, Slate drew his weapon and continued to follow her.

This room was more like what he had expected to find. Old and stained mattresses dotted the open floor. Empty and partially full bottles were stacked on various cardboard boxes flipped over to be used as tables. More bottles littered the floor. Discarded drug paraphernalia was scattered around the room as well as a vast snowfall of cigarette butts. The place reeked of spilled booze, unclean bodies, and rotting food. At least Slate hoped the putrid odor was rotting food. The place was a drug den, with a heavy emphasis on the den part, if Slate ever saw one. He glanced at Kaylen and noticed she didn't seem the least bothered by any of it.

She's probably lived in worse places, a small snickering voice in his head declared. Slate agreed the voice was probably right.

Kaylen wandered around the building, going from room to room in an unhurried, unobtrusive manner. The few people they encountered were startled at their sudden appearance but were either so stoned or drunk they didn't become alarmed. Slate knew what they were thinking. Here was some girl looking for her sister or brother or boyfriend or somebody and she didn't want to go alone so she talked a cop into playing escort. The addicts in this building knew when they were being rousted and when someone was looking for something. The former situation would have led to a mass exodus until things got quiet and the latter led to what Slate was seeing; a bored indifference to the strangers in their midst.

Finding nothing in the first building, Kaylen tromped to the second. She was worried she couldn't find Edward and annoyed that Slate was insisting on following her. She could have looked much more quickly and easily on her own. If she had been by herself, she would have asked the people here if they had seen Edward or heard of anything strange happening in the last couple days. They would have recognized her as a fellow street sleeper and would have answered some, but not all, of her questions. They would have given her just enough information to get her on her way. Having a detective at her heels had squashed that avenue of discovery. The people here might help her find Edward, but they weren't helping a cop find anything.

This building had a second floor and Kaylen went up the creaking, splintered stairs without a second thought. She saw that they were well traveled and doubted very much that everyone who had gone up and down were lighter than she was. She smiled when she heard a snatch of breath behind as one of the risers gave a warning squeal before accepting Slate's weight.

The second floor had three rooms with windows looking out towards the lot. She went to these first, thinking if Edward was keeping an eye on things, he would do it from high ground. The first two rooms held nothing more than the ones below. The third room made her stop in her tracks so fast, Slate walked right into her. He immediately shoved her aside and raised his gun, looking for the danger he was sure had stopped her.

"Put that away before you scare someone," Kaylen hissed.

Slate ignored her. "That's a lot of blood on that wall."

Kaylen nodded shakily and tried to take a step forward. Slate grabbed her elbow. "What are you doing?"

"Let me go. I want to see." She yanked her elbow free. Slate let her go, but walked right next to her, his eyes glancing in all directions.

"Calm down, detective. If there was anything dangerous here, I'd be the first to know."

"I'm glad you think so."

Deciding not to push his buttons and end up being thrown over his shoulder and carried back outside, Kaylen forced herself to speak in a civil tone. "They would be on edge if there was danger here. And look," she held out her arms and pushed up her sleeves. "No marks. We're fine."

"Only because you aren't in danger. That doesn't mean danger isn't close."

"It doesn't work that way," she said quietly but she had to concede he had a point. If they were sleeping or busy doing whatever they did when they weren't hunting, they usually kept invisible unless someone came right up close to her. If someone were in another room or part of the building, say, they might not be concerned enough to warn anyone. Especially if that someone wasn't hunting either.

"Look all you want but do me a favor and don't touch anything, okay?" Slate tried to sound pleading even though he and she both knew he wouldn't let her touch evidence.

"Why? Are you going to call this in?"

Did everything have to be a debate with this girl? "I should. That much blood means something very bad happened here."

"It could have just been a junkie on a bad trip who cut themselves."

"I hope to hell they got to a hospital in a hurry because they're gonna need a couple pints to refill what we're looking at."

He wasn't wrong. The corner near one of the windows was splashed with dark maroon streaks. A large puddle had dried on the floor beneath them and the center of it looked tacky. The puddle couldn't have been more than a couple days old, maybe fresher. It was hard to tell how long it had been there because the humidity was up, increasing drying time. Kaylen surveyed the floor all around the corner. The tracks in the dust showed only two sets of footprints.

"No blood trail," Slate observed.

"Huh?"

He gestured with the hand not holding the gun. "That much mess. Body must've been leaking like a sieve. There should be blood somewhere other than the corner."

"Maybe somebody wrapped it up. There's plenty of old blankets and tarps laying around here."

"True, but how would someone get a dead body out of here without alerting the local residents?"

Kaylen gave him a look. "You and I both know the people in these buildings have seen their share of shit."

He nodded, reluctantly. "That's what made my job so hard in Tampa. Lots of witnesses who didn't see a damn thing."

Kaylen sighed. "It's nothing personal. Just survival."

"Hard way to grow up."

She didn't answer, only crouched down next to the puddle of drying blood. It was thick and smelled awful. Her gorge rose but she fought it down. Whoever had lost all this was almost certainly dead. Could it have been Edward? What would he have been doing here? It wasn't as though he were shy about drinking or smoking. She had never seen him shoot drugs, but she knew he smoked pot and snorted a little coke now and then. What if someone had attacked him and he defended himself and killed the person? He would have been scared enough to hide the body rather than call the police. Was that what happened? It was possible, but it didn't jive with what she knew about Edward. The fact that he had been missing before the whole thing with Marco even went down was the biggest snafu with her speculations. Maybe he got in with the wrong dealer and things went south? Or maybe this had nothing to do with Edward at all.

She stood up. As she did, a wave of dizziness made her sway on her feet. Slate caught her. "I think it's time you got some food and some sleep. You won't find anybody if you're in the hospital for exhaustion."

Kaylen pulled away from him and lost her balance. She threw out an arm to catch herself and her hand slapped solidly in the bloodstain on the wall. They were instantly there, ripping out of her again and leaving her to fall back against Slate. She let Slate keep ahold of her this time, knowing if he was holding her up, he couldn't use his gun.

The creatures paid the humans no mind at all. The larger one was sniffing and licking the blood on the walls while the smaller one lapped at the sticky center of the puddle. Both tasted and paused and tasted again. They sniffed like hounds, drawing the scent deep into their lungs and holding their breaths for a second or two before exhaling. After thoroughly investigating the corner, they turned and began touching, tasting, and sniffing their way around the room.

Kaylen sagged in Slate's arms, her eyelids fluttering as if she were on the edge of a faint. He crouched down on the floor, careful to keep her out of the blood and let her stretch out. Her fingers were digging into his arms and he was glad she bit her nails or she would have been drawing blood by now. "Don't let them get too far away from me," she pleaded.

"I don't think they'll leave the room." At the sound of Slate's voice, both creatures turned and stared at him for several heartbeats. It was as though they were noticing him in the room for the first time. Slate felt his pulse quicken.

The larger one stalked over to the crouching man, dragging its pincher claws along the floor as it came. The smaller one scamper around behind Slate. Slate could hear that one's claws clicking on the hardwood. The larger one stopped a foot from the humans and hunkered down so it could look directly into Slate's face.

The creature was terrifying this close. The large, razored teeth barely concealed by the snarling lips. Its large nostrils flared, blowing a hot exhale into Slate's face. He could feel the smaller one's equally hot breath on the back of his neck. He was very aware either or both of them could kill him in an instant. Slate held as still as he could while keeping Kaylen's top half off the ground as the two creatures inspected him the way they had inspected the room. Their tongues left a wet stickiness wherever they licked his skin. Then they shoved their noses as hard as they could against his clothes to get his scent.

Movement from below caught his attention. He shifted his eyes slightly and saw the marks on Kaylen's exposed arms. They were fluctuating in color and pattern, sometimes dark and thick, sometimes thin and barely noticeable. Kaylen herself was breathing deeper and her eyes were open and focused on the two creatures. She looked at them with an almost adoring look on her face. *The face of a woman in love*, Slate thought. And why not? These things had practically raised her, had kept her safe her whole life. What better reason to love someone?

The creatures circled around until they were back at their starting positions. The smaller one, apparently losing interest, wandered back to the corner. The larger one held Slate's gaze for a moment, then reached out so fast the movement was a blur and clipped the side of Slate's jaw with one of its pinchers. Slate felt the sting of breaking skin followed by the warm drip of blood. The blood made a trail along his jaw and dripped onto the front of his shirt. Satisfied, the larger one gave a choked, barking command and the two creatures vanished. Kaylen drew in a sharp gasp and her body bowed up from the floor, then was limp again.

She looked at Slate with glassy eyes. "You're bleeding."

"No kidding." He shifted her so she was sitting up. She swayed a bit but remained upright. Slate ripped a piece of his shirt off and put it over the cut. He did not want any of his blood here in the event this place was investigated. He stood up and pulled Kaylen to her feet. "Let's get out of here. I've had enough of your pets for a while."

CHAPTER 18

"Have they ever done that before?"

Slate and Kaylen were back in the motel. It was early evening and the remains of a large pizza was on the table between them, along with several empty water bottles. Kaylen was slumped in her chair and nursing a glass of whiskey. Slate noted the slight tremble in her hand and didn't blame her. The return walk from the buildings had been an adventure in itself.

After their encounter with her friends, Kaylen could barely stand, let alone walk. Slate had half carried her down the stairs and out the door, then back to the parked car. He had thought about just leaving her in the building until he got the car and came back. He wasn't concerned about the residents bothering her. She didn't have anything they wanted and they wouldn't want to get tangled with a cop in any case. What made him keep her with him was the thought of her staggering out into the street and some good Samaritan calling the cops to pick her up. It hardly ever happened, but in this case it didn't hurt to be cautious.

He'd had a bad moment when a woman had noticed him putting Kaylen's limp body in the back seat. The lady had approached hesitantly, trying to look around him at Kaylen. He turned to face her and closed the door of the car abruptly.

"Is she okay?" This local Nosy Parker inquired.

"She will be as soon as I get her back home and in the ac. She's getting over a cold and the heat just took it out of her today." It was unfortunate how easily lying came to most cops.

The woman flapped a hand dramatically. "Oh, don't I know it. It's a warm one. You get her home and cooled off."

He gave the woman his most winning smile. "Will do."

"That's a nasty cut you've got on your face."

Slate had run a finger gently over the cut. "We may have run into a little trouble over on that street back there." He nodded toward the buildings.

"Oh, yes, that's a rough neighborhood. Does she need to go to a hospital?"

He shook his head. "No, she just got a little scare. She'll be fine."

Apparently satisfied, the woman strolled off to the grocery store in the plaza. Slate watched her for a few seconds before deciding he and Kaylen were fodder for the next bingo meeting, but not interesting enough to report to the local cops.

The first thing he did when he got Kaylen back to the room was pull off all her clothes and rinse off her sweat and dirt grimed skin. She had put up a brief struggle before submitting to his administrations. He scrubbed her, dried her off and then dumped back into bed. She had been asleep in seconds. Satisfied she wasn't faking, Slate took his own shower.

Standing under the nearly scalding water, Slate finally gave into the shakes he had been fighting since that ugly fuck had stared into his eyes back at the building. Over the years, Slate had become familiar with evil. He had cleaned up after it, arrested it, interrogated it, and seen it set free by people dumb enough not to see through its mask. In movies and on tv, they always say when you looked into the eyes of evil you only saw blackness looking back. Slate could testify under oath that was not the case. When you looked into the eyes of evil, evil looked right back at you, like Nietzsche's abyss. Looked back at you, and measured you. That's what that big bastard had done. Clearly, it hadn't seen anything worth killing Slate over, or maybe it was just biding its time.

He had looked longingly at the bottle of booze before deciding that he needed a clear head if he was going to get any answers out of her when she woke up. And he was going to get answers this time, no more screwing around. Before any kind of interrogation could happen, however, he needed his own shut eye. Not caring what the little lady would think about sharing a bed, Slate rolled her over to one side and crashed out next to her for several hours.

It was his good luck that he woke up first. When Kaylen's eyes flew open an hour after him, she was nearly hysterical. It took him almost twenty minutes of gentle stroking and soothing words to get her calmed down. Then she realized she was naked, cradled in his arms. Calm gave way to fury. She began kicking and hitting and cursing. Knowing it was panic and frustration fueling her rage didn't curve his own fury one bit. He was tired of her shit.

He caught her wrists and pinned them above her head, climbing on top of her to still her kicking and keep her from flinging herself onto the floor.

"Get the fuck off me," she snarled.

"Not until you calm the fuck down," he shot back.

"Don't tell me what to do."

"Somebody needs to. You're acting like a jackass."

She redoubled her efforts and tried to buck him off. Scrawny as she was, she nearly did. "You better not go to sleep anytime soon with me in this room."

"Are you threatening me?" He could hear the incredulity in his voice. "After everything I've put up with from you?"

"You wouldn't have to put up with anything if you'd stayed away, you asshole."

"Oh, I'm an asshole? Let me enlighten you missy. If I hadn't dragged your ass outta that lot after your buddies castrated your boss, you'd be sitting in a cell right now trying to explain how you ripped off his dick with your bare hands."

She didn't drop her eyes. "The others would have hidden me."

"Would they? The cook and the meth head maybe, but everybody else? I don't know if you're aware, but having some chick around who doesn't have a problem giving a man an impromptu sex change makes those of us of the male persuasion a tad nervous."

"They would not have turned me in," she insisted.

"Even if they didn't, the cops would've found you eventually if you were still on the lot." He cocked his head at her. "And I'm sure the actual circus boss wouldn't want a dangerous roustie working his show. What if you decided to go after a paying customer?"

To this she had no comeback. He let go of her wrists and got off the bed. He went to the bathroom and got her a towel so she cover herself up on her way to the bathroom to get dressed. As she wrapped the towel around herself, he carried her backpack into the bathroom, making a point not to look in her direction. While she was in there, he took the chance to order pizza so she would have something in her belly before she started drinking since he was sure alcohol was on the menu tonight.

"So," he prompted when it looked like she wasn't going to answer. "Have they ever done this before?"

"Which part?"

"Any of it."

Kaylen sipped her drink. "No, they've never shown themselves to anyone unless they were feeding. Or protecting me."

"What about the investigating?"

She rolled her eyes at his choice of words, but answered his question. "No, that was new. Usually when they hunt, they don't put much effort into it. They just seem to find people by some kind of radar or something. They've never come out and tracked anyone."

"Why do you think they did it?"

She threw up her hands, spilling whiskey on herself and swearing. "How should I know?"

Striving for patience, Slate put his hands on the table. "Look, you might just accept these things because they're like family, but this is all new to me and that big guy gave me one hell of a going over, so if it's all the same to you I'd like to try and figure out what the fuck is going on."

Kaylen took a long swig of her drink and Slate saw the tremble was back in her hand. That softened him and he went on more gently. "I know you're scared. If not for yourself then for this Edward guy, but the only way we're going to get answers is by asking hard questions."

"I bet you always played the good cop back where you came from."

"Actually, I was usually the hard ass."

"I believe that." She held out her cup. "Refill?"

He had no intention of letting her get herself shitfaced, but she could probably handle quite a bit. He filled her cup about a quarter of the way and waited.

She sighed at him and brought her feet up on the chair so she could wrap her arms around her knees. "Alright, what do you want to know?"

He had been thinking about this since he ordered the pizza. "First, I want to know what happens to you when they come out and then go back in. I saw what happened but I didn't understand it."

"It's like they pull themselves out of me."

"Does it hurt?"

She shrugged. "A little, but it's a good hurt. Like when you pop an abscess. Sure, it hurts when you do it, but afterwards it feels great to have all that pressure gone."

"Charming description."

"When they come back in, it's like getting filled up, like taking the biggest breath you've ever taken."

"Does that hurt?"

"Nope."

"How does it feel when they eat?"

A slow smile spread across her face. "Like the best orgasm ever."

Slate suppressed a shudder. He'd heard murderers say the same thing in interrogation rooms. For some people, killing was as addicting as eating potato chips. "So, even though you say feeding them is all about them, you get something out of it too."

"Every addict has a high."

"You like it when they hunt, don't you?"

For the first time, her steely gaze shifted away from him. "The people they feed on deserve it."

"So, they're just dealing out justice, is that it?"

"Maybe if the justice system didn't fail so fucking often, they wouldn't have so much to eat. Sometimes when I walk around my arms are literally on fire by the end of the day because of all the scumbags I've come across. And most of them are in little towns like yours, if you want to know the truth."

She was baiting him again and he refused to let her. "What are they? Do you have any idea? Ever researched them?"

"And what would I look under, self-help demons?"

He waved a hand. "Haven't you ever been curious if anything like them has ever been documented?"

"Okay, fine. I did get curious. I went on a search once a long time ago. It didn't last long. I looked up everything I could find on the paranormal, demon possession, familiars, haunts, poltergeists. You name it, I read about it. I went to every library in every town I passed through and couldn't find anything anywhere resembling these things. Not a hint, not a clue, nothing. I think the closest I got was familiars, or maybe spirit guides. But neither of those were as tangible as my guys. They were more ethereal, I guess. More an aspect of faith than real live monsters."

She took another sip. "My guys are more the B horror movie or comic book variety of fiends."

Slate was quiet for a minute, thinking. "If it's great when they eat, what happens when they're hungry?"

Kaylen shuddered. "It's no picnic. If they can make me feel good when they get what they want, you can bet they can hurt me if I leave them hanging." She looked down at the table. "I try to feed them as soon as they start wanting food. Mostly because after they feed I'm not much use for an hour or so."

"And they leave clean up and getaway to you, don't they?"

"Yes."

He ran a hand through his hair. "Just saying, from my point of view you're right up there with Dahmer and Bundy as far as being able to get away with murder."

"I don't think of it as murder, I think of it as balancing the scales."

"Getting the ones that squeeze through the cracks?"

"Something like that." She didn't sound very convinced despite her brave words.

"You don't like the killing, do you? Even though you get something out of it."

"It...depends. Sometimes the killing doesn't bother me one bit. Sometimes I feel like they're doing a good thing. Given what they show me, it turns my stomach to think that the prey has gotten away with so much and it seems they'll never get caught. And even if they do, half the time they get set free on a technicality of some kind. So with those people, I feel okay about it.

"But sometimes, I wonder. Sometimes it feels like the prey will get caught, that they will be punished, that killing them is just speeding up the process and I don't want anything to do with it. But then I think, if that were true they would have been caught already."

"You keep saying 'what they show me'. What do they show you?"

"All the bad that the prey has done and gotten away with. Horrible, horrible things. Things that give me nightmares even the best drugs and strongest booze can't even touch. Not that I do much of either to get to sleep. Not being able to wake up is scarier than going to sleep."

She looked so miserable and small, sitting in her chair. He wanted to go to her, to hold her and comfort her, but he knew she wouldn't accept it. Not yet, anyway. He reached across the table and took one of her hands. It was very cold. "Protection with a price."

"A very high one."

"When we were in the building and they were sniffing around, the farther away from you they got, the more distressed you were. Do they take something from you when they leave?"

Her hand flexed in his. "Yes. I'm not sure what. When they're out of me I feel really weak. Like I've had the flu or something. Then they come back and it's like getting an energy shot or something, but then I crash and all I want to do is sleep."

"I've noticed." He ran his thumb over the back of her hand. "Will they protect you if something happens while you're out cold?"

"I suppose so. It would be in their best interest to. I don't know because nothing has ever happened."

"Except now."

She frowned at him. "What do you mean?"

"After Lenoy, you couldn't just pass out on one of his designer couches. You didn't know if he'd be having company any time soon. So you took off. Must've been a hard go."

"Like running a 5K without ever even jogging a mile. I thought I was going to die in those woods if I didn't stop running."

The mention of woods made Slate jerk reflexively and he dropped her hand.

"What's wrong?" she asked, alarmed.

"Nothing, just a memory."

"About being lost in the woods? In a storm?"

Slate's eyes turned wary. "How do you know about that?"

Kaylen looked away from him. "I saw it. A little of it anyway. One of the times I saw you. Just a glimpse, but I saw the woods and the storm."

He reached for her hand again. "I was looking for you. I heard you screaming," he swallowed. "And then I didn't."

"Because I died."

Now he did get up and pull her into his arms. "I'm not going to let that happen."

Her voice was muffled against his chest when she spoke. "You weren't with me remember? You were looking for me."

"I know. But where were they? Shouldn't they have been protecting you?"

He felt her tremble in his arms. "I don't know where they were. And I don't know who was killing me."

"After we find your boyfriend we'll work on that problem."

"He's not my boyfriend." Her voice was slurred. The alcohol was starting to take effect.

"Whatever he is, we'll try to find him tomorrow. Tonight we should catch up on our sleep."

"Does that mean you want back in the bed?"

"Only if it doesn't bother you. I don't want to give your friends any more of a reason to tear me apart."

"If they were going to do that, you wouldn't be standing here."

He drew away from her slightly so he could look at her face. "Maybe they're saving me for later, like a midnight snack." His attempt at a joke had the desired effect.

She smiled up at him. "In that case, maybe you should sleep on the floor to make clean up easier."

"Maybe you should sleep on the floor, you've got more experience with that sort of thing than I do."

She punched him lightly. "Are you insulting me or paying me a compliment?"

"Take it however you like."

She rubbed a hand across her eyes. "I'm too tired to decide right now. Let's get some sleep and text Fred in the morning. Maybe Edward turned up before they pulled out tonight."

"And if he didn't?"

"You're the detective. Start detecting."

CHAPTER 19

Kaylen frowned at the building they had searched the day before. She had texted Fred that morning and Edward was still a no show. She did find out where the circus was headed next. It wasn't that far; she and Slate would be able to catch them by tomorrow night if they left this town tonight. Of course, they could always stay here until they found Edward and not go back to the circus, but Kaylen decided she would wait until tonight to make a decision.

"I don't think we're going to find out any more today than we did yesterday unless you can figure out what your friends were so interested in," Slate commented. "Any ideas?"

Kaylen wished Slate would give it a rest about them. He was like a terrier on a rat. "I told you, they've never done anything like that before."

"Which is why it's important to figure out why they're doing it now," he insisted.

She glowered at him. "Fine. Let's go over it again, since the horse might not be completely dead yet."

"Love your metaphors, don't you?"

"Keeps the conversation interesting."

"I was thinking it was more of a diversion technique."

"It usually works." Giving up on trying to dissuade him, Kaylen tried to focus. "Okay, so they came out and started sniffing around the blood and the room like they were tracking something. While they were doing that, I kept seeing flashes of things that had happened in that room. Lots of drug use, sex, arguing, typical activities found in any drug house. Nothing that could explain all that blood." She slapped a hand on her knee. "I'd be able to focus more on what happened yesterday if I wasn't so damn tired and disoriented."

"Why is that?"

"I've been having dizzy spells, blackouts and nausea for weeks." She glared at him. "And I am not pregnant."

He was studying her. "I didn't think you were. Other than the nausea, none of those are pregnancy symptoms as far as I know. When did all this start?"

"I just said a few weeks ago."

"Before or after you joined the circus?"

She frowned. That was something she hadn't thought of. "Definitely after. Before Lenoy I was fine, although miserable because they were starving, but normal enough. I didn't have my first dizzy spell until the day I started working on the show."

He tapped his fingers on the steering wheel. "Can I ask you a question without you getting pissy with me?"

"I make no promises."

"Was this Edward guy around every time you had an episode?"

"What are you getting at?"

"Just answer the question."

She rolled her eyes at him. "Yeah, I mean, probably. But I was around Fred and Mabel and Tony and Trips and Donna and Roger all the time too. And Marco. It's a small show and we all work and live together. It's hard to single someone out." She could hear the defensiveness that was creeping into her voice and wondered why she gave a damn about whether Edward was around her or not when she flaked out.

"Did your marks ever show around him?" Slate asked. He was peering out the windshield, miles away from the car, forming some kind of theory. Kaylen didn't like the way her body was heating up while she was looking at him. She turned to look out her own window, hoping he didn't see the flush that was rising to her cheeks.

"No, I don't..." she trailed off. Had her marks shown around Edward? They had certainly made an appearance whenever Marco was around. She was so used to her marks coming and going she didn't pay them much attention.

"You don't what?"

"I don't know, okay?" she snapped. "I know this is all new to you, but I'm used to being a freak so I don't pay much attention to my marks unless it's feeding time."

"Alright, alright. Arguing is getting us nowhere. Think, not just about him if you like that better. Has anything weird happened? Something that's out of the ordinary even for you."

She wanted to snap at him to make him back off, but knew that would only encourage him into the wrong direction. Besides, pretending to think would give her a break from his endless questions. She looked back out the window.

A woman was jogging on the sidewalk across the street. Farther down a truck was waiting at a stop sign. Unconsciously, she
scratched at her arms because they started to tingle. She glanced
down as a memory tugged at her. Hers arms had tingled like
this before, near the tent. Had Edward been around then? She
thought he had. She sat up straight in the seat. He had been in
the compartment the night she had the first nightmare too and
he had been there when she almost passed out before her first
fight with Marco. Of course, so had Roger, but on the nights
Roger had come over begging drugs or booze from Mabel,
Kaylen hadn't had nightmares or gotten sick.

"You look like something just hit you," Slate said.

"Something just might have," she replied slowly. "I can't say
for sure Edward was around every time I flaked, but I know he
was there at least most of the time. And he was definitely there
the night I had the nightmare the first time."

Slate cleared his throat and made a point of looking out the
windshield again.

"It wasn't like that," Kaylen said hotly. "He stayed over because I was sick. He and Mabel stayed on the bottom bunk and I
was on the top one. You must think I'm some kind of slut, don't
you?"

"I do not."

"Yeah, right. That's what all you cops think. You see a girl like
me and the first thing that crosses your mind is just what exactly
I'd do for enough money to get some blow or a bottle of booze.
Or maybe you'd flash your badge and try to scare me into giving
you a blowjob free of charge."

He rounded on her. "I would never do anything like that and most cops wouldn't either."

"Most?" Her eyes told him she'd had enough experience to disbelieve him.

"Yes, most. At least out of the ones I've worked with." He glared back at her. "You have to admit that given the places you hang out in you're not exactly going to cross paths with the best of us."

"And that makes it okay?" she countered.

Slate slammed his hands on the steering wheel. "No, it doesn't make it okay, it just explains how you only see the darkness of humanity."

"I only see the darkness of humanity, huh? Well, let me tell you something you self-righteous motherfucker. You know where they like to hunt best? Huh? Let me clue you in. They don't like to hunt in the underbelly of a city or down in crack-town or on poor row. No. They eat best when they hunt in the suburbs or in the better apartment complexes. You think the people you spend your time with are so wonderful? The most craven human beings they've ever fed on have had jobs and families and go to PTA meetings and host church socials and coach little leagues and have the neighborhood kids over for movie nights." Her voice dripped with venom as she delivered her final shot. "And they know all the local cops by first name."

He winced and wouldn't look at her. He knew she was telling the truth. Why would she lie? They had gotten used to each other over the last day or so and he had forgotten she knew more about the depravity of the human race than he could imagine. Even so, it still shook him. After a few seconds, he said, "I'm sorry. I forgot that you've grown up on the bad side of the world, but maybe you could give the good side a shot once in a while, deal?"

Kaylen looked at him, her jaw set. She wanted to make him squirm, knock him off his high horse for a few seconds, but he looked so miserable, she relented, a little. "Fine." She tapped her nails on the console. "So, now what, Mr. Detective?"

"Canvass the area, try to find someone willing to talk." He waved a hand. "Usually ask the local cops if anyone meeting his description has been found or arrested but I think that would raise more questions than get us answers given what happened to Marco."

"None of the people in those buildings is going to talk to us. Most of them have probably relocated for a couple of days until we go away."

She had a point, but Slate's mind was somewhere else. "You said when you saw me, you looked into me enough to know I wasn't a mass murderer or anything."

"Not my exact words, but we'll go with it."

He ignored this. "Do you get hits on most people you come into contact with or is it random?"

"With you, nothing like that ever happened to me before. Sometimes I'll get a hunch about somebody, not a glimpse, but something that makes my hair stand up. Like Marco. I didn't need to see my marks to know he was bad news. Or I'll feel at ease with people right off the bat, like Fred and Mabel."

"What about Edward?"

"The first time I met Edward I- ". She frowned. "That's weird. He didn't blip across my radar at all."

"You did say it was hit or miss."

"Yeah, but he was around enough, I should have gotten a feel for him. Been able to tell his moods or when he was around, stuff like that."

"And?"

She shrugged. "And I didn't."

Slate settled back in the driver's seat to get a good look at her. "And you didn't think that was odd?"

"I had a lot going on with me at the time," she said sourly.

"And since you've been with me?"

"Since I've been with you, what?"

He gestured. "Any blackouts, nausea, dizziness?"

Kaylen shifted uncomfortably. She didn't want to tell him that since she'd been with him, she felt more at ease than she had in years. "No."

Slate studied her. He had a question, maybe a very important question, he wanted to ask, but he knew it wasn't a question she wanted to answer. Especially, not in her current state. He decided to let it wait a bit. He didn't think it would change much but it might shed some light on the current situation. Instead of pushing her buttons, he asked, "What do you want to do? Keep looking or go back with the others?"

She looked away from him. For the first time in a long time, Kaylen was torn between what she wanted to do and what she should do. The survivor in her said leave and go back with the show, if she could, get some miles between her and here, then jump ship and never look back. The part of her that was tired of always being on the move and wanted to be accepted somewhere wanted her to stay and find Edward. If she found him and he came back with her the others would be more likely to let her back into the fold. She didn't think Fred or Mabel would turn her out, but Trips and Tony and Roger might start having seconds thoughts about her being around. Detective Slate was right about that.

"What are the odds of us finding him, do you think?" As if she didn't know.

"Slim to none if he doesn't want to be found. If he's anything like you, I bet he can go to ground with the best of them." No hesitation at all in Slate's voice. No apology either. He didn't want to spend time looking for Edward, he wanted to spend his time learning about her. Although Kaylen had no idea what he could get out of her that she hadn't already told him.

Her stubbornness at the detective made her decision. "Let's see if anyone wants to talk and if we get stone walled, we'll catch up with the show."

"Fine. This is your snipe hunt."

She got out and slammed the door without replying. He caught up with her before she went into the building. It was the same as yesterday with one exception; there were no people here. The place was abandoned, she could feel it in the air. She glanced at Slate and saw he felt it too. He kept his mouth shut, however, and followed her back upstairs.

They searched the second floor again, checking for signs of struggle or footprints with blood in them and found neither. Kaylen approached the blood splattered corner and turned her back to it, trying to see the room from the perspective of whoever had been standing here last. She didn't see anything in front of her, but she caught a flash of color from the corner of her eye. She turned toward the window. "Slate, look at that." She pointed.

From this vantage, she could see the whole lot, small as it was, and no one from down there could see up here. She saw the fence where Marco had been feminized, but more importantly, she could see where the cookhouse had been parked. Next to one of the trash cans that was still waiting to be picked up was a backpack. The show had pulled out last night and the people on it were generally particular about their stuff, so why had they left something behind? She didn't like it. It smelled like bait to her.

"That's bait," Slate confirmed. He looked around the room. Someone looking up could see him because he was in the window, but they wouldn't be able to see Kaylen in the corner and they would lose sight of him if he stepped back a foot or two. The backpack was wedged between two of the trash cans and couldn't be easily seen from the ground because it was closer to the wall the cans were in front of. Whoever put the pack there knew it would be seen from this window. "It's a setup of some kind."

"Set up by who?" Kaylen was behind him, peering around his shoulder, but being careful not to get too close to the window. "It seems a little devious for law enforcement."

You've never met some of the cops I've worked with, Slate thought but didn't say. Mostly because he agreed with her. Cops would leave something like that out in the open and try to get a bite. This was too hidden. "You think it's yours? Maybe the cook left it for you, thinking you'd wander around the lot?"

She shook her head. "No, I asked Fred to keep my stuff when I texted him. Besides, my pack is blue. That looks green to me."

"It is." He stepped back away from the window. She moved out of his way but kept in contact. She was jumpy, her eyes darting around. *What was wrong with her all of a sudden*, he wondered. "Whoever put that there knew the best place to spot it from would be up here." His eyes fell on the corner. "Which means they were up here at some point and knew someone would come looking for them."

"Are you trying to say Edward came up here, attacked someone, then knew I'd come looking for him and left a clue down there?" He could hear her disbelief.

"Maybe not him, maybe someone after you who knew you'd be coming after him."

"Why would anyone bother coming after me?" She tried to sound bewildered, but wasn't succeeding very well. She must have doubts as to having always covered her tracks. After all, he had found her, hadn't he?

"Are you sure everyone they eat is guilty?"

Her eyes hardened. "I've told you; they don't make mistakes."

"Alright, but what about the friends and relatives of the people they kill? Do they know their loved one is guilty?"

"I've never stuck around to find out." She threw up her hands. "Anyway, if someone suspected me of something I feel like I would have met one of your brethren a lot sooner."

Slate had to admit she was probably right. If someone suspected her of a killing, they would have gone to the police before stalking her on their own. "I don't like this," he said simply.

"Me either," she glanced at the stairs visible through the doorway. "Let's get out of here."

Back in the car, Slate asked her the question he had avoided earlier. "Just for the sake of argument. Have you ever thought they might be wrong about someone?"

"You aren't going to let this go, are you?"

"It's important. People make mistakes, sometimes get it wrong. If these things ever misjudged or misgauged or whatever you want to call it, they may have crossed a line."

"What are you talking about?" she was watching him closely.

He held up his hands. "Look, just bear with me a minute. You say these things sense darkness and eat evil. If that's true then they must serve some kind of purpose, uphold some sort of balance. If they didn't, they could just kill anyone."

"I suppose..."

"What if they got it wrong sometime? What if that mistake threw the balance off and something came looking for them? And you because you're the vessel they live in."

"Vessel?"

"You know what I mean," he said through gritted teeth.

Kaylen thought about it. "If they did make a mistake, I don't know how they could have done it. They always show me what the prey has done to deserve being hunted and there's always plenty of prey to be found. If they messed up, they would have had to show me a lie and what would be the point? They don't see people the way you and I do, so why bother playing a game?"

"I don't think they'd do it on purpose. It wouldn't be in their best interest to put you in danger. Then they'd lose their house or whatever you want to call yourself. If anything, I'd say you're some kind of sanctuary they go to when they hibernate or whatever."

"Again, what's the point?"

It was his turn to frown. "I don't know, but I'm telling you someone left that pack out as bait and the only real way to see it is from that window."

Hating to agree with him, but getting more nervous the longer they sat here talking, Kaylen strapped into her seatbelt. "Let it be bait. Whoever set that trap won't get me that easily. Let's blow this town, catch up with the show. I don't want anything bad to happen to Edward, but if that room means anything it's that either he did something to someone or they did something to him and I want no part of any of it anymore."

Slate put the car in drive. They had already packed the trunk with their belongings. Even if they had stayed another night, it was time to move on to a different motel. The manager of the one they had been in was getting too nosy about their comings and goings. "We should catch up with them at their next spot. Do you want to go back to them or stay with me?"

"Does that mean you're tagging along?"

"I think I need to. I had the same dream remember."

"And you showed up too late." She felt instantly guilty when she saw his jaw tighten. "Oh, hey, that was a low blow. I'm sorry. I'm just edgy right now. I don't know why. I just want to get miles away from here."

He relaxed a little and looked at her. "Me too. Something doesn't feel right about this town anymore. It feels like something's got its eye on us."

"Or like something's hunting."

There wasn't anything he could say to that. Kaylen settled back in the passenger seat, watching the town dwindle in the side mirror. Somehow, even though they were leaving, it felt like whatever was in that town was coming with them. She reached inside herself and felt for them. They were there, but not sleeping as usual. They were on alert; she could feel it. Something was hunting them and they were waiting in the stillness for it to reveal itself. Kaylen shuddered. It had been a long time since she had been the one who was hunted.

CHAPTER 20

"Damn, honey, we thought we'd seen the last of you." Mabel was leaning over the counter of the concession trailer. The show was on, still in the first half, and it was a small crowd. They didn't buy much before the show and would purchase even less at intermission. The town was just a little burg on the way to bigger populations, but as Kaylen knew, it was the smalls that got you through when you were waiting for a hit.

"Did you really think I'd let you keep all my priceless heirlooms?" Kaylen leaned on the counter. "Truth is, I just couldn't stay away from you numbwits. Us losers need to stick together."

"See, Mabel? She left for a few days and now she preaching gospel and spreading the word." Trips was leaning against the opposite counter and grinning. "Yo, Rails, I don't know how in the hell you womanized Marco, but why the fuck'd you wait so long?"

Kaylen cast an innocent look over to Slate standing at the corner of the trailer and surveying the grounds. "And you thought they wouldn't want me back."

"Wouldn't want you back?" Roger said incredulously coming around the back of the trailer. "Shit, we need to up your pay and you can be the lot bouncer." He grabbed her around the waist and swung her around. Surprised, Kaylen held onto his shoulders to keep from falling. She needn't have bothered. Roger lost his balance almost as soon as he picked her up and the two of them ended up on their butts next to the trailer, laughing like a couple of asylum escapees.

Mabel cocked an eye at Slate. "You sure you want to stick around, law man?"

"I guess I better until things get back to normal."

"Depending on your definition of normal, you might be around for a long ass while," Trips commented.

Kaylen was untangling herself from Roger and got to her feet. "Is Fred around?"

"In the cookhouse makin' chow." Mabel was still watching Slate. "Since Marco's weaving baskets, Fred's in charge of the rousties. If you want to stick close, law man, you better get on the payroll." She whacked Roger in the back as he stood up. "Guess you and me are bunkmates again, unless you want to sleep in the truck."

"Why don't you sleep in the truck for once?" he grumbled.

"Because I've been here longest next to Fred and I get a bunk. Help Trips with the break. I'm gonna go move my stuff."

"Ain't we gonna talk about this?" Roger pleaded.

"Why? I'm pretty sure you don't want to bunk with a cop." She marched off in the direction of the bunk trailer.

Slate watched this whole scenario with a detached sense of amusement. They had just lost one of their own and here they were making room for the next recruit. It was slightly unsettling to see how fast they could all move on. Slate guessed it came with the territory.

Kaylen gestured to him. "Let's go talk to Fred. I'm pretty sure I still have a job, but you might not be a sure thing." Leaving the others to their squabbling, Kaylen and Slate headed to the cookhouse.

"Wondered when you were gonna turn up again, girly." Fred was leaning in the doorframe of the cookhouse when they strode up.

"Don't call me that," Kaylen said absently. "I still got a job?"

"If you want it. What about the big man here?"

"It would be easier to keep an eye on her if I was on the lot as part of the work crew," Slate said with a shrug.

"Would be. Could be we might need some more manpower with Edward gone."

"Have you heard anything? We didn't find anything promising." Kaylen let her eyes shift to let Fred know they needed to talk but not out here where every trailer had ears.

"Nope, but I don't expect to. People like Edward jump ship when the cops get too close." Fred looked at Slate when he said this to make sure the other man got the point. Slate couldn't have missed it if he tried. "Far as you joinin' on, I doubt it's a problem. The boss is always lookin' for rousties. I expect sleepin' arrangements have already gotten under way?"

"Mabel is handling that," Kaylen said with an eye roll.

"Then the only other problem is your car."

"My car?" Slate asked.

"Boss ain't keen on the crew having their own vehicles."

"I'm not getting rid of my car."

"Can you haul a trailer?" Fred was scratching his chin.

"It's been a while but I can manage," Slate said evenly.

Fred nodded. "Good. You drive one of the rigs so we ain't got to double haul and let Kaylen drive your car and I can probably get the boss to come around."

"Do you have a license?" Slate asked Kaylen.

"Does it matter?"

"Yes, it matters. I'm a cop and you'll be driving my car. If you get caught, it'll be my ass."

"Mabel's got a license."

"Really?" Kaylen and Slate said together. It was pretty unbelievable.

"Current and everything." Fred sighed. "Look, let Mabel drive your car and Kaylen can ride with her. She'll be clean on the road. She only uses once we're stopped for a date."

Looking less than satisfied, but not seeing an alternative, Slate agreed. "Fine, but you two don't trash my car."

"We're clean," Kaylen quipped. "Enough."

"Just don't look in it right away when they get to the lot," Fred explained. "They junk my truck up sometimes on the ride, but they always get it clean again."

"It was one carton of fries and I wouldn't have dumped it if you hadn't slammed that pothole," Kaylen grumbled.

Fred rolled his eyes, mockingly exasperated. "Lord, child, you take everythin' so damn personal. Go on and store your gear. Boss wants out tonight and you know what that means."

"Yeah, no sleep 'til dawn."

The cook nodded. "Get settled then go on and help Tony like always. What's your name, son?"

"Adam Slate."

"You lock up your car and come on back here so I can figure out where to put you."

Slate nodded and followed Kaylen over to the bunk trailer. Mabel had already moved all of her things over to Roger's compartment. She held up a half-filled grocery bag. "Rails, what do you want to do with this?"

"What is it?" Kaylen asked cautiously. Someone finding a plastic bag filled with who knew what was always cause for suspicion on a road show.

"What's left of Edward's stuff. Looks like he cleaned out before he left."

Slate and Kaylen exchanged a look. "You want to check it out?" she asked.

He held out his hand to Mabel. "I'll go through it, but I still don't think we're going to find him unless he wants to be found."

Mabel was nodding. "Smart man. Why don't you go grab your stuff?"

"So the two of you can talk about me?"

"We don't need you to leave to do that around here," Mabel cawed. She hopped down from her new compartment, waited for Slate to set the bag inside Kaylen's compartment, then hopped up on her old bunk. She waited until Slate was out of earshot before talking. "You need to have a care with that one. He's not going to come easy into this crew."

"Tell me about." Kaylen was going through her things, not because she was worried anyone had taken anything, but because they were a touch of familiar. She held up her old backpack. "He brought this for me from the town I left. And brought the money I left behind. I think he's a lot too straight and narrow for this bunch."

Mabel was still watching Slate in the parking lot. He was on his cell phone and rearranging things inside his car. "He have a problem with me driving?"

"He'll get over it." Kaylen handed Mabel one of the Mountain Dew she adored so much. "Get a hit about that or just logical deduction?" She climbed onto the top bunk.

There was silence. Kaylen frowned and leaned over the edge of the bunk. Mabel's face was pensive, her eyes narrowed as she watched Slate. She held the bottle but hadn't made any move to open it.

"Mabel? You alright?"

The other woman shook her head, as if she were clearing it, and twisted the cap off the bottle. She took a long drink before answering. "Been gettin' a lot of hits, just lately. Good hits. Like back in the before."

"Since Marco?" Kaylen asked quietly.

"Since before Marco. Started happening when you starting screaming at night." Mabel fidgeted with the lip of the bottle. "I didn't think about it at first. We got into that bad booze, then I know I got a laced rock, so I didn't pay my hits much mind. Thought I was just tweakin'." She craned her neck to look up at Kaylen. "But I barely been on the pipe the last week and nothin' stronger than beer at night. And the hits are getting worse."

"What are you seeing?"

Mabel shrugged. "Different stuff from different folks. That's why I've been runnin' stock and dippin' corndogs. Tryin' to keep away from the rubes. The crew, I can deal with what I get from us."

"How about me?"

Mabel leaned back against the wall. "You're funny, Rails. From the first time I met you, when I look into you all I see is nothing."

Kaylen nearly sighed with relief. So, they could hide themselves, even from psychic prying. She had often wondered about that. If people who had a little of the sixth sense could pick up on them at all. Apparently, they could and they couldn't. Mabel knew the nothingness meant something, but she couldn't see what it was. "What did you see when Edward was around?"

"You mean did I get a hit he was going to cut and run?"

"Something like that."

"When Edward was around I was still pretty high most of the time, but the few times something hard got through it wasn't anything about him leaving. That didn't surprise anyone. He had a record, he said, but never told anyone what it was. I guess if we ever bothered to get his real name, we could have looked it up, but all of us got records. Comes with the territory." She sipped her soda. "The last clear hit I got on Edward...I saw trees."

"Trees?"

"Trees and rain. Like a storm."

Kaylen felt a shudder twist through her. Had she told Mabel or Edward what her dreams had been about? She couldn't remember. Trying to clear her mind, aware that Mabel in her heightened state might pick something up Kaylen didn't want her to know, she said, "Did you guys meet Edward when it was raining or something?"

She felt a tap on the bottom of her bunk. "You know that's not how it works. What I see is what's going to happen, not something that's already happened." Mabel's voice brightened. "Maybe it means when we pick him up again, it will be rainin'." She cackled. "Ol' Edward will look like a drowned rat if that's the case."

Kaylen rolled over on her stomach and hung her head over the bunk. "And what about my tagalong? Anything I should know about?"

"Nothin' you don't know already."

Kaylen frowned. She knew Mabel was lying. Before she could press the issue, Slate's voice made her jump. "I am not sleeping on the bottom."

"You'll sleep wherever we say," Mabel snapped back.

Slate dropped his duffle bag on the ground and held out his hands. "Ladies, I'm not being an ass about this. I'm not going to fit down there."

"You'd be surprised," Mabel commented. She got off the bottom bunk and stretched. "Guess we better get back at it." She tapped Kaylen's foot. "You with me or Tony?"

Kaylen slid off the bunk. "Tony."

Mabel cocked her head at Slate. "Where are you goin'?"

"Cookhouse, after I get my shit stowed. Fred says he'll find something for me to do."

"Lugging poles and packin' canvas," Mabel said as she and Kaylen tromped off to the concession trailers.

Slate shook his head, climbed into the compartment and started putting his few items away. He didn't want anything to do with the bunk Mabel had been sitting on until he wiped the whole thing down with the disinfectant wipes he found in a cabinet. It was only then that he realized unless he was willing to use a borrowed blanket from someone, he would have to hit a Walmart or something and get his own. The idea of sharing a blanket with any of the crew he had seen or met made his skin crawl.

Satisfied that nothing in the compartment was a great loss to him if someone went snooping, Slate closed the door and went back to the cook trailer. He had left his sidearm in the car. No point giving any of these yahoos as chance to blow their own toes off.

Fred was setting out paper plates and plasticware. He gave Slate a slight nod, then raised his voice to one of the crew. "Trips, y'all come and get chow before we start tearin' down. Boss says he'll give us an hour before we get movin'."

The other man gave a wave and disappeared behind a trailer.

"What do you want me to do?" Slate asked.

"Right now I want you to tell me what the hell's going on."

"Good, I was hoping someone around here would be direct." Slate sat down in one of the camp chairs in front of the trailer. Fred sat in the one opposite him. They could hear the sounds of the music and the crowd from inside the tent. Despite the unfamiliar atmosphere, Slate felt himself finally start to relax. He had been on edge since they left town that morning.

"I think something or someone is after her."

"Mabel says the same. What I want to know is what the hell happened to Marco."

Slate met the other man's eyes. "I think you should ask Kaylen about that. It's her business and I'm not at liberty to discuss it."

"Cut the bullshit. You and me both know that little girl isn't telling anybody anything unless torture is involved. She's a hard one, that one. I know you saw what happened. He didn't rape her, did he?"

"He didn't have time. When I came around the corner something already had him pinned to the fence and his dick was in the dirt. Literally."

Fred's eyes narrowed. "What do you mean 'something'?"

"I mean I don't know what they were. And neither does she, not really. She accepts them and their help, but she doesn't know what they are."

"No surprise about that. When you grow up on the street, you have a tendency to be more accepting of the strange than most."

Slate threw up his hands. "What is it with you people? Do you just accept the unbelievable as a matter of course?"

Fred spread his own hands. "Take a good look at where you are, boy. This is the circus life, the carnival tour. We've been makin' people believe the impossible since the Roman days. Unbelievable is commonplace around here. This ain't polite society. We're the outcasts, the unwanted, the shadows in the shadows. We don't get a life; we have to make one."

"What about the performers? They seem pretty well adjusted to normal life."

Fred waved a hand. "Performers are different. They got careers and goals and their own rigs and dreams for the future. The rest of us, we get by and travel light. You aren't going to find a whole lot of dreamers in this crew."

"Stoners and drunks, more likely."

"No doubt. But we accept our lives and how we live them. If you're gonna make it farther than the next lot, you better wise up and leave that self-righteous shit at the door."

Slate ran a hand over his face. "Sorry. It's just been a crazy few weeks. What I saw the other night...there's nothing in this world like them."

"You mean there's nothing on this plane like them."

Slate rolled his eyes. "Please don't start with the supernatural shit. I've had enough of that in the last few days. What I'm trying to focus on are the things I can do something about."

"You want to save her."

The two men looked at each other. It was Slate who spoke first. "Don't you?"

"Hell, of course I do. But that's not to coming me, it's coming to you. At least that's what Mabel thinks. She's the one who was yapping loudest for you to join up. Said she thought you were gonna be important."

"You don't agree?"

"I'm not sure yet." Fred looked out over the lot. "Thing is, I've always thought life is half chance, half fate. Some things we can change based on the choices we make. And sometimes, the universe decides the river's gonna roll on all the way to the sea no matter what we think or do. You dig?"

Slate nodded. He dug it, but he didn't like it. If that were true, how could anyone change anything? Although, Fred did say he believed life was half chance. "So, do you think fate or chance brought me here?"

"Said I wasn't sure yet. But either way, you being around will warn the other idiots off and I think Rails could use some quiet."

They'd had quiet at the motel, but Slate knew it wasn't the same thing. In the room she was restless and agitated, fretting at the feeling of being held prisoner even though she was free to do as she wanted. Slate had no intention of arresting her or holding her captive. Now that she was back on familiar territory, she was already more relaxed and getting back to her usual self.

"Guess you'll start out helpin' get the seat wagons ready to roll. Stick with Tony and Trips after the show and they'll get you through. You know who they are?"

Slate nodded.

"They'll get you a set of gloves. Might want to get a baseball cap next town. Sun off the canvas is a bitch when we set up in the morning. You'll learn quick enough. Rails might or might not help you."

"I think she'd enjoy watching me get brained by a stake right about now."

"Starting out on the right foot, then."

Slate turned away toward the concession trailer where Tony was already taking down the signs and putting up and locking the unused outside counters up for travel. He looked back at Fred before he got too far. "Hey, did this Edward guy have a green backpack, do you know?"

Fred thought about it. "Might've, but if he did, I never saw it. Only one I saw was black. Said he got that one so the dirt wouldn't show. Why?"

"No reason, just wanted to know." He headed off.

Fred watched him go. The game was set. All the players were holding their hands close to the vest and everybody wore poker faces. It would take a few days for them all to get used to each other and loosen up a little, maybe share what they all knew and what they thought they knew. Turning back to setting out dinner, Fred hoped they'd have a few days before the storm. He doubted they would. When fate started to roll it became an avalanche in no time, burying anyone and anything that got in its way.

CHAPTER 21

"So, how're ya likin' the carny life?" Kaylen didn't even try to hide the smile in her voice.

Slate for all his gym time, run time, and handyman around the station time, had gotten his ass handed to him today. The boys had showed him the ropes, sorta, but had made sure he worked twice as hard as they ever did. Kaylen and Mabel had kept on eye on the situation, but didn't interfere. If Slate wanted to get in with the crew, he'd have to do it on his own. Every single person here had been through the same wringer. They'd all started on the bottom and worked their way up. It was different if you'd already been broken in; they accepted you then. If you were newbie, you had to go through it all.

Slate rolled his shoulders. They were stiff and sore in way they hadn't been since he'd played football in high school. "You don't have to sound so smug about it."

Kaylen leaned back against the wall on the top bunk. "Kinda pissy about it, aren't you?"

"It's been a while since my rookie year."

"Oh, are we upset about being lowest man on the totem pole for a change?" She raised an eyebrow and sat up cross legged. She had already taken her shower and gotten into clean clothes.

Slate was still dirty and wet from the small downpour that had begun while they tore down last night. He didn't smell all the greatest either. At least he wasn't hungry. Even though Fred had fed them all before they tore down, when they had stopped to fuel up, he had run into the service center and gotten a burger and fries. He couldn't remember the last time he had been hungry like that. "How long does this initiation last?"

"Usually the crews move on after the first week or so." She grinned down at him. "But you're a cop. And they all know it. My guess is they'll ride your ass for a while before they get bored."

"Perfect. Am I going to have to arm wrestle someone for the shower?"

"I doubt it. They'll all be sleepin' now. The shower's on the other side. Bathrooms are by the concession house. The fairgrounds guy unlocked them for us."

He collected his shower bag and a clean set of clothes. He tried to think of this whole experience as being at camp back when he was a kid. It wasn't working. How did people live like this? Always in a different place, owning the bare minimum to survive, and never making any kind of plans past the next town. It was a nomadic lifestyle he didn't understand. "I'll be back in a while." He stepped out the door. Dawn was breaking behind him. "Lock this door until I get back."

"I'll do what I damn well please," she sniped.

He waved a hand at her in apparent disgust and slammed the door. Kaylen heard his heavy tread stomping off around the trailer. She sighed. She knew why she was jerking his chain. She had spent the entire ride here listening to Mabel lecture her about how she needed to accept the fact that Slate was here for a reason. No matter how much Kaylen had argued that she'd been getting along fine without a man around, Mabel had stuck stubbornly to her conviction that Kaylen needed the detective. The last hour had been very long indeed, with both women barely speaking to each other. Getting back around the rest of the crew had loosened them up again and by the time they went to their bunks they were joking and laughing like always.

Kaylen knew in her heart of hearts that Slate had some role to play in whatever was going on, but his being here scared her in a way she had never been scared before. They had always been enough; they had always taken care of her. Why did she need his help? It was the not knowing that scared her. And being scared made her edgy and angry.

She hopped off the bunk and dug around in the small cabinets. Hardly eating for three days had left her ravenous. She pulled out a bag of chips and found a can of soda in the little refrigerator. Turning around, she appraised the sleeping situation. Slate was right, he wasn't going to fit very comfortably on the bottom bunk. He had wanted to swing by a Walmart to pick up a blanket but hadn't had the time and Kaylen doubted he'd want to drive anywhere when he got back from the shower. Well, they had shared a bed at the motel and he had behaved himself. Kaylen was in no mood for romance, but even she could admit it had been nice sleeping wrapped in strong arms, and she doubted Slate would object.

Putting her stuff on the scant counter, Kaylen rearranged the pillow and blanket on the bunk and was about to take her predawn snack to the bottom bunk when someone knocked politely on the compartment door.

She suppressed a grin. Kaylen had never shared a compartment with a man before for longer than one night, but she knew the protocol. "It's open."

Fred looked at her from the opening. "Brought you two an extra pillow." He handed it through the door. Kaylen took it and tossed it on the top bunk. "He had a go of it today."

Kaylen shrugged. "We've all been there."

Fred scratched his head. "No arguments about that. Think he'll duck out?"

She rolled her eyes. "I couldn't get that lucky."

"I think you got lucky when he hunted you down and I think you know it. Whatever the reason, he's gonna be around for a while. When the show gets going, I'll put him in with you and Tony. You run the stands and leave him in the trailer. He ain't a bad lookin' dude. The ladies'll like him, but not with you in hangin' in the trailer. The men'll buy in the stands, but not with him keepin' watch."

"Divide and sell?"

"Took the words outta my mouth. We all gotta make money." He stepped back from the opening. "Here comes your knight in shining armor. Be nice to him, girly. He just might have to take a hit for you." With that, he closed the door. She heard him hail Slate and Slate said something back.

Swearing under her breath, Kaylen slumped onto the bottom bunk and opened the bag of chips. Slate came in, clean and refreshed but still tired, and glanced at her. "Are you seriously going to get chip crumbs all over my bed before I go to sleep?" He started putting his stuff away.

"I figure you were right about not fitting down here and I also know you don't have your own blanket, so I thought until then we could share the top bunk."

He paused only briefly, then continued putting things away. When he had the cabinet organized to his satisfaction, he turned to her. "Can I have one of those?" He nodded at her soda.

"In the fridge. If you can sneak away later, I've got a list of stuff. I need to stock up since it looks like Mabel ate everything I left behind."

Slate took a sip of his soda. "Apparently, you've decided I can be useful as long as I'm running your errands."

"Don't worry. If you really want to get in good with the crew ask them if they want you to pick shit up for them when you go into town."

"That's if I can sneak away."

Kaylen shrugged and crunched a chip. "You're a grown ass man and the show don't start until six. Set up won't take that long and you've got your own car. The boss can't keep you here."

"And what am I doing at showtime?"

"According to Fred, you're working concessions with me and Tony."

"Tony seems like the only guy around here that isn't trying to get me killed."

Kaylen drained her soda and put the empty can on the counter. "We won't let you get killed. Just a little maimed is all. Nothing you can't live through," she paused, "Or without." She crumpled her empty chip bag, tossed it next to the soda can, and hoisted herself onto the top bunk. "I'm just gonna assume you want me next to the wall and away from the door."

"You're a quick study, aren't you?"

"Never had any other choice." She pulled the blanket up to her waist and sat watching him. "Fred brought you a pillow. He thought you might not have gotten around to getting essentials."

"He seems like he's got the run of things around here. He looks out for you." Seeing her frown, Slate continued, "Looks out for all of you. Especially, Mabel."

Kaylen's frown deepened. "You see a lot, don't you?"

"I am a detective. It's my job to notice things."

She leaned forward. "Alright. What else have you noticed on your one night with us?"

He put his empty can next to hers and pulled off his shirt. "In my professional opinion, I have observed that you guys are dysfunctional, crude, loud, obnoxious, addicts." He climbed up on the bunk and got under the blanket. "I have also noticed that you are loyal, hardworking, compassionate, although no one wants to admit that last one, and a good group of people."

Her green eyes found his gray ones and for the first time since meeting her, he didn't see one of them looking back at him. "You really think we're good people?"

"I think if they weren't your little buddies would be more active. But even if they were around, the people here, the crew at least, are exactly what you said they were. The outcasts of society. And if they've found a place where they can be themselves and they aren't hurting anyone, I'm not gonna judge them."

"That might be the most intelligent thing you've said since you started stalking me."

"Stalking is a strong word."

"It's the right word." They were very close now, their lips almost touching. Before Kaylen could think about whether this was a good idea or not, he moved closer and his lips were touching hers. It was a gentle kiss, not forceful or hurried. He took his time, giving her all the time in the world to pull away from him if she wanted. She didn't want to pull away, didn't want to be alone, but she didn't want him to get hurt either. So many people around her got hurt.

Hesitantly, not wanting to commit and committing anyway, Kaylen brought her hand up to touch his face. He hadn't shaved and his stubble pricked her fingertips. She moved her fingers higher to the smooth skin of his cheekbone. He smelled like good soap and clean water. Her other hand moved to his shoulder, feeling the muscles flex and move as he put his arm around her to draw her closer. His other hand slid under the blanket, coaxing her leg across his lap so he could stroke her strong thigh.

His lips moved against hers, his tongue seeking entrance. Kaylen opened her mouth letting her own tongue explore and taste. She could feel her marks starting to show across her skin. This happened sometimes, and it was always something she was aware of. That's why if she planned on having sex, even a quickie, she made sure it was always in the dark. No man had ever seen her marks during sex.

Slate was kissing her jawline, his lips making a trail down her neck and then up to the sensitive skin below her ear. The hand on her thigh moved up to caress her breast. Kaylen gasped and felt heat between her legs. It had been so long since she'd been with a man, too long. The marks on her arms shifted and changed faster. Slate pulled away from her and reached for her sleeve cuff, meaning to push it up.

"Don't," Kaylen said. "I've never let anyone see them like this." She turned her hand under his so she could grip his wrist.

"It's okay," Slate said quietly. "You don't have to hide them from me." He waited, letting her make the decision.

Kaylen took a deep breath. "Okay, but I'm not sure how many of them are going to show up." She pushed him away a little and pulled her shirt up over her head. She wasn't wearing a bra and when she tossed her shirt aside and looked down at herself, she saw that her marks were swarming across her chest and breasts as well as her arms.

Slate traced an ornately looping line that curved over her shoulder to form a spiral around her breast. Kaylen shivered with pleasure as his finger glided over her erect nipple. "I'm starting to get used to them. They're kinda pretty actually."

"Are you just saying that to make sure I'll sleep with you?" Kaylen smiled. She was thoroughly enjoying the way he was tracing the lines and patterns across her breasts.

"I'm pretty sure I don't have a choice anymore. You're gonna get laid whether I want to or not."

Kaylen burst out laughing. Her laugh turned into a gasp when his lips closed around the nipple he had been tracing. He sucked hard, pulling the nipple between his teeth and biting down just enough to make her gasp again. Kaylen's hands clasp the back of his head, encouraging him to keep going. Her whole body was focused on what he was doing. Somewhere deep inside her, she could feel them taking note of what was going on, but giving it the indifference they usually gave when she was with a man. They couldn't give her complete privacy but they tried to give her as much as they could.

Even if one of them showed up at this point, Slate couldn't care less. He had been fighting even touching her for days and he had no intention of stopping now that she was encouraging him. He shifted them both on the bunk, pulling her under him, but making sure his back would be to the door if someone tried to come in. Aroused as he was, his cop instincts wouldn't let him be entirely careless. Kaylen was squirming against him. Her hands stroking and caressing. Her breath was coming in quick gasps. She wrapped her legs around his waist, felt his erection pushing against her and pulled herself tight to him.

"Please," she breathed into his ear. "Please make everything just go away for a while."

Slate nodded against her. He brought her legs back down and pulled off her pajama pants and panties. He tossed them on the floor and yanked off his own pants, throwing them down to join hers. She was ready for him when he moved back on top of her, her legs immediately wrapping around him again. He only had to shift his position once before thrusting forward into her.

Kaylen cried out against his chest, her legs tightening around him. Her arms held onto him like a life preserver as he thrust again and again. Feeling his rhythm, she began to move her hips in counterpoint. The resulting sensation made them both gasp.

"I don't know what you're doing, but don't stop," Slate panted.

"I wasn't planning on it until I get what I want." She began to move her hips faster, her breath coming in harder against his chest. Then she cried out, her back arching underneath them both, her thighs twitching on his hips. Slate felt her orgasm and it pushed him to his own. He cried out into the pillow, trying to muffle the sound, as he exploded within her. Kaylen tightened her legs around him, pulling him as close as she could get him. It caused another spasm and he gasped against her neck, his body trembling with the after effects.

They lay that way for a few seconds, catching their breaths. Kaylen wanted nothing more than to melt into oblivion for a few hours and not think about the consequences of what they had just done.

Slate was taking deeper breaths. He rolled off her, moving her over at the same time so they could lie next to each other. They could accomplish this as long as she lay on her side with her head on his chest. Kaylen, not usually a cuddler, molded herself along his side without comment. He pulled the blanket up around them and put his arm around her. He was tired and sated. He hoped she'd just go to sleep. He didn't want to have any kind of heart to heart at the moment. When they woke up and got something to eat, he'd be more than happy discuss their new dynamic.

Kaylen held her arm up so he could see it. "My marks are going away."

He blinked, trying to focus. "Do they always do that after?"

She snuggled closer. When she spoke, her voice was groggy. "I don't know. It's always too dark to see them."

Slate felt and heard her take a deep breath, her body relaxing against his. *Thank God*, he thought. He put an arm behind his head and closed his eyes. He was almost asleep when he felt a breath on his face. Slate slowly opened his eyes.

The big one was hanging down from the ceiling somehow. That was why he hadn't felt the bunk shift. The creature stared at Slate, breathing shallowly, it's muzzle inches from Slate's face. It sniffed him as it had before then cocked its head to look at Kaylen. Slate had thought these things used her as safe haven, a place where they could hide and feed, and they took care of her to help themselves. Watching the creature, he reassessed his earlier assumptions. The creature wasn't looking at her like she was a means to an end, it was looking at her the way she had looked at it in the abandoned building. It had the same expression of love and compassion.

The creature swung its head back in Slate's direction. Its eyes shifted to Kaylen, then back to Slate's. To Kaylen, back to Slate. Slate cleared his throat. "I understand. I'll do my best." He paused, wondered if he were pushing his luck and spoke again. "Why do I have to protect her? Why can't you?" He glanced down at Kaylen. "She's scared."

The creature looked back at Kaylen, its eyes soft. When its gaze came back to Slate it seemed to have come to a decision. It reached out with its pincher and touched Slate's forehead, drawing a slight line of blood. Slate closed his eyes.

A vision bloomed in the darkness. Slate could see them, the two creatures, one large and one small. They were sitting in a cave like structure that reminded Slate of a womb. No wonder they felt safe with her. They seemed content. Then their heads turned, tuning in to something Slate couldn't hear or see. They changed then. They went from being content and almost lazy to sly and stealthy. They were hunting. Slate watched them stalk, kill, and feed. He saw what they saw, knew what they knew. He understood why they did what they did, the purpose they served. Then the scene changed. They were lost, unable to get back into their womb-like cave. They were keening too, their calls desperate, their panic evident. Slate felt himself start to shake. Before he could react to the vision enough to wake Kaylen, his eyes opened and he was looking at the creature again.

"Locked out?" he whispered. "The two of you can be locked out of her?"

The creature nodded slowly.

"Can you get back in?"

The creature nodded, but not very convincingly in Slate's opinion. Maybe they didn't know if they could be get back in once they were locked out. Slate did not find the idea of them not knowing what was happening comforting. He had hoped they would at least know what was going on. Seeming bored, the creature disappeared. Slate felt Kaylen take another deep breath and shift against him.

Despite his misgivings, Slate felt himself sliding into sleep. The last day and night were catching up to him. Besides he couldn't do anything about what was going to happened until he had more information. As he was drifting off, he thought he needed to get Mabel alone. She might be a meth head tweaker, but that woman knew something. She might not want to tell Kaylen, but she was going to tell him.

CHAPTER 22

"'Bout time you got a piece of ass."

Kaylen rolled her eyes. "Is that what everybody's talking about? How I finally gave it up?"

Roger stretched and yawned. "Don't know 'bout everybody else but all of us in the bunk house got an earful."

"Oh? You pick up any pointers, Rog?"

He grinned at her. "I ain't never got any complaints."

"That's because all the women you get are just screwing you for drugs."

"Hey, whatever works."

Kaylen tried to keep a straight face, but she just couldn't, not with Roger sounding so sincere. She burst out laughing. "You know that's what I like best about you, Roger. You're the most honest person here."

He laughed with her. "Yo, I got a parole officer, an ex-wife, and a couple of very disappointed parents. I got no reason to lie to you losers."

Kaylen gaped at him. "An ex-wife? Really?"

"Misspent youth, bad decisions, booze. Pick your excuse."

"So did you guys get a do-it-yourself divorce or did you have to get lawyers and shit?" They were sitting on the back of one of the pick-up trucks drinking water and waiting for Mabel and Slate to get back from the store. When Slate had asked Mabel and not Kaylen if she wanted to go to town, Kaylen had covered it up by saying she wanted to nap after the morning's vigorous exercise. Mabel didn't buy the excuse at all, but the guys all laughed it off and accepted it as a job well-done on Slate's part.

"Please, Rails. Lawyers? We just signed papers and filed them with the clerk of court. Done and done."

"How long were you married?"

"About six months."

"A record for you, I'd imagine."

Roger took a swig of his water. "Nah. Before her I was with a girl for a couple of years. Didn't work out."

"Obviously." Kaylen cocked her head so she could look at him from under the brim of her cap. "I think you're more of the bachelor type anyway. You seem happy without any commitments."

"Totally." He waited a few minutes before saying, "You and this cop a thing or just company?"

"Why? You still holding out for me?" She smiled sweetly at him.

"If I was, you better believe I'll wait for him to be gone. A pissin' contest over a piece of ass with a cop is somethin' I don't need."

"Glad you hold me in such high regard."

Knowing she wasn't going to answer the question, he changed the subject, and asked, "What do you two think happened with Edward?"

She frowned. "I don't know," she said, surprising him. "It was weird. We thought maybe something happened to him, but even Dick Tracy couldn't pick up his trail." She took a sip of her water. "Hey, Roger?"

"Yeah?"

"Does anyone on the show or in the crew have a green back-pack?"

"Is it important?"

"Just wondering."

He thought about it. "I can't say offhand about the perform-ers or the riggers. Pretty sure none of us has a green pack. Mine's red and Mabel's is purple. Tony don't have one and Trips lives out of that stupid suitcase of his."

"Doesn't that thing have Mickey Mouse or something on it?"

"Bugs Bunny. He got it at a Goodwill last year. He loves that thing, no one knows why."

"Trips is the weirdest of your little clan."

"I'll tell him you said that. He'll love it." Roger hopped off the tailgate. "Want to see if Fred wants to play cards 'til they get back? He won't be cookin' yet and we got at least two hours be-fore we have to get goin'."

"Sure. Ain't like we got anything better to do."

#

"So, you ever going to ask me whatever the hell it is you want to know?"

Slate glanced over at Mabel. She was sitting in the passenger seat munching corn nuts and drinking a Mountain Dew. On top of the drugs, Slate couldn't imagine how the woman could eat anything normal and keep it down, let alone the battery acid soda she was slurping up. "I've been trying to find the right moment."

"Bullshit. You've been trying to get up the balls."

"Not much for subtlety, are you?"

"What's the point? Hey, if you still don't want to ask about whatever it is you want to know, we can talk about you gettin' Rails off right and proper this morning."

Gritting his teeth, Slate fought for control. He didn't want to be dragged into a conversation about his sexual prowess, particularly not with Mabel of all people. "If you and Kaylen want to have share time, that's up to her, but I'm not discussing it."

"You don't have to, sugar. We all heard it." She grinned at him, gapped teeth and all. "Everybody hears everything in the bunkhouse, babe. Better get used to it 'cause I don't see you two rabbits stopping anytime soon."

"Why am I here, Mabel?" he snapped. "I know you know more than what you've told Kaylen."

If he thought he was going to throw her for a loop, he was mistaken. "What makes you think I'll tell you anything?"

"Because you may not like me, but I know you like Kaylen. I've seen the two of you together. She's like a lost girl and you're Wendy. You look out for her. You and Fred. You don't want anything to happen to her and you know the things that protect her can't save her from what's coming." He took a breath. "So, what's coming, Mabel?"

"Pull over up there, in that park or whatever."

"What about the groceries?"

"They'll keep. You want to know or don't ya?"

Slate pulled into the park without comment. He drove until they were under a large oak, put the car in park, powered down the windows and turned the car off. "Alright. Start talking."

She was quiet for a minute. Slate watched a couple of young moms. They were sitting on a bench together talking while their toddlers played on the miniature jungle gym. The women didn't look much older than Kaylen, which reminded him of something he had conveniently forgotten until he had picked up a box of condoms at the store.

"She ain't pregnant, so don't worry about it."

Slate stared at Mabel. "How the hell would you know that?" Especially this fast, he thought but didn't add.

"Just know. Better wear a raincoat from now on though."

"Thanks for the advice."

"Ain't you I care about, like you said. And don't give me that look. I know you won't leave her in the dust if you get her knocked up. But do you really think Rails would want a kid right about now?"

"Can we change the subject? I got the safe sex lecture when I was about fourteen."

Mabel waved a hand. "Fine." She took a deep breath, settling herself. "I don't see everything. I just get glimpses. Hunches. Some stronger than others. I know you have to be here because I've seen the woods too. And when I see them, I feel alone. I don't know why whatever hiding inside Rails can't help her, but it can't, not in the woods."

"It's a they, not an it. There's more than one."

"However many, they can't help her." Mabel ran a hand through her tangled hair. "And you're not with her either. She's all alone." She gripped his hand. "But you're looking for her. You're in the woods and you've got to find her before he does."

Slate stared into her eyes. He got the very real sense that Mabel was gone, that whatever happened to her when she saw things, when she was in the zone so to speak, was happening right now. "Who's after her, do you know? Can you see him?"

Mabel's eyes clouded, her brow furrowed. "I can't see his face. I don't know who he is."

"Have you see him before?"

Her fingers tightened on his hand. "I don't...know. I think maybe I have. He feels familiar, but I can't see him."

Changing tack, Slate said, "What about Edward? Do you know what happened to him?"

Her voice dropped, taking on an ominous tone. "He's served his purpose. He's not useful anymore." Her eyes grew soft, her voice sad. "Oh, Edward. You should have told someone. We could have helped you."

Not wanting her to get sidetracked, Slate squeezed Mabel's hand. "What purpose, Mabel? What purpose did he serve?"

"Used him to find her."

"Who used him? Who is looking for her?" Slate released her hand and grabbed her upper arms. "Mabel, who is looking for her?"

The woman blinked at him. "Looking for who?"

"Kaylen! You said someone was looking for her. Who is it?"

Mabel frowned. "I don't know. I told you that."

He let go of her arms and slammed his hands on the steering wheel in frustration.

She reached out and touched his shoulder. "I'm sorry, dude. I told you. I get glimpses of things. I can't ever get a whole picture."

He took a deep breath. "It's okay, Mabel. I know more than I did before and that's something." He looked at her and kept his voice calm, what he thought of as his telling-people-their-loved-one-is-dead voice. "You told me Edward is dead, do you remember that?"

Mabel put her hand to her mouth. "Oh no. I really said that?"

He nodded. "Not exactly, but close enough for government work. I'm sorry."

She looked out the passenger window. Slate saw her shoulders start to shake as she began to cry. He reached passed her and opened the glove compartment. He pulled out a couple of the napkins he always kept stashed in there and handed them to her.

He turned away, trying to give her privacy, and watched the young mothers again. One of the toddlers had apparently fallen off the jungle gym and was having a sniffling fit about it. The kid's timing was perfect. The moms were so concerned about getting the kid calmed down, they wouldn't notice the crying woman in the parked car.

After a few minutes, Mabel pulled herself together. "Did I say anything else important?"

"Yeah. You said 'he served his purpose'. You said he was 'used to find her'."

"But I didn't say who was doing the looking?"

He shook his head.

"Well, that's a real kick in the balls, ain't it?"

Slate grinned at her. "You said it. But at least we know Kaylen isn't in the woods being chased by some random psycho. Someone is hunting her."

Mabel nodded. "But why? If it was a law thing, another one of you guys would have already shown up. And if not yet, then if somebody does come, wouldn't they want to talk to the cop on the lot?"

"It's not a cop," Slate said. "A cop wouldn't risk chasing her down. They'd find some reason to take her down to the station." He was quiet, debating how much Mabel knew against how much he should tell her. Deciding being cryptic would get them nowhere fast, he said, "The things that help Kaylen."

"The things that look back at you?"

He nodded. "One of them showed me something this morning. It showed me that they can be locked out somehow. I think whoever or whatever is after Kaylen is really after them."

"But why would they hurt Kaylen? Wouldn't they know that these things need her as much as she needs them?"

"Maybe they don't. Or maybe they don't care. Maybe they want to get rid of them and they think by killing Kaylen they'll accomplish that."

Mabel rubbed her arms. "Let's get back to the lot. We need to talk to Fred about this and see what he thinks."

Slate turned on the car. "Is he like you?"

"Nah, but he's seen his share of weird shit. And the more eyes we have looking for someone with an axe to grind, the better chance Rails has of staying alive."

"You guys really pull together for one of your own, don't you?"

"We have to. It's not like anyone else will."

CHAPTER 23

"Holy shit, Rails. Did you see who showed up at the show?"

Kaylen was leaning on the counter, thinking about the conversation she and Slate had had when he got back from town earlier. It had been elusive and frustrating because she knew there was a lot he wasn't telling her, but she hadn't pushed the issue. They were still a little hesitant around each other due to recent events. She knew eventually she would wear him down but then hadn't been the time.

Pulled out of her musings Kaylen snapped, "Who, Rog? It can't be another cop 'cause Slate would have headed them off at the pass."

"Fuck no it ain't no cop. It's Edward."

Kaylen stared at him. "What?"

"It's him. He's standing over by the sound guy like he always used to."

Slate hadn't said anything about Edward when he got back from town but Kaylen had gotten the idea he had asked Mabel a thing or two about Edward's abrupt absence. It would have been the cop in him coming out to solve a case. He hadn't said anything, but Mabel's downcast appearance and red rimmed eyes had said plenty. Besides, Kaylen herself had seen the blood.

"Roger, have you been hitting the pipe at showtime again?"

He threw up his hands and glared at her. "No, I have not. And I don't know what your problem is. You should be happy he's back." His look turned sly. "Can't wait to see his face when he finds out you're banging a cop."

Ignoring the jibe, Kaylen tried to get Roger to focus. "How did he look?"

Roger shrugged. "Like he always does. Pale, skinny, mind off somewhere on a smoke break. If you want to know so bad go have your own look. I can keep an eye on things here. Still two acts before curtain."

Grabbing her hoodie, Kaylen left the concession trailer and headed for the tent. Before she could get more than a dozen steps, Tony came around the corner of one of the trailers. "Hey, Rails, you see Edward's back?"

Out of the corner of her eye, Kaylen saw Mabel's head pop up in the other concession. "What you talkin' about, Tony?"

He looked at Mabel. "He's standin' right next to the sound guy. Holy hell, this is gonna be good when he finds out about the cop."

But Mabel was still fixated on the other part. "He can't be here, Tony."

"Well, he is."

Kaylen touched his arm and they both walked over to Mabel. Kaylen didn't like the way Mabel had come over all pale and she noticed the other woman was holding onto the counter with white knuckled fingers. "What's wrong, Mabel?"

"Nothing if you think seeing a ghost is normal."

Tony and Trips exchanged a glance, then laughed. "Who's seeing ghosts, Mabel?" Trips asked, patting Mabel on the back. "Edward just ducked out for a while and now he's back. Probably a little worse for wear, but he'll be same as always in a few days."

Mabel shrugged off his hand. "No, you don't get it. Earlier today I flaked out when I was with the cop in town and I told him Edward was dead so it's pretty fuckin' weird that he's up and walking around, ain't it?"

The other three looked at each other and her, their puzzlement clear. Kaylen spoke first, "Maybe you meant dead in another way, Mabel. Depending on what you mean, dead could be a lot of things."

"He does look a little shell shocked," Tony offered. "Maybe he got some bad rock and lost his memory or somethin'. Weird shit like that does happen." He smiled at Kaylen. "That's why I stick to drinkin'."

"You're a regular role model."

Trips, apparently bored with the speculations, tossed his rag on the counter. "I'm gonna go say hi. Talk to him right up close and see what you guys are all talking about."

Tony grinned. "I'll go with you. With all the sleepin' arrangements being what they are, he'll probably have to bunk in a truck and keep his stuff in our compartment." They started off toward the tent.

Kaylen assessed Mabel, saw that the woman was getting her wits back, and said, "I'm going with them."

Mabel's hand shot out and grabbed Kaylen's arm hard enough to hurt. "You stay right here. Get in this trailer until that cop comes out."

"Mabel, you're hurting me." Kaylen twisted her arm loose. She pulled back the sleeve of her hoodie. Red marks were already blooming on her forearm. "I'm gonna have finger bruises. Slate's gonna love that."

Mabel's voice came out in a hiss. "Get your skinny ass into this trailer now!"

Stunned by this new assertiveness, Kaylen stowed her sharp reply and went around to the door at the back of the trailer. She opened the door and felt the hair on the back of her neck stand up. At the same time, she felt them come fully awake and on edge. She turned around and surveyed the immediate area. There was no one around. Still, she felt eyes on her, marking her. Shuddering, she almost jumped into the trailer and slammed the door.

Mabel was leaning on the counter, squinting into the semi-gloom surrounding the lighted tent and trailers. She had closed and locked all the service windows except the one she was peering out of. "Lock that door."

Without questioning her, Kaylen reached back and locked the door. The lock was a flimsy thing, easily broken if someone was determined, but it would stall the person trying to get in long enough for help to arrive. Kaylen joined Mabel at the window. "Mabel, what's going on?"

"Don't know, but I feel something out there." Her eyes raked over Kaylen. "You feel it too and whatever's inside you, they feel it."

Kaylen nodded. Where the hell was Slate? He had been her constant companion for days and now when that gun he always carried would come in handy, he was nowhere to be found.

Mabel patted her hand. "It's okay, Rails. He'll be here soon and I think we're safe in the trailer."

Kaylen let out a long breath. "Mabel, what did you mean when you said Edward was dead?"

"Just what I said. I told your cop friend he was."

"But how can he be here?"

Mabel frowned, the burnt-out workings of her brain trying to explain a complex thought. "You could have been right. There's dead and then there's dead. Maybe what I saw showed that the Edward we know is gone, that it's just a shell walking around."

"Like a zombie? C'mon, Mabel."

"Like a shell. Tony's right. You can get a bad rock. Somethin' mixed in that shouldn't be there. It can, like, short-circuit your brain and you do act like a zombie. Can't really do a whole lot of real thinking."

"Mabel, you're talking about catatonia." Kaylen leaned against one of the counters. "It happens, and you don't even need to be on drugs to have a nervous breakdown, but those people couldn't track down a traveling show. They're more or less walking mannequins. If they even walk at all. They usually need be led or directed."

"You a shrink now?" Mabel asked shrewdly.

"No, but I have my own reasons for reading about shit like that."

Mabel sighed. "Maybe he only shorted out for a few minutes or something, who knows? I just think it's better if me and you stay here until your bodyguard shows up."

"I don't need him to take care of me," Kaylen said hotly. She was suddenly furious that everyone was under the impression she needed a babysitter. "I've been doin' just fine in life without him around. Me and mine are perfectly capable of taking care of ourselves."

"Don't you mean they're perfectly capable of taking care of you?" Mabel shot back.

"It's not like that. I have to make sure they don't get caught because they'd starve to death if we all got thrown in solitary confinement. Of course, it wouldn't matter to me because they'd drive me batshit crazy long before that."

"Don't you think once you weren't useful to them, they'd just leave you?" Mabel snapped.

Confused by Mabel's attitude and wondering how in the hell the woman knew so much all of a sudden, Kaylen narrowed her eyes. "Seems to me I didn't have any of these problems when I was on my own." With that, she spun on her heel and stormed out of the trailer. She heard Mabel calling to her as she stomped to the compartment, but didn't turn around. If they all thought she couldn't get by without a goddamn man around then she'd show them.

Throwing open the compartment door, Kaylen climbed up the steps and went inside. She quickly filled her backpack with her money and a few necessities. She didn't need these people, she didn't need anyone but them, and she certainly didn't need that fuckin' cop coming in here and telling her she needed his help. A voice in her head, not them, this one was the one she liked to think of as her Common Sense Voice, whispered that she was making a very bad decision. Kaylen shut out the voice. She was tired of doing the right thing, tired of listening to all the voices, both inside and out. She hadn't really been herself since that damn Lenoy thing. She needed to go to ground somewhere away from people so she could get her own head straight. Slinging the pack over her shoulder, Kaylen left the compartment and disappeared into the darkness surrounding the lot.

#

Slate stood with one hand on the back of the bleachers trying not to look cataclysmically bored while the dogs were doing their thing in the ring. He normally liked dogs, but these little yappers were getting on his nerves. Even working their act, a couple of the furry bastards wouldn't stop barking. It was giving him a headache. Tony had said the dog act was the longest five minutes of the show and he hadn't been lying.

The dogs were annoying, but Slate had already been in an irritable mood before the show started. He had talked to Kaylen briefly when he got back from town, but he hadn't told her everything he and Mabel had talked about. That had got her wind up. The girl wasn't stupid; she knew he wasn't being straight with her and a coolness had sprung up between them. He knew he was going to have to smooth things over with her tonight or he was apt to end up sleeping in his car. And after this morning, that would be a damn shame since he knew she'd enjoyed herself as much as he had.

Not wanting to start an argument with her before she'd be locked in a trailer with Roger for an hour or more, Slate had gone off to find out from Fred what he was supposed to do during the show. Fred had originally said he would be in the food concession with Mabel, but she had chased him out saying that he needed to keep an eye on things. She had been vague on what 'things' Slate was supposed to be monitoring. Deciding that hanging around Kaylen would just piss her off more than she already was, Slate had stationed himself just inside the opening to the tent. That was when he caught the eye of one of the spectators.

His stomach had dropped and his jaw had tightened as soon as he saw her looking in his direction. He knew the type. Ten or, in her case, maybe twenty, years older than she thought she was, wearing clothes that screamed street tramp and enough make-up to make Tammy Faye raise her eyebrows, she had spotted him immediately after he took up his position. Before intermission she had passed him at least four times. Slate wasn't sure what the hell she kept leaving the tent to go do, but on her last pass, this would have been her sixth, she had made a point of brushing up against him, accidently of course, and then laid her hand on his arm to steady herself on her stripper spike heels while she got her balance.

Slate had endured her attentions because a) he didn't want her to cause a scene, women like her always liked to be the center of attention not matter what the attention was, and b) he had enough on his mind without Kaylen thinking now that he got a piece of ass from her, he was looking for fresh meat. The town slut, taking politeness for a green light, had tried to start a conversation with him, while still holding onto his arm. He disengaged himself and told her she better take her seat since her moving around was distracting the performers. She had left, but not before giving him a full once over that made him want to slap her cross-eyed. He supposed some men, as well as some women, liked being ogled like a piece of choice steak, but he didn't like it and because he didn't like it, he never looked at women that way.

The slut had taken her seat, but kept glancing his way to make sure he knew she was planning on pursuing him after the final bow. Slate knew he would be in the trailer with Kaylen by that time whether she liked it or not. In his experience, nothing got your woman back on your side, at least temporarily, like finding out another bitch was sniffing around her man. That sudden territoriality came under the heading of he might be an asshole, but he's my asshole so back off, bitch.

Ignoring the woman and trying to tune out the barking dogs, Slate ran a hand over his face and turned his attention to back of the ring. He blinked. Was that Edward standing next to the sound guy? Slate squinted in the shadowy interior of the tent. It sure as hell looked like the guy he had seen when he had staked out the lot while following Kaylen. His surprise was followed by chagrin. He had learned time and again not to trust people's accounts of events. Eyewitnesses were notoriously unreliable and that was why detectives always continued to search for hard evidence. A witness's memory was too chancy when they got up on the stand. And to believe Mabel of all people. Both Kaylen and Fred and then even Mabel herself had told him her visions or whatever weren't totally clear. They were pretty open to interpretation.

Still...There had been a lot of blood in that building. Too much for anyone to have walked away without immediate care. It had nearly gone to the ceiling for Christ's sake and the puddle on the floor was almost an inch thick and still wet in some spots.

A person simply couldn't walk away from that, not alone at least. Yet here Edward stood. Well, swayed was a better description. He looked like a sailor just off the boat for shore leave, leaning one way then over compensating and leaning the other. It was almost as if he were in a trance of some kind. Slate saw Trips and Tony walking up behind Edward.

Wanting to get his own assessment, Slate turned to leave the tent and come in through the back opening. The slut was standing outside the tent, blocking his way. "Hey, you got a cigarette?"

And she was a smoker. Perfect. "I don't smoke." He ducked his head, meaning to get around her.

She shifted on her stripper spikes and stuck out a hip. "Bummer. I didn't want to walk all the way back to my car just for my smokes." She said 'all the way' as if her car was parked in the next town over.

"Show's almost over. You won't miss anything if you leave now and you'll beat the traffic."

She pouted. "Does that mean if I ask you out for a drink the answer's no?"

Not even trying for courtesy anymore, Slate said with no small satisfaction, "Definitely a no. My girl's around here somewhere and she's the only one I buy drinks for."

The pout turned into a frown. "I bet she wouldn't want you buyin' her any drinks if she found out you were eyeing the spectators."

Oh, no, we are not doing this, Slate thought. "Look, I don't know what you think is going on here, but I've got somewhere to be." He pushed passed her, not touching her, but getting close enough for her to know he was not amused by her small-town debutant bullshit.

She stumbled back on her spikes, nearly fell, grabbed a tent rope to keep from ending up on her ass, and swore at him. Slate didn't even give her satisfaction of defending himself. She could call him whatever she wanted, all of a sudden his cop instincts were on high alert.

He came around the back of the tent, heading for the opening, when Mabel stumbled into him. "I'm so sorry. I've done somethin'. Somethin' really bad, I think."

Slate grabbed her upper arms to steady her and looked into her tear-streaked face. "What are you talking about, Mabel? Do you know Edward's here? You told me he was dead."

"I thought he was. But that ain't what I'm talking about."

Slate felt an icy finger slide slowly down his spine. "Mabel, where's Kaylen?"

"That's what I'm trying to tell you," she sobbed. "I said something I shouldn't have and she stormed off to the compartment. I went to look for her, but she's gone."

"Gone like she needed to walk it off or gone like she left the lot?"

Mabel blinked back fresh tears. "The cabinets were open and her pack was gone."

Slate didn't wait to hear what she said next. He raced through the trailers to the bunk house. The door was open, he guessed Mabel hadn't thought to close it. He hurried up the steps and gave the compartment a quick going-over. She was gone alright. It was the same as in Karl's apartment. She just took what she needed and walked out the door. "No, you don't, sweetheart. Not this time."

Slate nearly jumped out of the compartment. He saw Fred trotting toward him with Mabel right on his heels. Giving them no notice, Slate closed his eyes and tried to focus himself. He took several deep breaths and turned in a slow circle, waiting for the ping. It came on his left. He spun and ran in that direction. Fred and Mabel followed him.

He followed the pinging in his head through the back of the lot to the road that connected the parking area back into town. Slate stopped at the entrance to the lot and waited for the ping again. It was there, but felt more distant. She was in a car, had to be, she hadn't been gone long enough to walk that far. "God damn it!" Slate yelled in the inky darkness.

He whirled to face a panting Fred and Mabel. Striding passed Fred, he grabbed the front of Mabel's shirt. "What the fuck did you say to her?"

Dark hands gripped his wrists gently but firmly. "Easy, now, what's done is done and yellin' ain't gonna git us nowhere."

"It'll make me feel better," Slate growled, but he released Mabel. He walked off a few feet and swore viciously at no one in particular, kicking an empty plastic Coke bottle so hard it sailed across the road to vanish in the bushes on the other side.

While Slate had his tantrum, Fred spoke calmly to Mabel. "Alright, now, what happened? Rails was moody before the show, but I figured she was just pissed at Casanova over there."

Slate snorted, but walked over to hear what Mabel had to say.

The detective hulking so close had Mabel cowering next to Fred. It was easy for the big man to see how Detective Slate got the guilty to confess. The man could have been a witch hunter in a past life. "I'm sorry. I didn't mean to piss her off."

"C'mon, Mabel," Fred coaxed. "What did you say?"

Not looking at Slate, Mabel mumbled, "I told her she needed him to watch out for her. I told her those things that are with her would leave her as soon as they figured out she couldn't help them anymore."

Slate threw up his hands. "And that pushed all of her damned Wonder Woman buttons, I bet."

Mabel nodded.

Fred sighed. "I'm not entirely following this conversation, but it sounds to me like Rails just needs a breather. Too many people have been minding her business just lately. I can't figure she'll go far with Edward showing up. She'll probably get a room in town and be back in the morning. She knows we're staying here a couple days."

"If she wanted to get away, I would have driven her to town."

"And then gotten a room right next door if she wouldn't let you stay with her." Fred shook his head. "No, she wouldn't have wanted you to give her a ride anywhere, not if she had her Rails up."

"I am not staying here while she's alone only God knows where."

"Then you'd better start canvassing motels or do whatever it is you do." Fred shot him a look. "But you know that's only going to piss her off more."

Slate glared at Mabel. "You always make a point of giving wrong information and then running off the people who need help."

Mabel stood up straight. "I've had about enough of your Captain America shit. Yeah, I get it wrong sometimes, but that ain't my fault. I told you Edward was dead because I thought he was."

"If you've gotten a look at him, he ain't exactly lively," Fred muttered.

Mabel held up a hand and continued her tirade at Slate. "And as far as Kaylen's concerned, I didn't tell her nothin' that wasn't the truth. She does need your help and those things will leave her if she doesn't hold up her end of the bargain."

Slate thought of the way the big one had looked a Kaylen, the affection pure and open on its face. That thing wasn't going to leave her unless it had to, but Mabel didn't know that. She hadn't seen that. She only saw what her visions showed her. "They won't leave her as long as she needs them," Slate countered.

"Well, she shouldn't with you around, should she?"

Slate waved a hand at the deserted road. "You don't see me around her, do you? And I'd say she definitely needs them now. She needs something familiar to calm her down."

Fred put a hand on Slate's shoulder. "She might be back tonight. She may have gotten into town, went to a bar, got a drink and started thinking she made a rash decision."

"Do you really think she'd come back and admit it?"

"Not to Mabel, but as far as Rails knows, you have no idea what's going on so why should she be pissed at you?"

"Because she's a woman," Slate said tiredly. He looked at the road into town. He wanted to go look for her. Even if all he did was find out where she was staying it would calm his nerves enough for him to sleep. Of course, he'd sleep in his car in the parking lot of wherever she was holed up. He thought of how comfortable she had been in the abandoned buildings with the addicts and shuddered.

"Look, let me get the crew fed. Talk Donna into cleaning up the kitchen and then you and me'll take drive. Might be we'll see her marching her skinny ass back this way."

"How long will that take?" Slate fell into step beside Fred. He needed to go back to the trailers to retrieve his car anyway.

"'Bout twenty minutes. Food's already cooked and if I ask real nice, I can probably get Donna to dish it out."

"Twenty minutes and I'm leaving."

Fred nodded. He looked at Mabel. "You want to ride along, see if you can spot her?"

Mabel glanced at Slate. He was looking straight ahead, his jaw set. "I think I'll hang back. Talk to Edward and try to find out where he's been hiding."

"Good idea." They were approaching the tent. Audience members, intent on getting home, passed by them on either side. Slate didn't see the town slut and was glad. In his current mood, if she came up to him again, he'd knock the shit out of her just to make his point.

They parted ways at the trailers. "Give me a few minutes and we'll be on our way," Fred told Slate. "Don't leave without me if you can help it. She might not come back with you, but I think I can get her to come around."

Slate nodded. He walked over to his car and opened the driver's door. Slumping behind the steering wheel, he pulled out his sidearm and checked the chamber and the clip. He didn't think he was going to need it, but his nerves were still buzzing. He drummed his fingers on the steering wheel as he waited for Fred, hoping like hell they weren't already too late.

He saw Fred walking across the lot. Tony intercepted him before he made it to the car. Knowing something was up, Slate got out of the car and joined them.

"—just up and vanished," Tony was saying.

Slate asked a question with his eyebrows.

"Tony says Edward's gone again," Fred explained.

"Where could he go?" Slate asked.

Tony shrugged. "Must've caught a ride with someone. He was standing by the ticket shack last I saw him. I had to close up the stand and when I went back to get him for chow, he was gone."

"He's not somewhere on the lot?"

Tony shook his head. "Could be he saw you were here and ducked out again. Edward's always been real edgy around cops."

"Probably a good reason for that," Slate grumbled.

Fred cleared his throat. "We got things to do, you and me."

Tony stepped away from them. "I'll keep an eye out for Rails too. She's just pissed. She'll be back by morning."

Slate and Fred got into the car and Slate turned on the engine. "I don't like this."

"Me neither." Fred scratched his head. "Let's just find one of them and then maybe we can figure out what the hell is going on."

CHAPTER 24

Kaylen motioned to the bartender. "I'll do this one more time. You bring my tab with the drink?"

He nodded and started off down the bar. Kaylen watched the room behind her in the mirror on the back wall. It was filling up in here. She saw couples, singles, men here to blow off steam, women looking for a place to bitch about their lives, everyone getting happily lubricated. On a night like this, in a room like this, Kaylen could have easily made close to five hundred bucks if she were on her game. But that wasn't tonight.

Tonight, she felt as if the whole world was some crazy carnival ride and she was two twists from puking all over the side. The bartender brought her drink, whiskey on the rocks, and her bill. She handed him some cash, enough to cover the tab and give him a decent tip. Not too much or he'd remember her as a good tipper, not too little or he'd remember her as cheap. She sipped her drink and watched the prey come and go.

What was she doing here, really? It wasn't like her to storm off like a teenager who couldn't borrow the car for the weekend. She was much more reserved than that, more aware of her decisions. That's what kept her out of trouble and alive. Although, she chided herself, a lot of really weird shit had been going on just lately. She should behave like a grown-up and go back to the lot. She could give Mabel the cold shoulder for a few days and then relent. She was sure Slate had been clued in as to why she had left by now and was probably driving up and down every street in town looking for her. The thought of him going out of his mind trying to find her made her smile despite her self-pity. He was going to be mad as hell that she'd walked off, but for perhaps the first time in her life, Kaylen understood that his anger was born out of fear and worry, unlike the people in her past who got pissed at her because they needed a handy target.

Kaylen drank the last of her whiskey. She needed to get back, or at least start walking in that direction. She slipped off her barstool and reached for her backpack. A hand got to it before she could. She looked up and saw a smiling man. Terrific. This was just what she needed, some asshole looking to get laid. She fought hard to curb her tongue and put on a nice, but not encouraging smile. "Can you hand that to me, please?"

His fingers tightened on the pack strap. "Only if you let me buy you a drink."

She reached for the pack. "Sorry, I already had my limit and I've got somewhere to be."

He held the bag out of reach. "One more won't kill you."

Kaylen's eyes narrowed. "How would you know?" She darted forward and grabbed a pack strap with one hand, bringing up the palm of her other hand to slam into the bottom of his chin in the soft spot between his jaw bones.

He fell back more in surprise than pain and let go of the strap he was holding. "What the hell's your problem?"

"Just getting tired of people not taking fuck off for an answer." She slung the pack over her shoulder. "Maybe you'll have better luck with the locals."

She strode to the door. The few people who had noticed the incident at the bar moved out of her way. The night air was brisk with a wind that had blown up while she had been in the bar. Trash, mostly napkins and straw wrappers from the restaurant on the corner, blew down the sidewalk and across the street. Kaylen pulled her hoodie up over her head and turned in the direction of the lot. She had gotten a ride into town, but town was only a mile or so from the lot. An easy walk if she kept up her pace and with the night getting chilly, keeping up the pace wouldn't bother her a bit.

People passed by her while she was on the main street, going to dinner, going to drinks. Most of the them were chatting about the circus and laughing about this clown act or that one. Several teenagers were twirling around a lamp post, mimicking one of the web girls. Kaylen saw them all and saw no one. This seeing without seeing was something she had honed over the years. In this way she could easily pick out the ones that didn't belong; the ones that were looking for someone like her. A girl, alone, at night walking farther away from lights and noise and safety. Kaylen actually pitied anyone dumb enough to follow her tonight. If Slate didn't find her first and vent his frustrations on a would-be rapist, they would get a quick meal to tide them over for a while. For her it would be a win-win.

She followed the main street out of town and was walking along the shoulder when she heard someone coming up behind her. Kaylen had been walking with her knife in her right hand, she didn't like to get them riled if she didn't need to, and she turned to face whoever was following her with the knife open and down by her right thigh. "What do you—Edward? Is that you creeping up behind me?"

Edward stood about twenty feet away, swaying gently on his feet. His face held a fixed expression and he kept blinking slowly as if he were trying to clear his eyesight. Even in the yellow light from the street lamp between them, Kaylen could see how white he was. He didn't look like he had any blood in his body.

She put her knife away and took a step toward him. "Edward? Are you okay?"

He cocked his head slightly as if trying to find her by sound. "Kaylen? Is that you?"

Kaylen stopped abruptly. What was going on? Edward had never called her Kaylen. He always used her nickname. Something was very wrong here. She gave back the two steps she had taken and shifted her weight, ready to run. They were turned toward Edward as well and she could feel their perplexity coursing through her. It was as if they couldn't really see him.

"Kaylen, I'm in a bad way." Edward took a step forward, lurched on his foot, nearly fell over, and righted himself. "I can't see too well and my legs feel all weird."

Not wanting to get close to him and wishing Slate would come looking for her, Kaylen held out a hand. "Just stay put, Edward. Maybe you should sit down for a minute. I can run back to the lot and get the guys to come help you. You look like you need to go to an ER or something."

"Don't want a hospital." He wavered on his feet. "How come that cop's still around?"

"He's just hanging for a while. Wants to know if I know anything about some murder. I told him I didn't, but you know how cops are."

"That's bullshit," he shouted. His words were slurred and he staggered forward another step. "Why should he leave when you're so happy to fuck him?"

Kaylen's mouth dropped open. Was he drunk? Was that what this was? Drunk and jealous over another man? "What does it matter to you? It's not like we had a thing going." she shot back, her anger rising again.

"How could we? You show up acting like your snatch is made of gold, don't want nothin' to do with nobody and then this cop shows up, the one you've been runnin' from, you say, and you can't wait to wrap your legs around his ass."

"What I do with who is none of your business. And how do you know what's been going on? You've been out to lunch for days. How did you find us so quick anyway?"

He gave her sly look she didn't much care for. "I've been in this business a while, girly. I know how to find a roadshow."

"What was in the backpack?"

He blinked slowly at her, reminding her of a sloth. "What?"

She put her hands on her hips. "The backpack. The green one. The one you left behind the trash cans as bait?"

He was staring at her. Kaylen had the distinct impression he was hearing her, but the information was going on a scenic detour before it got to his brain. "There is no backpack."

"Edward, it was jammed behind the trash cans. You could only really see it from the window in that building with all the blood."

At the mention of the building, Edward shuddered. It was a full body twisting motion that almost sent him sprawling. "I don't want to talk about that."

Taking a breath, Kaylen reined in her anger and spoke softly and slowly. "Edward, what happened in that room?"

He shuddered again and shied back from her.

Taking a different tack, Kaylen said, "Okay, why were you gone the night Marco came after me?"

Watching him try to think was painful. His brow furrowed and his eyes fixed on something she couldn't see. When he started talking, it was like he was rehearsing lines. "I saw the cop. I wanted to get away for a while. If he saw me, he might ask me questions. I thought I'd just hang out somewhere else for a while."

"So, you leaving had nothing to do with Marco creeping around?"

He shook his head. "I was going to be gone until morning. I went to the building, sat next to the window so I could see everybody." He fell silent.

When it appeared he was done talking, Kaylen prompted, "And then what?"

He seemed to shake himself back to the now and blinked at her. "It all went dark."

Realizing they had been standing here for quite a while and no traffic had gone by, Kaylen wondered how long it would be before Slate came looking. It couldn't be much longer. She had to keep Edward talking long enough for someone, at this point anyone, to come cruising by. "Are you sure you aren't hurt?"

"I'm fine." His voice was dreamy, drugged, far away and getting farther.

They were completely focused on Edward. Kaylen could feel them ready to spring out of her at the slightest provocation. She glanced around again, up and down the road. Where the hell was everybody? It was a small town, but it couldn't be much passed eight thirty and this was a cut-through road. Someone should have come by. She decided standing here was accomplishing nothing. "C'mon, let's get back to the lot. I'm starving and I'm sure Fred and Mabel are pulling their hair out wondering where we've got off to."

Edward took a step toward her, in the direction she wanted him to go, and then a strange expression crossed his face. He focused in on her, really seeing her for the first time since he'd come back. Kaylen took a step back, stunned by the pure fury in his face. They leapt out of her immediately, raising clawed hands directly for his throat. Edward opened his mouth and said something in a language Kaylen didn't know. Instantly, they were thrown back, sliding across the dirt shoulder, the bigger one knocking Kaylen's legs right out from under her. They regained their feet almost as soon as they stopped tumbling and crouched in front of her, forming a wall.

"Do you really think your pets can save you from me?" The thing in Edward's body hissed.

"What are you?" Kaylen demanded. The two creatures flexed their muscles, ready to spring again.

The Edward-thing cackled. "Did you really think you were the only person who had friends of a questionable persuasion?"

"Not really, law of averages and all that bullshit, but I didn't figure someone else like me would come after me. What do you want with me anyway? I'm a nobody."

It looked at her quizzically, as if the answer was obvious. "To eliminate the competition, you stupid twit." The voice was grating, hard to make out. It was as if something was playing Edward's vocal cords like some sort of musical instrument as opposed to speaking naturally. The sound set Kaylen's teeth on edge.

"Really?" Her disbelief was clear.

The Edward-thing narrowed its eyes. "Are you surprised?"

Kaylen got to her feet. "Disappointed really. I mean, you expect the sheep to take each other out over something as stupid as territory. I just always thought my friends here were above all that, since they've never indicated otherwise." She shrugged. "And given how much prey there is to go around, why bother picking a fight?"

It cocked its head. "Why not?" It shifted slightly, moving one foot behind itself and turning sidelong. "Anyway, what makes you think we're above the pettiness you humans display so well?"

"There never was anything in that backpack, was there?"

"Of course there wasn't. I was hoping it would be enough enticement to get you into a more...secluded area where your friends wouldn't already have their hackles up."

"What about Slate?"

It cocked its head again. "What about him?"

"He would have protected me."

It grinned so wide Kaylen half expected the top of Edward's head to topple backward like the old toothbrush commercial. "He would have tried."

Kaylen shuddered despite herself. "And Edward? What's he? A means to an end?"

It nodded.

Feeling a chill, Kaylen said, "How are you controlling him?"

"We can always control our shells, if we want to."

Kaylen's eyes dropped to them. The creatures hadn't moved. They were still on guard. "They've never tried to take control of me."

The Edward-thing sighed, put upon. "They've never had the ambition most of us have. Those two are rather lazy, if you want to know."

Kaylen stood straighter. "I think they're pretty smart. We've got a good deal going on here. So why don't you get lost?" She was becoming more and more nervous with the casual way the thing was speaking, as if controlling its human partner was simple. Something Slate had said flitted through her mind. "If you're in control, do you openly hunt bad people?"

"Why only hunt the bad? The good taste just the same." Kaylen swallowed. Slate had been onto something and he hadn't even known it. "So that means there isn't any kind of balance or reprimands for killing the wrong person?"

It raised a hand and waved it lazily, composing phantom music. "Oh, there's a balance, but not enough of us care to impose it."

"These two seem to care." Kaylen gestured to the two creatures in front of her. "They both seem to care a great deal about the people they hunt down."

"That's only because they're weak," it hissed. "If you really wanted them gone, you could throw them out anytime you feel the urge." Its voice lowered with mock sadness. "And then they'd be lost, vulnerable, and easy picking for one of us."

"I don't believe you." And she didn't. She knew only too well what happened to her when they were too far away.

"Believe what you want. It doesn't matter to me either way." It uttered another of those foreign words and the creatures slid back a few inches, brushing up against Kaylen's shins. What was happening? How could this thing be pushing them back with just words? Then she saw Edward's chest panting. Not a lot, but the panting was definitely there. So, this thing wasn't as strong as it wanted them to believe.

Without moving, Kaylen reached out to the creatures in front of her with her mind. She had always been able to contact them to some degree and she hoped she could do it with them outside her body. In seconds, she felt the familiar brush of their minds. Using images, she quickly showed them what she wanted to do. It would be risky, but she didn't think the Edward-thing could yell at both of them if they were split up.

"Alright, time to stop fucking around. If you're gonna do something, I guess you better come on and do. I ain't got all night."

"Such strong words, from such a pathetic little thing." It threw out an arm. Kaylen instinctively ducked. The arm extended to much longer than it should have been able to reach, swiping over her head and snatching a handful of hair. At the same time, the creatures darted outward to either side, flanking the Edward-thing.

It spun, keeping its eyes on the larger creature while the smaller one circled its back. Kaylen took the opportunity to try and run. She got about fifty feet before collapsing along the road. Her breath was gone and her legs felt like rubber. The same weakness that had drained her in the abandoned building was depleting her again. She heard the thing cackle again. "Did you really think you could just run away, little rabbit, after being with them so long?"

It started to laugh again, but the laugh was cut short and then it shrieked in fury. Kaylen didn't turn to see what had happened. She forced herself up and started limping down the road, praying for headlights. Behind her, the sounds of a vicious struggle filled the night. Growling, snarling, and squeals of pain echoed down the deserted road. She kept going, knowing if she stopped she'd be done for good. Of all the times for Slate to have better things to do...this would be the perfect hero moment.

Behind her, the sounds became more primal. She could hear crashing, as if they had rolled off the shoulder of the road and were in the trees on the side of the road. Branches snapped and something heavy fell over. Kaylen paid it all no mind. She kept lurching along, fighting the urge to lay down and give up. It felt like she had a huge rubber band around her middle and for every step she took forward, she slid several inches back.

Then the sounds stopped. Kaylen risked a glance over her shoulder, but couldn't see anything in the light from the street-light. She turned back to the road and the Edward-thing was standing right in front of her. Before she could jump back out of its range, a bloody hand, more exposed muscle than skin, shot out and fastened around her arm. She opened her mouth to scream, but the other hand slapped her hard enough to rattle her teeth. The thing whispered something and then Kaylen felt as if she were being constricted by invisible cables. The feeling was there and gone in less than a second. Breathless, Kaylen slumped to the ground.

The Edward-thing regarded her. "Let's see what they do, now that they're locked out." A flash of lights down the road made the thing swing unsteadily to look. It grabbed Kaylen's shoulder with fingers that felt like talons. "We need to go somewhere more private. Somewhere we won't be easily interrupted."

As she was dragged off the road and into the woods, Kaylen saw headlights moving slowly down the road from the lot. She opened her mouth to scream again in a vain hope whoever was driving had their windows down. The thing dragging her turned, almost casually, reached down with the skinned hand, and pinched Kaylen's windpipe shut like a vise. "None of that now." It said something Kaylen couldn't understand and then her voice was gone and she was dragged silently into the forest.

CHAPTER 25

"We should have brought flashlights."

Slate nodded at Fred's astute observation. He hadn't realized how thick the trees along the roadside were until it got dark. They were planning on going into town to check the local watering holes but Fred had suggested they keep an eye out on their way in.

"She coulda had a couple drinks during the last half, thought about what a jackass she's being, and is on her way back already." He had given Slate a measuring look. "No point in not checking since we have to go that way anyway."

Since they had forgotten to grab flashlights, Slate was creeping along the road and both men had their heads craned out the windows looking for Kaylen in case she was walking just inside the tree line. If she were trying to avoid getting picked up on her way back to the lot, she would be camouflaging herself in the shadows.

Slate was about to suggest they get moving and go into town when he saw scuff marks on the shoulder. He braked hard enough to throw Fred against the dashboard and got out. Fred scrambled out of the car behind him. "What's up?"

Slate was crouching by the marks. "There was some kind of struggle here." In the illumination of the street light, the two men could see grooves in the dirt where someone or someones had been shoved around, their feet fighting for purchase. Small splatters of blood speckled the ground as well and glinted in the light like wet paint. Slate touched one of the splotches. It was not only wet, but still warm. "If this was her she can't be far." He stood up.

Fred pointed. "Look, there's footprints leading that way." The footprints were small, easily Kaylen's size, but not clear. It was evident that she was limping heavily, dragging her left leg, but she had kept going. The men followed the prints until they disappeared into the woods. Slate made as if to go in headlong and Fred caught his arm.

"You go in there without a light and not only will you not find her and fuck up any trail she might have left, but you'll get lost and then you'll be no good to nobody."

Slate whirled angrily. "Then what the fuck are we supposed to do? You and I both know time is short. We can't go back, dig around for a light, and answer a bunch of stupid questions. Kaylen will be dead by then."

"I know all that, but you have to think for a second or she'll be dead anyway. You can't go crashing through the woods. Whoever took her is going to have a fight on their hands in any case and Kaylen is tiny but she ain't Tinker Bell. Someone dragging her through those woods is going to have a tough time of it, so they can't be that far. Just listen for a second."

Swearing because he knew Fred was right, Slate held still and listened to the night air. He was hoping for breaking branches or screams or the sound of thrashing. He heard nothing. No. He cocked his head. Not nothing.

Gesturing Fred back a step, Slate walked slowly to where the struggle had taken place. He went a couple steps into the trees, just far enough to be hidden from the road and listening. Whimpering, low and intermittent, from his left. He looked over. The two creatures were huddled against the base of large tree. The larger one was crouching in front of the smaller one, shielding it from Slate's view.

"What's in there?" Fred called.

"Don't come over here," Slate shouted back. "It's not Kaylen but I'm not sure how they'd like more company."

Anyone else would have asked several questions at that response, all the while walking right up to the back of Slate to get their own look see. But Fred had seen a lot of strange shit in his day and when someone said stay put, he stayed.

Slate moved cautiously up to the creatures. He knew they were wounded. He could see blood glistening in the flickering light filtering through the leaves, but he didn't know how bad and animals and people in pain could be dangerous. He stopped a few feet away, close enough for the big one to reach out with its pincher and take his head off if it had a mind to do so.

The creature bared its teeth and shifted to shield the little one even more.

Slate reached out a hand. "Hey, big guy, you know who I am." The creature stretched out its neck and sniffed the extended fingers. Slowly, too slowly for Slate's taste but he kept his cool, the creature rose up to its full height. The smaller one stood up behind it and peered around its back at Slate. Slate could see both creatures had slashes along their torsos but the blood was clotting and none of the cuts looked particularly deep although there were a lot of them and that made up the difference.

Reminding himself to be patient, getting in a fight with these guys would certainly not help Kaylen, he said, "What happened? Where's Kaylen?"

The larger creature reached out with its pincher and pushed lightly against Slate's chest. At the same time, Slate felt an odd tickling sensation in the middle of his forehead. Acting on instinct, Slate took a deep breath and forced himself to relax, opening his mind to the creature.

The contact was instant and aggressive. Slate's hands curled into fists and he grit his teeth, willing himself not to fight the invasion in his mind. He knew he would never look at another rape victim the same way again. This must be exactly what those people felt, a complete and utter helplessness while a foreign and unwanted presence tore through them.

Images flashed behind Slate's eyes. Everything that had happened leading up to this point. Edward being off kilter, the building, the backpack, Kaylen sensing something was wrong, her fight with Mabel, the bar, her confrontation with something that looked like Edward but wasn't: it all flooded his mind. When the creature showed him the fight, Slate took control of his own mind again and asked the thing to slow down so he could see exactly what happened. The creature complied, but Slate could feel its anxiousness to get moving, to find Kaylen. He felt that they were as depleted as Kaylen when the three of them were separated.

"Why did that thing have so much power over you?" Slate asked.

The creature huffed, thinking, then more images. Cats then lions, dogs then wolves, cuddly black bears then a huge grizzly. Slate got the point. "Okay, so this thing is a lot tougher than you two, but we can still get her back. Did you guys hurt it at all in the fight?"

The smaller one stood straighter and puffed out its chest. Slate saw the slashes it had made against the Edward-thing, the slice that had gone home over the throat before the thing had managed to throw them both off. Exhausted from the struggle and from being driven away from Kaylen, the two creatures had hidden in the brush to regroup. When they came back out, Kaylen was gone and they saw the car coming.

Slate held up his hands. "Alright. So this thing is tired and wounded like you guys. It's also dragging a struggling woman through high brush which is going to exhaust it even more. We need to find her before the thing gets a second wind. Can you two lead me to her?"

They exchanged a look. Slate felt the tap on his mind again. What he saw scared the hell out of him but he knew it was the only way to find Kaylen and have these two for backup. He took a deep breath to settle himself. "Okay, fine. But only because she needs us."

The creatures nodded curtly and leaped. Slate felt the wind knocked out of him as they filled him. In that moment the three of them were one, he could hide nothing from them and they could hide nothing from him. In that moment, he saw the little girl Kaylen had been, the teenager on the streets, the young woman riding her thumb over all the highways. And he saw the ones they hunted, the ones they killed. He saw what the prey had done to deserve that punishment and felt his gorge rise. No wonder Kaylen had nightmares. He was shocked the woman wasn't in a psych ward somewhere living in a padded room.

He staggered out of the trees to a very concerned Fred. Slate held up a hand before Fred could start the barrage of questions. "Give me a second. I gotta catch my breath."

Fred waited a full minute before asking, "So now what?"

Slate straightened. "Now me and her friends have some business to settle."

Fred didn't ask what friends. "What do you need me to do?"

Slate barked a harsh laugh. "The right thing to say is call the police but I don't want any of my buddies getting involved yet. It would only freak them out and delay us more. Go back to the lot. Get whoever is in the mood for a night hike through the woods and as many flashlights as you can find. Bring them back here and start looking."

Fred nodded. "I'll be back with the troops as soon as I can. I'll grab bandages and shit too. Who knows what we're gonna find. When you finish what you gotta do, stay put. It'll be easier for us to find you two if we're not all circling each other."

Slate nodded, hearing but not hearing what Fred was saying. He was rechecking his sidearm, making sure his phone was on silent, and preparing himself for a full-on confrontation. And they were ready too. Rested and reenergized with his own vitality, they were annoyed with the conversation and impatient to get going.

Slate turned back to the woods. Before he started walking, he held out his hand. "If I don't, I want you to know it's been a time."

Fred grasped the hand and shook it firmly. "You will and you ain't seen Mabel dance around the fire yet. That's a time." He eyes grew sober. "Find her. And let them rip apart the bastard that's got her."

Slate nodded. Somewhere in the distance, thunder rumbled. As Slate started back into the woods, the trees began to rustle in the rising wind.

CHAPTER 26

Kaylen knew she couldn't get away, not until this thing let go of her shoulder. She could feel warm blood oozing out of the puncture holes where the Edward-thing had pierced her skin. Pain radiated from her shoulder, down her arm all the way to the tips of her fingers. She was having a hard time staying conscious too. The farther she was pulled from them, the more her whole body ached and the more exhausted she became.

Since escape was on the back burner for the moment, she decided to make it easier for Slate to find her if he picked up her trail. Kaylen used her remaining strength to swing her legs out, catching as much brush and small trees as she could to both mark her passage and slow the Edward-thing down. It realized what she was doing and dug its fingers deeper into her shoulder, but it didn't stop to punish her.

Kaylen could hear the deep wheezing coming from the thing's mouth and it lurched heavily to the right with every third step. If she wasn't so damn tired, Kaylen knew she could wrench herself away and scurry into the heavy overgrowth. But when she tried to pull away from the hand holding her, her body refused to put forth any real effort.

The thunder she had heard a few seconds before was getting closer. The wind had picked up, and the trees swayed, slowing their progress even more. Kaylen could smell rain on the wind and the déjà vu of her dream almost paralyzed her. Somewhere up ahead in this chaos was a stake with her name on it.

The Edward-thing broke through a thicket of thorned bushes, unmindful of the scratches and cuts that began bleeding on its arms and face, and stood swaying for a moment, seeming to get its bearings. Kaylen took the chance to lunge up from her prone position. The Edward-thing was stronger than she thought and easily slammed her back down on her ass. It twisted its fingers in her shoulder, making her cry out.

To her surprise, sound did come out. Apparently, whatever it had done to her only had a temporary effect. She drew in breath to scream and the Edward-thing swung around and drove a heel down into her stomach. Her breath went out of her in a rush and Kaylen gasped for air.

"Behave yourself," the Edward-thing rasped. "We've still got a ways to go."

"Why not just kill me?" Kaylen gasped.

The Edward-thing offered her another ghastly smile. "And ruin the fun? You need to be punished first, then I can set you out as a warning for anyone coming along looking for a fight."

"You won't last much longer in that body whether someone comes looking or not. What was the deal with all that blood anyway?"

Finding its direction, the Edward-thing started lurching again, dragging Kaylen behind it like a hunted deer. "The takeover isn't always painless. This skin sack had to learn his place."

Fury made her struggle against the hand. "What did you do to him?"

The hand tightened, but this time the thing swung around and punched her in the face. Pain exploded on the left side of Kaylen's face. "I made him realize death can take a long while if you know what you're doing." It started moving again. "Something you'll be finding out shortly."

Kaylen relaxed in the thing's grip, making herself as heavy as possible. She wasn't giving up, but she needed to rest herself so that when the opportunity came, she could give it all she had. She knew she had to keep an idea of where they had come from because that was direction she had to run. The closer she could get to them, the better chance she would have. She hoped whatever the Edward-thing had done to them to keep them out of her had worn off the way the voice block had. If not, she had better come up with a plan b pretty fast.

The Edward-thing stopped abruptly. "First stop on your last journey."

Kaylen craned her neck and saw a beat-up old car parked in a clearing. The car was covered in mud to the windows and the front fender had a large dent in it. A junker for sure, and not something someone would report stolen. If the Edward-thing had stolen it. The thing could just as easily have killed the owner and taken the damn car.

It was dragging her toward the trunk. "It might be a little cramped in there but you won't be in for long."

Knowing the trunk was certain death, her body would never function if the Edward-thing drove any distance away from them, Kaylen readied herself. She had to wait for the perfect moment because she would only have one shot.

The Edward-thing kept a tight hold on her while it opened the trunk. Then it turned to pull her up and in. It needed both hands to do this. They had wounded it more severely than it had thought and the body was starting to break down. That wouldn't be a concern once this was through. It could find a weak enough mind to bend as it had the Edward person and then sleep for a few weeks or months inside its new, unknowing host. Once rested, it would begin its own hunting, finding more of its own kind to destroy.

Kaylen stayed limp as the Edward-thing hefted her up to the edge of the opening. She could see various objects certain to cause pain she couldn't imagine. A tire iron, ropes, several knives of varying length. Those items were bad enough, but the one that froze her breath was the tent stake laying against the seat at the back of the trunk. The tent stake that would kill her.

It was the jolt she needed. Drawing on everything she had, Kaylen lunged forward in a roll. The Edward-thing, caught by surprise, flew over her back and onto the ground. It had lost its grip in the tumble and Kaylen was staggering back against the car as soon as she stood up.

The Edward-thing rolled to its hands and knees and hissed. Kaylen saw it was getting ready to speak again. Not knowing what it could with its voice and not wanting to find out, Kaylen lashed out with a foot and caught the Edward-thing in the side of the neck. It fell to the ground and started coughing, clawing at its throat and glaring up at her.

She spun, meaning to grab some weapon out of the trunk to defend herself and a wave of dizziness almost sent her sprawling. Lightning set the clearing in stark relief and thunder crashed directly overhead. The wind had become a gale and Kaylen gripped the car to keep from falling. She took a deep breath and pushed away to the left, giving herself plenty of distance to get around the Edward-thing still gasping on the ground.

She turned to run and felt something wrap around her ankle, pulling her down to one knee. Panic flared in her as thought it was the Edward-thing, but when she looked down, she saw it was a bramble that had tangled around her jeans. Desperately, Kaylen ripped the bramble loose, cutting her hands. She shot forward as the Edward-thing lunged, missing her by mere inches. Then she was up and running as best she could back the way she had come to them and safety.

Low branches and thorn bushes whipped at her face and arms, cutting her cheeks and snagging on her sleeves. She stumbled on, grabbing tree trunks and pulling herself every time her legs felt too heavy to move. The lightning was flashing faster, disorienting her, making her turn slightly instead of going straight. She yelled, calling out for help, but the thunder buried her cries and she saved her breath. She needed it.

Kaylen swung herself around a smooth-barked tree as the sky opened and the rain came down in a deluge. She was soaked in seconds despite the heavy foliage. The weight of her clothes made it even harder to run. She slowed to a fast walk, not daring to look over her shoulder to see if the Edward-thing was coming.

She tripped over a root and went sprawling. Her knee, the same one she had injured in her last gamble through the woods and whacked on the stake, of course it was, landed solidly on a jagged rocked pushing up through the soil. Kaylen cried out as pain exploded through her joint. She rolled onto her back and gripped her knee, cradling it as best she could while the rain formed hurrying streams around and beneath her.

Lightning flashed and Kaylen looked to her right and left, searching for a hiding spot. The left was no good. That way was blocked by a huge boulder slick with rain. To her right was another tangle of brambles, but they had grown over a fallen tree. The fit would be tight, but Kaylen wriggled under the tree. Mud squelched through her fingers and her jeans were plastered to her legs making it hard to squirm completely under. She got under enough to pull her legs up and hide herself. Claustrophobia tried to smother her, but Kaylen fought it back, trying to calm her mind enough to reach out to them and help them find her.

Tuning out the storm as best she could, Kaylen slowed her breathing, fought the chills that racked her, and opened her mind. She had never done anything like this before and wasn't sure what she was looking for until she felt the familiar touch of their minds with hers. Something was different though, a strangeness, she shied away from it, afraid it was the Edward-thing trying to lock onto her mind. The feeling had been them, but not them.

Scared and miserable, Kaylen huddled under the tree and brambles and tried to figure a way out of her situation. She couldn't reach out to them without opening herself to the Edward-thing and she wasn't running or even walking fast on her knee. With the storm around her increasing in intensity, for the first time in her life, Kaylen decided to stay put and wait for rescue.

CHAPTER 27

The rain pelted Slate as he thrashed through the trees and brush. He wasn't concerned about making noise; the wind and thunder were drowning out all sound but the steady rain. They were trying to target on Kaylen, but they kept losing her. It was like she would pop up on their radar and then disappear again. Slate compensated for this by trying to keep in one direction, but it was hard going with the wind and rain.

He came to an abrupt stop as he felt another mind brush against his, or more accurately, theirs. He knew it was her but she shied away before they could make permanent contact. He felt their frustration twisting inside him. He and they all knew that Slate was the reason she had backed away. She had felt the strangeness of his mind and had fled, thinking it was the Edward-thing trying to find her.

Cursing soundly, Slate continued on, slipping and sliding on the muddy ground. He didn't call out to her, not because he was worried about that monster coming for him, but because she wouldn't hear him unless he was right next to her.

He fought his way through a thick tangle of brambles and found himself in a small clearing. A car was parked in its center, the trunk open. He crouched down, flicking the safety off his weapon and proceeded with caution. They were on high alert. He could feel them twisting inside him, anxious to rejoin the fray as so as they found their target.

Slate circled the car from a distance, ascertained no one was hiding on either side and sidled up closer. Even with the rain he could tell no one was in the car. The trunk was filled with a brick-a-brack of shit that told of the plans the thing had in store for Kaylen. It made Slate's skin crawl.

He looked around. The trunk was open, which led him to believe someone had been here. The rain had washed away all signs of a struggle if there had been one and the brush around the clearing thrashed and danced so much in the wind and rain it was impossible to tell what direction Kaylen had gone in.

Feeling like he had a spotlight on his back, Slate slammed the trunk closed. He shut his eyes and tried to use his own method for finding Kaylen. They stirred within him, unsure of what he was doing, but they kept their peace. After a few seconds, Slate felt a ping off to his right. Hoping it wasn't some trick by the Edward-thing, who knew what it was capable of, Slate turned in that direction and started slogging through the woods more cautiously. They weren't in a chase anymore. Now they were in the hunt.

\#

Kaylen stayed under the tree until she was sure the chattering of her teeth would give away her hiding spot, storm or no storm.

She couldn't feel her fingers and her knee had gone completely numb. She was also having a hard time keeping her eyes open and she had read somewhere that tiredness in extreme cold was a warning sign of hypothermia. She wasn't sure if that were true but she had no intention of proving the theory.

Slowly, she pulled herself out from under the tree. The rain slashed at her face and chest and she almost slid back under. It was cold and wet under there but at least the wind couldn't get her. What got her moving was the thought of falling asleep and dying under this tree when Slate could be just a few feet away. In the dark and the rain, he would never see her.

She stood carefully, using the tree to brace herself. The knee wasn't going to hold her, that was obvious as soon as she tried to put any weight on it. That was going to make this a lot harder. Kaylen staggered to the closest upright tree and gripped the ragged bark. She was starting to get feeling back in her fingers. She sighted on another tree and hobbled to it. She moved this way, from tree to tree, until she tried to hop too far, lost her balance and tried to use her injured leg for support.

Pain exploded up and down her leg. Kaylen cried out and crumpled to the ground. She swore viciously at the knee as if yelling at it would make it behave itself and work again. She glanced around nervously and saw a shadow, dark against a light-colored tree trunk, moving her way. It was staggering, fighting for balance, and Kaylen knew it was the Edward-thing.

She forced herself to her feet and tried to limp away, dragging her injured knee behind her. She thought she might be able to out distance the Edward-thing enough to find another hiding spot when something hard hit the back of her head.

Kaylen fell face first, not even noticing the complaint from her knee as she landed. Her head felt like it was about to burst and her vision had come over all red. She reached back tentatively and touched the area of impact. She bit her lip to keep from crying out in fresh pain and she could feel warm, slippery blood coating her fingers. Refusing to give up, Kaylen tried to get her good knee under her, pushing herself up with her hands.

Something else hit her in the side like a golf club. She screamed and fell over onto her back. She knew what had hit her, knew what was next. Hadn't she been dreaming of this moment for weeks? Kaylen looked up at the dark figure above her, its face split in that same hideous grin and the tent stake swinging by its side.

"I had hoped for more," it said in its cracked voice, "but you did put up a good fight." It glanced over its shoulder, then back at her. "Who can say? If you had known I was coming it might have been me laying there in the mud, whether they helped you or not."

"Are you gonna end this or what?"

The Edward-thing shrugged. "A fighter to the end. Well, at least you won't die begging." It raised the stake, aiming the point between her breasts. Kaylen closed her eyes; she didn't want that deteriorating monster to be the last thing she saw. She felt a deep sense of calm overcome her and for the first time in her life she was at peace with herself.

A peace that was shattered with a gunshot and the front of her right shoulder just above her breast bursting into a pain that made her knee injury feeling like a stubbed toe. Kaylen's eyes flew open and she screamed as the stake, pushed down by the Edward-thing's weight as it used it for a crutch, penetrated her skin and muscle. It lodged in the joint, stuck fast.

The Edward-thing had turned toward Slate, who was continuing to fire into the thing's side and chest. Even in the rain, Kaylen could see the spray of blood from the exit wounds. Shrieking, the Edward-thing wrenched the stake free of Kaylen and threw it. The stake arced end over end twice before hitting Slate squarely in the chest on its long side. Lucky for Slate, as the point was sharp enough to have shot through his chest and into his spine with the force the Edward-thing had put into the throw.

Slate was knocked off his feet, his gun thrown from his hand and the wind knocked out of him. His chest was on fire and it was excruciating to draw breath. The solid iron bar hadn't penetrated him the way it had Kaylen, but it felt as if something was broken inside him. Slate gasped for breath, one hand searching the ground for his gun and the other trying to push himself up.

The Edward-thing, furious at being interrupted, this was not at all how it had imagined this going, was holding itself up using a tree and kicking at Kaylen's huddled form, trying to stomp the life out of her. It could have retrieved the stake, but this body was well on its way to dying and it still needed to get back to the car and find another host.

Slate had almost gotten his breath back when he felt the pull Kaylen had described. It was like something being ripped out of the very fiber of his being and he flopped back down into the mud.

They tore free of the man and split, flanking the Edward-thing from either side. It saw them and drew breath to use its words, black curses learned from the tortured damned to enslave and destroy, but before it could utter them, the smaller creature darted forward and bit down hard on one of its legs. The razor teeth clamped hard, severing the leg just below the knee. With a quick twist of its head, it snapped the bone and pulled the leg free.

The Edward-thing howled in pain and fury. It reached out with its clawed hand and slashed at the attacking creature. The creature danced back a few steps and shook the severed leg like a puppy shaking a rag.

A challenging snarl made the Edward-thing swing back to Kaylen's quivering body. The larger one was crouched over her, its hate-filled eyes fixed on the Edward-thing. It raised its pincher deliberately and snapped the claw rapidly. It grinned, showing all its sharpened teeth.

"Alright," the Edward-thing panted. "Enough hiding. Let's decide this as we are meant."

The husk that was all that remained of a man called Edward who had once served out God's justice when man's had failed and been hunted for it ever since, making his haunted mind the perfect place for evil hiding as salvation to take root, burst like a bomb filled with blood and organs. The thing inside destroyed the shelter it had created and slammed into the large creature crouch over Kaylen.

The two creatures rolled off Kaylen, biting and tearing and clawing. The smaller one tried to find an opening so that it could join the fray but the two were locked so closely it was impossible to discern one from the other.

Slate, having regained his breath, found his gun in the rain-soaked bushes and raised it, trying to get a good shot. Like the smaller of the three creatures, he knew that would be impossible. He couldn't risk hitting the one trying to help Kaylen. Swearing, hoping the two would separate and give him an opening, Slate made his way over to Kaylen.

Kaylen was in a very bad way. She had pulled herself as much into the fetal position as she could. Her body was wracked with shivering and she was moaning deep in her throat. He touched the wet spot on the back of her head. The blood was beginning to clot, but he had no idea if she had cranial swelling or hemorrhaging.

Unmindful of his own pain, Slate struggled out of his jacket. It was nearly as wet as Kaylen's hoodie but it might give her some protection from the wind. He tucked it gently around her and then took up his own crouch, waiting to see which of these things would win.

The two creatures came apart, each backing as far away from the other as they could get. The one from Kaylen was torn and bloody in several places, but still looked ready to carry on the fight. The Edward-thing, perhaps because Edward's body had protected it from the initial attack and the gunshots, looked far more hale. It grinned and ducked its head, trying to watch both of Kaylen's creatures and Slate at the same time.

Slate drew a bead on it and fired three times in rapid succession. He was running out of bullets and he tried to make each shot count. Two of the rounds found their mark. The Edward-thing was knocked backward against a tree. Immediately, the smaller creature was on it, pouncing on its chest like a cat and slashing at it throat and face. The Edward-thing reached for the attacker with razor-edged huge claws that would rip the smaller creature in two.

Before it could grab the little one, the larger creature launched itself, knocking the Edward-thing away from the tree and down to the ground. On its back and unable to rise, the Edward-thing fought with everything it had to dislodge the smaller one, while slashing at the larger one to keep it at bay.

Knowing if the thing got up, it would try to run, Slate pushed himself to his feet and limped over to the swarm of three creatures. He raised his gun, aiming for the Edward-thing's face and fired. The gun clicked, out of ammo. Slate tossed the weapon and staggered over to the stake, laying where it had fallen. He hefted it, almost fell, felt something inside him flare in pain, and dragged it over to the Edward-thing.

The two creatures from Kaylen were keeping it down, but they were having hard going. As his limped, Slate could see the Edward-thing readying itself to spring. They would only have this one chance. If it got away, Slate had no doubt it would hole up somewhere until it was healed and then come hunting again.

Slate got as close as he could to the snarling trio, spread his legs to brace himself and gave a sharp whistle. The two from Kaylen looked up and drew away from what they knew was coming. The Edward-thing, sensing its chance, thrust itself up. At the same time, Slate brought the stake down, driving the point through the Edward-thing's chest and bearing down with all his weight.

The Edward-thing threw its head back and howled. It fell back on the ground convulsing and shrieking. It clawed at the iron stake impaling its chest and Slate could see wisps of smoke rising from around the stake where it touched the creature. The other two backed away, positioning themselves between the smoking, dying creature and Kaylen.

Slate backed up too, not sure if the Edward-thing was going to melt or explode. It did neither. After several eternal seconds, it lay still. Blood oozed out of its mouth and around the hole in its chest. As Slate watched, it disintegrated, falling apart like wet ash and then soaking into the ground.

Slate stood where he was for a few heartbeats, oblivious to the rain, which had slackened considerably, and his own pains, which had increased remarkably, before stepping close to the stake. It was still standing upright, driven as it had been several inches into the ground by Slate's weight. He reached for it and the larger creature growled.

Slate looked at it. The creature looked at him, then the stake, then the ground beneath the stake, then back at Slate. "Does this have to stay here?"

The creature nodded slowly. Leaving the stake alone, Slate went to check on Kaylen.

She was still conscious, so that was a plus, but she was freezing to the touch. She needed a hospital. The rain had slowed to a drizzle and Slate was pretty sure he could find the car again. He would have to carry her. He didn't know if he could. The adrenalin in his system was starting to wear off now that the immediate danger was passed and he was pretty sure the broken feeling he had inside was at least one if not two broken ribs.

Crouching down next to her, Slate wrapped his jacket around her as tightly as he dared. He wanted to keep her as compact as possible when he lifted her. They circled the humans, making odd crooning noises in their throats. They each sniffed Kaylen and nuzzled her briefly, then looked at Slate.

"Go ahead. I think she'll settle more if you guys are back where you belong." He looked at the dark forest. "I don't think anything else is going to bother us tonight."

The creatures sniffed at him, then disappeared like they had before. Slate felt Kaylen's body rise and expanded slightly, then lay still. He gently pushed her hair out of her face and prepared himself to lift her. It wasn't going to happen. Little as she was, she was still too much for him to lift, let alone carry, with his broken ribs.

He dragged her over to the lee side of a tree where they would be sheltered from the rain and the wind as long as the storm stayed docile. He gathered her up into his lap and hoped Fred and the others were already looking for them. He shifted Kaylen slightly, dug his phone out of his pocket and turned the flashlight function on. During the heaviest part of the storm it wouldn't have shone enough to make any difference, but in the drizzle the light would be a beacon if anyone was looking in this direction. Slate put the flashlight on a rock and positioned it to reflect off the tree, then he hunkered down with Kaylen in his arms and waited.

He didn't have to wait long. No more than fifteen minutes passed before he heard crashing and yelling in the woods. Ignoring his ribs, Slate hollered as loud as he could until he saw Fred's large form shove through the brambles like an angry bear. The big man had a flashlight in one hand and a gun in the other.

"You guys okay?" He asked but didn't look. His eyes were scanning the immediate area, looking for a threat.

"The fight's over, but she's not okay." Slate shifted slightly, wincing, and then Fred was kneeling in front of them and gently pulling Kaylen away from Slate.

The others were coming. It sounded like Fred had brought the whole cavalry. Panic flared in Slate as he thought of one of them inadvertently knocking the stake loose. "Fred, tell them to be careful. There's a tent stake in the ground over there and it can't be moved."

Fred nodded. "They're over here. Y'all be mindful of the tent stake. It has to stay exactly where it is."

Slate heard the crashing sounds grow quiet as the others picked their way more cautiously. He looked at Fred. "Did you find the car?"

"Yeah," Tony answered. He had come up behind Slate and was casually swinging a sledgehammer in one hand. "That was a murder car if I ever saw one."

"None of you touched anything, did you?" Slate hated the cop he heard in his voice but he couldn't help what he was. He hoped none of them would get defensive.

"Of course, we didn't, you big jackass. How stupid do you think we are?" Mabel's voice chimed from somewhere off to the side.

"You can argue later," Fred ordered. "Right now, we got to get Rails to a hospital." He picked the girl up carefully and she gave a soft cry. "It's alright, honey, we're gonna get you some help." He turned to Slate. "I'm gonna get movin'. Tony and Mabel can stay with you. I might need Trips to help get her through brush."

Slate nodded and watched Fred and Trips blunder back through brambles. Tony reached down and gripped him under one armpit. "Alright, soldier, on your feet." He pulled with a surprising amount of force. Slate wasn't so much helped and yanked to his feet. He ribs protested but he clamped his mouth shut on the pain.

Mabel was standing in front of him with a flashlight in each hand. Slate didn't doubt for a minute she had a weapon stashed somewhere. "You ready?"

"It a minute. Tony, I need you to use that sledge for a minute."

"Want me to knock you out? It's gonna be a lot harder to drag your ass out of here than if you at least try to walk."

"Not for me. We have to hammer that stake down as far as it will go."

Tony and Mabel exchanged a look. Mabel shrugged. "Fine," Tony said, resigned. He handed Slate off to Mabel, who staggered under his weight for a second before steadying. The three of them walked over to the tent stake. Slate was alarmed to see it was leaning to one side. Another onslaught of rain would knock it right over.

Sighing dramatically, Tony righted the stake, tapped it a few times with the hammer to get a good set then stepped back and swung hard. In the rain slicked woods, the sound of the sledge hitting the stake was very loud and final. Tony kept at it until the stake was barely an inch above the ground. "I've never driven a stake that far. If you'd have asked, I would have told you it was impossible."

"Stack some rocks around it so no one will trip over it and wonder what it is and what it's doing here," Slate directed.

With another sigh, Tony did as he was told. He had seen his own share of shit in his day and this whole damn situation was too weird to warrant asking questions. Besides, driving the stake and hiding the head felt like the right thing to do. When he was finished, he gestured to the stake, completely hidden by a small pile of rocks. "Satisfied?"

Slate nodded and slouched against Mabel, the last of his strength giving way.

"We better get you back to the lot before you pass out big guy," Mabel said. Tony gripped the hammer up by the head and put an arm around Slate's waist, taking the other man's weight off Mabel.

"I want to go to the hospital," Slate grumbled as they walked.

"And you will. But not before we get you cleaned up and decide what kind of story we're going to give the cops," Mabel said patiently.

Slate laughed, then winced. "You guys are turning me into a regular felon."

"You want to go to jail for slaying the monster and saving the princess, be my guest," Mabel quipped.

Slate sighed against Tony and almost tripped over his own feet. "First, don't ever tell Kaylen you said that because she would just blame me and second, what kind of cop would believe a crazy story like this?"

"I know one who would," Tony muttered.

CHAPTER 28

"Mabel, I swear if you don't stop mothering me, I'm going to get up out of this chair and kick your skinny ass all the way across the lot."

"Promises, promises." The other woman did take a prudent step back, however.

Kaylen was sitting in a camp chair in front of the cookhouse with her right leg propped up in another chair. The cast she wore was one of the flexible kind, not that she was supposed to be flexing her knee too much, but it still itched like hell. She had been reaching for a chopstick out of the box of takeout they had ordered for lunch to use as a scratching stick for her damn leg when Mabel caught her.

Mabel handed her the chopstick and sat down opposite her in another camp chair. "You are still not supposed to be moving much."

"I am perfectly capable of reaching for a stick," Kaylen fumed. She pulled the chopstick out of its wrapper and pushed it into the gap between the cast and her leg. Scratching was bliss.

"At least it's not one of those fiberglass kinds. They itch worse. And stink."

"Isn't there something you should be doing somewhere else?"

"Nope. I'm under strict instructions to keep an eye on you until Fred gets back with the shopping." She stretched back in her chair to show she had no intentions of going anywhere.

Kaylen glared at her then looked away across the lot, still scratching absently. It had been three weeks since the night of the Edward-thing. Kaylen had spent several days in the hospital, a time she barely remembered. She had been heavily drugged during her stay. It cut down on the screaming in the middle of the night while sane patients were trying to recover.

The trip to the hospital had nearly been a disaster in itself from what Fred had told her. Roger had stayed at the truck in case she or Slate wandered back to the road. When Fred and Trips arrived the Kaylen, unconscious and breathing heavily, he had sprung into action as the hero of the moment, insisting on driving them all to the emergency room. From what Fred told her, Kaylen was very happy she had been knocked out during that crazy ride.

The story they concocted had been that Kaylen had stormed off toward town during the last show. She had gone to a bar, maybe gotten a little tipsy, and then decided, for her own reasons, to march back to the lot through the woods instead of down the road. The storm had broke, she had gotten disoriented, panicked, and had run straight into a jutting tree branch, thus impaling her shoulder, and then fallen down a slope hitting every rock and tree root on the way down.

The doctor, an older gentleman who seemed to only want to be done with the whole business, asked only one question. "If you hit a tree branch, why did we find flecks of rust in the wound?"

To which Kaylen had replied. "I don't know man, meth is a hell of a drug."

Disgusted, the doctor had treated her, given her pain meds, sleeping pills, put her arm in a sling and her leg in a cast and sent her on her way as soon as the paperwork cleared.

Slate hadn't been seen at all. Fred had checked the bruising from the stake, declared two of Slate's ribs were probably broken, and gave him a bottle of pills from inside the cook trailer.

Slate had picked Kaylen up from the hospital. She had taken a couple of the sleeping pills, stretched out as much as could in the back of his car and slept the whole ten hours it took to catch up with the show. The show owner hadn't been thrilled with their arrival, but Fred eventually got him talked around to letting Slate and Kaylen stay since they had the space and Slate at least could still work.

"Where are you gonna go?" Mabel asked, bringing Kaylen back to the present.

Kaylen shrugged. After the hospital found out she had no insurance, no address, and no way to be tracked, they settled on a bill she could afford. She paid the whole thing outright with cash, but it had drained her entire nest egg. Not that it was much of a problem. Kaylen had spent most of her life broke and on the streets.

"You know Fred's got it worked so you can stay here as long as you want." Mabel took a deep breath when Kaylen didn't answer. "Oh, for Christ's sake, how far are you gonna get with a bust knee and a fucked up shoulder, anyway?"

"Farther than you think," Kaylen answered.

"And what about him? You just gonna pack up and limp outta here while he's gone cleaning up his business?"

Slate had flown back home not long after he and Kaylen returned to the show, to settle up a few things and officially file for a leave of absence. He said it would take few days and he'd been gone for ten. Kaylen was starting to believe he wasn't coming back, car or not. "What makes you think he's coming back?" Mabel gave her a look.

"Okay, fine, he's coming back, but I can't wait around much longer."

"They gettin' hungry?"

Kaylen nodded. After she had come back, Kaylen had insisted that Mabel stay with her in their old compartment for a few days. Slate had been crestfallen until Fred took him aside and explained to him that in her current state Kaylen might need help with things she'd rather not have the man she was sleeping with know about. It took a minute or two for the idea to get through, and to his credit, rather than yap about how her bodily functions didn't matter to him, Slate had given her space.

It had been the right decision, but it had left Mabel to pick up the shattered pieces of Kaylen's psyche. There had been many sleepless nights during which Kaylen had unloaded nearly all her secrets to Mabel. Many more nights of Kaylen waking up shrieking and struggling with an unseen attacker. For a little while, Slate, Fred, and Mabel had quietly discussed the possibility of putting Kaylen in a psych ward just to keep her from hurting herself. They decided to give her another week. The nightmares lessened and her waking mood improved with the much needed sleep.

"It's not bad yet, but it will be soon enough." Kaylen rubbed her temple.

"How will you do it, the way you are right now?"

"They'll find a way. They always do." Like how they had used Slate to get back to her. She didn't think they could enter just anyone, not like the Edward-thing had, but she thought it was easier for them because she and Slate had a bond. She wondered if Slate would be willing to explore that bond further now that their real purpose was at hand.

"You think he'll go for it?"

Kaylen shrugged again. "I can't say that I care either way."

"That's a bald-faced lie and you know it." Mabel got up and started cleaning up the take-out cartons. Her anger was clear as she slammed cartons together or smashed Styrofoam cups before tossing them in the nearby trashcan.

"Okay, maybe that wasn't the right way to say it." Kaylen took a deep breath. "But, Mabel, I've discovered I'm more miserable without these things than I am with them. And there are a lot of really bad people that get away with some really bad shit."

Mabel's jerky movements slowly smoothed out. After a moment she said, "It's your life and your decision, but I still think you need him around. What if another one of those bad ones comes looking for you?"

That was something that had been on Kaylen's mind. She answered carefully, "Well, this time, when I start with the dizzy spells and black-outs, I'll know what to look for. And my friends have learned from this too. Another bad one won't get the drop on them the way this one did."

"You can hope."

"Mabel, either with Slate or without him, I can't stay."

The other woman nodded mutely and finished her cleaning. She had been sober, more or less, since that night and the clarity of her visions was coming back. And the memory of her lost family. It was a hard road and Kaylen wouldn't judge her at all if she went back to the pipe and booze. Sometimes life was too much to bear and that was the bottom line.

"Hey, ladies, look who I found in town." Fred's baritone rolled across the lot making Kaylen and Mabel jump. The quick movement sent a spasm of pain through Kaylen's shoulder and she winced.

"Don't make me jump like that, Fred. Don't you know I'm still healing?"

He walked up to the table with a bag of groceries in each hand, Slate right behind him and similarly encumbered. "Rails, the only thing that didn't get broke that night was your mouth."

"Fuckin' right it didn't."

They all laughed. Fred gestured Mabel. "C'mon, Mabel, help me get the laundry out of the back."

"Why didn't you take Donna with you?"

"Because Donna has better things to do than wash your underwear."

Slate and Kaylen watched them go, then he sat down in Mabel's chair. "Think I walked out?"

"Flew out would be more appropriate. And I did consider it."

"Me too," he said quietly.

They looked at each other. Inside herself, Kaylen felt them stir in their sleep. "Come back for the car, then?" She tried to keep the hurt out of her voice. She didn't need anyone, no matter what Mabel thought, and she hated herself for feeling hurt by this man she barely knew.

"That depends."

"On what?"

"On whether you're coming with me or whether I'm going to have to track you all over the damn country. If I have to follow you around, I want something with more gas mileage."

She blinked at him. The corner of her mouth tried to come up in a smile and she forced it down. They were out here in front of everyone and she had a reputation to uphold. "I would think stalking tendencies would be something they would test for when you join the force, officer."

"I'm a detective and stalking is what makes me good at my job."

"Sounds like a smooth way to hide your mental instability."

He shrugged. "Call it what you want. If I didn't have it, you wouldn't be here."

She shuddered before she could stop herself. Pain shot from her healing head all the way down to her toes. Slate was out of his chair and next to her in an instant. "Hey, I'm sorry. I didn't mean to bring up bad memories."

Kaylen put her good hand on his arm. "It's okay. I'll deal with it eventually."

He put his hand over hers. "So? What's it gonna be? Do we stay here with the circus or strike out on our own?"

She took her hand away and rubbed her temple. "We can't stay here. And you shouldn't stay with me. Being with me will put you in real, legal danger."

"They getting hungry?"

She nodded. He took her hand back and kissed it. "I think I know how to get around law enforcement. And I can tell you from a cop's perspective that most of us can't stand it when someone we know is guilty has been set free." He ran a finger down the side of her face where the bruising was still faint. "I'm pretty sure that's the main reason why I was the first one to track you down. Cops want justice as much as anyone else and even we understand that sometimes that justice is beyond us."

"Okay," she agreed softly, "but I can't put any more of these people in danger."

"Fair enough."

"You do understand that if you hook up with me, we'll be on the move and off the grid almost all the time. No permanent place to stay, no permanent friends, basically living out of a backpack."

He nodded. "I think I've got it figured out. I did have to find you, didn't I?"

"We'll see how you feel the first time you have to wait out a hurricane under an overpass."

"I'll risk it." He looked at the crew walking around or hanging by the trucks and trailers. "I guess we should tell everybody and say our thanks and good-byes."

"We will, but we should make it quick and get on the road."

"Need a change of scenery?"

Kaylen gave him a razor-edged smile and he could see them looking out from behind her eyes. "The daylight's going fast and tonight, we hunt."

Rebecca McCullough grew up on a traveling show. She is a
fourth-generation performer.
Her experience has shown her how tough and rewarding that
life is for those who work at it.
She currently lives with her daughter in south Florida.

Her website is herrmannsroyallipizzans.com.